Hearts **racing.**

Blood **pumping.**

Pulses **accelerating.**

Falling in love can be a blur...
especially at 180 mph!

So if you crave the thrill of the chase—on and off the track—you'll love

ALMOST FAMOUS
by Gina Wilkins

For the first time since his accident, Jake found himself thinking about romance.

He genuinely liked Stacy in addition to being increasingly attracted to her. He couldn't even say why exactly. It wasn't as if she had been completely forthcoming with him. And that apparently innate reserve of hers made it difficult to get to know her quickly.

So maybe it was the puzzle that intrigued him. Maybe once he got to know her better some of the fascination would wear off. He regretted to say that he'd shown a rather short attention span in his past affairs. When it came down to a woman or a race car, he had always chosen the latter, which hadn't led to lasting relationships.

But maybe it would be different with Stacy. From what little he had seen, she seemed like the steady, settled, home-and-family type. Maybe this initial attraction could blossom into a great deal more. Or maybe he was just getting carried away because of his boredom and restlessness....

Dear Reader,

I've been trying to decide how to say that writing a romance novel is like driving a race car—just because it would be so cool to make that claim. The problem is…well, they aren't at all alike. Drivers perform before thousands of people; writers work in solitude. Drivers receive cheers and applause for every clever maneuver; writers wait for months between finishing their books and actually seeing them in print and hearing from their readers. Drivers are daredevils, taking risks every day; writers fuss about eyestrain and repetitive motion aches. Okay, so writing isn't nearly as glamorous or exciting or dashing as racing. And yet…

Both writers and race car drivers know what it's like to follow their dreams into careers that aren't the usual nine-to-five professions. Both businesses are difficult to break in to, and only a fortunate few actually get to make a living doing them. Both understand that to stay ahead in their respective fields, they have to struggle to get better all the time at what they do. Both are always looking over their shoulders at the talented, ambitious and impatient young people waiting to take their places. And both thrive on praise and respect from their fans, always striving to please the people who support them in their careers.

I have the greatest admiration for the men and women who dream of a future in NASCAR, and are willing to devote the effort and the commitment and the sacrifices to make that dream a reality. Is it any wonder I've had so much fun writing about them in two books now—and have new ideas already brewing for future books about people with a shared passion for racing? So maybe writing isn't exactly like racing—but that doesn't mean I can't imagine what it must be like to follow that dream, just as I have been following my own for so many years.

Gina Wilkins

//////// NASCAR®

ALMOST FAMOUS

Gina Wilkins

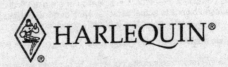

HARLEQUIN®

TORONTO • NEW YORK • LONDON
AMSTERDAM • PARIS • SYDNEY • HAMBURG
STOCKHOLM • ATHENS • TOKYO • MILAN • MADRID
PRAGUE • WARSAW • BUDAPEST • AUCKLAND

ISBN-13: 978-0-373-21776-2
ISBN-10:   0-373-21776-5

ALMOST FAMOUS

GINA WILKINS

Bestselling romance writer Gina Wilkins has written more than eighty books for Harlequin and Silhouette Books, yet she still finds excitement in every new idea. A lifelong resident of Arkansas, she is a four-time winner of the prestigious Maggie Award for Excellence presented by Georgia Romance Writers and has won several awards from the reviewers of *Romantic Times BOOKreviews,* including a nomination for a Lifetime Achievement Award. She credits her enduring career in romance to her long-suffering husband and her three "extraordinary" children, all of whom have provided inspiration over the years.

For my mother, Beth Vaughan, whose amazing courage
is an inspiration for everyone who knows her.

CHAPTER ONE

SOLITUDE. It was exactly what Jake Hinson had craved the most when he'd borrowed a friend's cozy cabin in the Arkansas Ozarks National Forest on the banks of the White River. He had told everyone he needed some time alone, away from cameras and microphones, intrusive questions and sympathetic gazes. He needed a chance to heal, both physically and emotionally, and he'd said he couldn't do either in the public eye.

Three days into his self-imposed vacation, he was already becoming restless and lonely. He had spent half of his thirty years pursuing fame and attention, he thought wryly. He didn't even know how to live anonymously anymore.

As for the lazy relaxation that had seemed so appealing a few weeks earlier...well, he didn't know how to do that, either. He was accustomed to having every minute of every day scheduled. To going 180 miles per hour on the racetrack and 200 in his personal life. Inactivity was a foreign concept to him, and the novelty had worn off quickly.

At least the late-September weather was nice. After the first couple of days nursing his wounds alone indoors, he ventured outside to the long front porch of the cabin. The last in a row of similar, privately owned vacation homes facing the river, the cabin sat on perhaps a quarter acre of rocky ground, separated enough from the neighbors to provide plenty of privacy. Behind the houses, the land rose to a wooded hillside, perfect for hiking.

Jake felt the draw of that hillside, but he wasn't sure he was ready yet for a strenuous walk over uneven ground. He would give himself another couple days of strength-building exercises and then he would give it a try, he promised himself.

All the cabins, including this one owned by one of his friends back in North Carolina, had boat garages on their property. A couple of empty trailers still hitched to parked pickup trucks sat at the public launch area on the other side of the road, evidence that their owners were out trying their luck with the fish on this Saturday afternoon. Jake didn't even like to think about getting back into a boat just yet, though he hoped there would come a time when he could do so again without remembering the horrific accident that had changed so much in his life.

Sitting in one of the four wrought-iron spring rockers arranged on the front porch, he stretched his jeans-clad legs in front of him, wincing when the position pulled at his healing scars. To distract himself from his discomfort, he looked across the narrow asphalt road toward the river on the other side.

An older couple floated past in a flat-bottomed aluminum boat, their faces shaded by straw hats, their fishing lines drifting lazily along beside them. Seeing Jake sitting there, the man at the controls raised a hand. It was a congenial, generic greeting having nothing to do with recognition. He'd have waved at anyone sitting there, Jake realized as he returned the salute with a nod.

He turned his attention to the row of four cabins leading up to the one in which he was staying. There had been little noise from his neighbors while he'd been there. He saw people coming and going, but other than the occasional nod of greeting, there was no interaction between the cabins. He had done nothing to

call attention to himself, staying inside most of the time since
he'd arrived. He hadn't emerged until today.

Closing his eyes, he let the quiet sounds around him seep into
him, soothe him. The hum of the small boat motor as it traveled
downriver. The lapping of the water in its wake.

A sudden burst of high-pitched barking made his eyes open
again. It seemed to be coming from the cabin closest to this one.
Turning his head, he spotted the source of the sound—a hairy
little black-and-brown dog tethered by a baby-blue leash to a
petite, slender young woman with long, dark hair and a sling on
her left arm. They appeared to be returning from a walk, and had
apparently just stepped onto their front porch when the dog had
spotted Jake.

A Yorkshire terrier, Jake decided, amused by the attitude ra-
diating from the compact critter. Not just a wanna-be dog, he
thought wryly. A wanna-be guard dog. Never mind that a good-
sized cat could probably make mincemeat out of the little mutt.

Smiling, he raised a hand in greeting to his neighbor, her sling
eliciting a tug of empathy from him. He identified all too well
with the signs of a recent injury.

Apparently, she didn't feel the same sense of kinship. Maybe
because his own wounds weren't as visible to her. Or maybe she
just wasn't the friendly type. Whatever the reason, she gathered
her dog's leash more firmly in hand and disappeared inside her
cabin with only a quick, rather chilly nod in response to his
gesture.

Okay, he thought, dropping his hand, his practiced smile
fading. So much for being neighborly.

He wasn't used to being so decidedly snubbed by an attractive young woman—just the opposite, actually. Aware that his
pride was stinging a bit, he chuckled ruefully as he limped
through his own door. Maybe he had gotten a bit spoiled by the

celebrity that had accompanied his rise in the ranks of NASCAR racing. He had become more accustomed to being pursued by pretty women than rebuffed by them.

It was probably good for him to be hit with an occasional reality check. Just to keep him from getting too conceited—not that his teammates would let him get too full of himself. He could count on his no-nonsense crew chief and blunt-spoken team members to keep his ego in check.

Suddenly, almost overwhelmingly homesick for his friends and his temporarily stalled career, he sank into a chair and allowed himself to slide into an uncharacteristic and totally self-indulgent bout of self-pity.

STACY CARTER LOCKED the door of her brother's river cabin, then pushed the dead bolt into place, just for good measure. For the most part, she felt perfectly comfortable staying here with only her pet Yorkie for company. The solitude was greatly preferable to the ordeal she had been through back home, giving her a chance to rest, recuperate and catch up on the piles of work that had accumulated during the past couple of weeks.

Her family had been concerned about her coming here alone, but she had assured them she would be fine. Her brother had owned this place for several years without a single unpleasant incident. The locks were sturdy, the grounds well lit, and she had a strong signal for her cell phone.

And she had Oscar, she thought with a smile, glancing down at the dog who was chewing on his favorite fire-hydrant squeaky toy at her feet. Oscar believed he was as fierce as any Doberman pinscher, and he made sure she was aware of every odd or suspicious noise.

Even with one arm temporarily out of commission, she wasn't worried about staying here, and had no doubt about her ability to take care of herself. Still, it didn't hurt to take extra precautions. Like keeping the doors locked. And not encouraging the attentions of the unknown man in the house next door.

She had been aware that the other cabin was occupied, though she hadn't seen anyone until today. Now she knew her elusive neighbor was a good-looking man with dark hair and a flashing smile.

She hoped he hadn't recognized her. She had tried to keep her face averted from him, hoping he'd gotten the message that she wasn't here to socialize. All she needed was to have some reporter show up on the front porch of her hideout, hoping for a filler feature story for a slow news day.

It wasn't as if there was anything left to write about her, she thought grumpily, but that had never stopped the local newshounds before. Not where her family was concerned, at least.

Oscar dropped his toy and headed for the kitchen, his body language inviting her to follow him. He'd made it clear he thought it was snack time, and he was right, she decided, thinking of the bowl of fruit waiting on the kitchen table. She ordered herself to forget the neighbor, forget the problems back home and concentrate on the more pressing dilemma of whether she wanted an apple or a pear.

THE MORNING AFTER Jake first glimpsed his reclusive neighbor, he sat outside again, this time on the deck that spanned the back of the cabin, overlooking the woods. It was a spectacularly beautiful day. The sky was a brilliant blue dotted with fluffy white clouds, and a light breeze kept the temperature comfortable.

A bird feeder sat on a pole in the neighboring backyard, and an interesting variety of birds fluttered around it, chirping and singing from the surrounding treetops. A couple of playful squirrels chased each other around the trunk of a big oak tree, and a trio of deer wandered briefly into sight, then disappeared silently back into the woods.

Though he couldn't see them from where he sat, he heard an occasional vehicle pass on the road on the other side of the cabin and a few boats puttering past on the river. He thought he heard a small dog yap a couple of times, but he caught no glimpse of the dog or its owner. He had peace, quiet and privacy—exactly what he had come here to find. And he was going slowly out of his mind with boredom.

The cell phone he kept clipped to his belt vibrated, and because any distraction was a welcome one, he lifted it to his ear without checking the caller ID. "H'lo?"

His crew chief, Wade McClellan, greeted him with typical brevity. "Hey, Jake."

"Hey, Ice. Aren't you too busy getting ready for today's race to talk on the phone?"

Wade chuckled. "Actually, yes. I just wanted to check on you. How's paradise?"

"Let's just say I'd be climbing walls if I had all my limbs back in climbing commission."

"Ready to come back home?"

Jake thought of the reporters who would be waiting there to ask him how his recuperation was proceeding. When he would be back in top form. How soon he'd be back behind the wheel. How he felt about losing his shot at this season's championship. And, oh, yeah, how it felt to lose a longtime friend in the tragic accident.

"No," he said, somewhat reluctantly. "Not quite."

"Doing your exercises?"

"Obsessively." It was pretty much all he had to do here.

"Hurting much?"

"Nah." Pain was something a professional athlete—and as a

race car driver, he counted himself among that group—learned to live with. Just the physical stamina required to spend four hours or more stuffed into a cramped, overheated, tension-filled cockpit was daunting, and that didn't count the jarring crashes and dizzying spins that were inherent to the sport.

"You keep following your doctor's orders, you hear? Don't try to rush it or overdo it."

Jake couldn't help but smile a little in response to Wade's admonition. He spent so much of his life with Wade's voice in his ears—usually through headphones—calming him, encouraging him, preaching patience, demanding his best efforts.

But another driver would be hearing that voice this afternoon, he thought, his smile dying. Another driver would be hanging on to the wheel of the Number 82 car, pedal to the metal, a monster engine between his legs, blood pounding in his ears and forty-two other drivers doing their best to leave him in their dust.

"How's Pete?" he asked, reminded of that other driver.

"Oh. You know." Typically, Wade conveyed a great deal with those few words.

"He's giving it his best?"

"Hundred percent. He's working as hard as anyone here. And the team's determined to provide him with all the support they can give. Everyone likes the kid—but he's not you."

Swallowing hard, Jake spoke brusquely. "Give him my best, okay? And tell him not to get too comfortable in my car. I'm coming back to claim it in a few weeks."

Wade chuckled again. "I'll tell him. You okay there? You need anything?"

"No, I'm good. How are things with you and Lisa?"

Wade had been nicknamed "Ice" McClellan for his ability to keep his feelings hidden even under the most trying of circumstances. When all hell broke loose on the racetrack, his was the voice of calm. When the team struggled in the points race or had a run of bad luck, everyone but Wade would get tense. Testy. Wade's tone never changed.

It changed now, at the mention of the woman he loved. The woman who had broken his heart years ago, but with whom he had reunited in the middle of this eventful racing season. "Things are good," he said, and though the words were rather prosaic, the deep satisfaction in his tone was so obvious that Jake had to smile again.

Wade had a hard time showing his emotions—one of the reasons he and Lisa had split up all those years ago—but that didn't mean he was unfeeling. He had a bigger heart than just about anyone Jake knew. Wade loved his coworkers, his employer, the fans who had been so supportive of him and Jake, and he quite simply adored Lisa. Something she understood now as she hadn't the first time they were together—and returned in full.

Jake was genuinely pleased for them. Wade was as close as he'd come to having a brother, and Jake wanted him to be happy.

Seemed as if just about everyone he knew these days was happily hooked up with someone, he thought as he disconnected the call a short time later after wishing Wade luck for the race. Wade and Lisa planned to be married during the winter break, as did another Woodrow Racing driver, Mike Overstreet, to his fiancée, Andrea Kennedy.

Another team driver, Ronnie Short, was expecting his first child in early December with his wife, Katie. NASCAR took pride in being a family-oriented sport, and Jake was surrounded on a weekly basis by the spouses and offspring of other drivers and team members.

People sometimes teased him about being a confirmed bachelor at thirty. They thought he liked playing the field, dating lots of women, staying footloose and unentangled. And while he wouldn't deny that he'd had fun as a single, popular NASCAR driver, the truth was that he hadn't led quite the swinging lifestyle many people assumed.

Racing was a career that required intense focus and dedication if one wanted to reach the highest levels, and Jake had always been driven toward the top. From the day he had secured his first full-time ride, he'd aspired to a NASCAR NEXTEL Cup championship title, and he had worked and sacrificed accordingly.

Marriage and family had also been on the life plan he had drawn up for himself more than ten years ago. Having never had a real family of his own—just himself and his often absent single mother—he had always envied the apparently happy families he had observed around him during the years. Moms and dads and kids. Pets. Real houses to spend holidays in, not rent-by-the-week motel rooms or cramped, colorless apartments.

So maybe his mental image of family life was a bit too heavily influenced by idealistic old television programs. And the career he had chosen was one spent mostly on the road, every weekend booked through ten months of every year, leaving little opportunity for soccer games or dance recitals or PTA meetings or family camping trips. But plenty of others were making it work, and he had no doubt that he could, too. When he set his mind on something, he didn't let anything get in his way—barring the occasional unforeseen circumstances of life, he added, glaring morosely at his game leg.

He would survive the disappointment of being sidelined for a crucial part of this racing season, he assured himself. And while it would be a longer process, and one he never expected to get over completely, he would eventually recover from the loss of a longtime friend in the boating accident that he himself had survived only by a stroke of luck. Next season would start with a clean slate, with him back on track both literally and figuratively.

Once his career was under way again, he could focus on the personal side of his mental to-do list. Look more actively for someone with whom he could settle down and start a family. Someone who would be there to cheer him on during the races and celebrate or commiserate with him afterward, who would share his luxurious motor home at the tracks and his palatial estate on Lake Norman in North Carolina. Someone who would understand the joys and demands of high-level stock car racing. Someone like Wade had found. And Ronnie. And Mike. And all those others who made up the huge and cheerfully obsessive NASCAR family.

Letting himself drift into that admittedly self-serving fantasy future, he closed his eyes, sprawled more comfortably in the canvas-cushioned outdoor lounge chair and felt every muscle in his battered body start to relax. He had just drifted into a light doze when a faint cry of distress, accompanied by what sounded like frantic barking, brought him quickly and awkwardly to his feet.

PAIN SHOT through Stacy's entire right leg when she tried to free herself from the shallow hole she had inadvertently stepped into while walking Oscar through the woods. She wasn't injured, she assured herself, taking a quick inventory. Her sneakered right foot was lodged beneath a fallen log that had shifted when she'd stepped into the leaf-hidden hole in the soft dirt.

The log had slid over her ankle, trapping her foot and leaving her sprawled, half sitting, half lying down, with her sprained left arm beneath her. Her ankle twisted painfully every time she tried to pull her foot free, but she decided that was due mostly to her awkward position. Once she was freed, she was sure she would be fine.

If only she could free herself....

Had she not been hampered by her temporarily weakened left arm, it would have been relatively easy to get back up. As it was, the heavy log really required two hands for leverage. This could take a while.

She looked at the little dog who stood nearby, barking fiercely at the log as if ordering it to release his companion. "You're not helping, Oscar. Maybe instead you could run tell Timmy that I've fallen into a well?"

Oscar wasn't amused by the old Lassie reference—but someone was. A man's deep chuckle came from behind her, causing her to gasp and twist uncomfortably to see who was approaching. She recognized him immediately, though she had seen him only from a distance before. This was the guy staying in the cabin next door to her brother's place.

Up close, she could see a few more details about him. His near black hair was longish around his face and almost touched the collar of the green-and-white-striped polo shirt he wore loose over an old pair of jeans. It looked as though he hadn't had a trim in a while—nor had he made use of a razor for at least a week. His square-jawed, probably handsome face was covered in stubble and decorated at his right temple with a fresh-looking red scar. He might have appeared somewhat dangerous, had it not been for the dimples that bracketed his smile and the twinkle in his long-lashed brown eyes.

He limped rather noticeably over the rocky, uneven hillside. Great. Between her sprained arm and his apparent injuries, they made quite an outdoor-adventure team.

"Did you fall?" he asked as he came closer, ignoring Oscar, who had gone into another round of fevered yapping.

One of her favorite stand-up comedians had based much of his career on routines about stupid answers to stupid questions.

She was tempted to respond with a sarcastic, "Nope. I just sat down for a rest and this big, old log crawled right onto my ankle."

Because such rudeness would have been completely out of character for her—at least outwardly, despite the evil little voice that spoke so often in her head—she said, "Yes. My foot's lodged in a hole under this log. I couldn't push it off because of the position I landed in and because one of my arms is out of commission."

"So I see." He took another careful step toward her. "I'm a little battered myself, but I think I can help get you out of there."

"I would really appreciate it."

Still smiling, he took hold of the log and tugged upward. Even as she freed her foot and quickly scooted backward, she could see that the effort caused her rescuer some discomfort.

A hint of relief crossed his face when he dropped the heavy log. Straightening, he moved toward her again. "You okay? Can you stand?"

She had already flexed her foot experimentally, grateful to feel no pain when she did so. She would probably have a few new bruises as a result of her carelessness, but on the whole, she'd been fortunate. "I'm okay. My pride stings more than my ankle."

He laughed and held out his right hand to give her a boost up. "No reason to be embarrassed. Everyone gets into a jam once in a while—some of us more than others."

Studying his devilish smile as she regained her footing, she murmured, "Sounds like you're speaking from experience."

His smile turned wry. "Honey, it takes a whole crew to keep me out of trouble."

It sounded as though there was some truth in his statement, which made her wonder what he did for a living, but she was more rattled by that casual "honey." He seemed like the type to drop such familiarities often and easily.

Her first impression was that this was a guy who had made an art of lazy charm, probably using it to get him out of more than a few tight spots. Because she was all too painfully familiar with that sort of man, she pulled her hand from his rather abruptly and made a show of brushing crushed leaves from her clothing.

"Thank you for your help," she said, then sighed. "Oscar, would you please be quiet?"

"You're welcome," the man replied, glancing at the dog barking up at him. "He is a yapper, isn't he?"

"Not usually so bad back at home. He's just overexcited by being on vacation."

The man bent to offer his hand for Oscar to sniff. "You've proved that you're a real tough guy, pup. You take good care of your friend here. But I can assure you I'm not going to give you any trouble."

It was no particular surprise to Stacy when her dog stopped barking, sniffed the offered hand, then began to wag his tail and allow himself to be scratched behind his flowing ears. Despite his bluster, Oscar was a very friendly dog who liked people. It didn't take him long to make a new friend.

Not that she trusted his instincts entirely. Scratch behind his ears and Oscar would make friends with a cat burglar. She, on the other hand, had learned that even people who offered friendly hands and charming smiles were often quite capable of sticking a knife in an unwittingly turned back.

She reached down to take firm hold of the baby-blue leash dangling from Oscar's matching collar. "Again, thank you for your help," she said, her tone indicating that the encounter was at an end. "I'd better take him back to the cabin now. He's probably hungry."

The man's smile faded a little, but didn't disappear completely. "You're sure you're okay? You aren't having any trouble walking?"

She took a couple of steps away from him to prove she was fine. "I told you, I wasn't hurt. I was just having trouble getting up. I'm sure I'd have managed eventually, but I appreciate your help."

He seemed to be holding his smile with an effort now, but his tone was still friendly when he said, "Glad I could help. My name is Jake, by the way."

He watched her closely as he gave his name. She figured he was trying to understand why she was suddenly trying to brush him off.

Because it was expected of her, she tried to hide her reluctance as she introduced herself in return. "I'm Stacy. Thank you again, Jake. Come on, Oscar, let's go find something to eat."

The dog knew the word eat. His ears perking, he trotted eagerly toward the cabin with such enthusiasm that he would have been dragging her along behind him had he weighed more than a loaf of bread. As it was, she didn't try to slow him down.

Aware that Jake watched her rather ignominious retreat, she hurried along behind her pet, grateful that at least her neighbor didn't seem to have recognized her. Maybe he was visiting from out of state, and hadn't caught any local news for the past couple of weeks. Maybe he would never realize why she was hiding out alone here in the boonies.

For some reason, she was particularly relieved she'd never had to have that particular conversation with the disconcertingly intriguing man she knew only as Jake.

CHAPTER TWO

JAKE SAT on his back deck again Monday afternoon. Stacy could see him from the kitchen of her brother's cabin, though she was pretty sure he couldn't see her in return. Just to be sure, she stood to one side of the window, looking out at him.

He certainly added to the appeal of the scenery, she thought wryly. The man was undoubtedly attractive. Despite her efforts to keep to herself here, she couldn't help being curious about him. Why, she wondered, was he over there all alone? He seemed to be the outgoing type. A people person. Yet he hadn't left his cabin all week, nor had he had any visitors.

Of course, the same could be said about her. But at least she had Oscar for company. And she had a good reason for wanting to get away from home for a couple of weeks.

Thinking of the evidence of his own recent injuries, she guessed that he was here for reasons similar to her own. To rest, maybe, and recuperate. If he was anything at all like her, he was tired of being hovered over. Or maybe his was the opposite situation, she mused. Maybe he didn't have anyone to take care of him, so he'd come here to heal in solitude until he could return to work, whatever it was he did.

There was something about his posture as he sat in the deck chair. His head was down, his shoulders just a little slumped. As if his thoughts weren't happy ones. She couldn't see his expression from here, but something made her suspect she would see sadness in his dark eyes.

Sadness. The word lingered in her mind, making her study him more closely. She knew someone back home who claimed to see auras around people, an assertion Stacy had always taken with a large grain of salt. Yet she suspected that if Amelia were here now, she would see a dark aura wrapped around Jake. It didn't take any special abilities to see that his thoughts were not happy ones.

Chiding herself for letting her imagination get away from her, she turned away from the window. She doubted that he would appreciate her spying on him.

She had come into the kitchen because she was restless. Work was piled up in the other room, but she'd been having trouble concentrating. After chatting with her mother and her brother on the phone, assuring them both she was perfectly well and getting lots of work done, she had decided she needed a break. Opening a cabinet, she spotted a boxed brownie mix, and immediately developed a craving for chocolate.

She frowned at her left arm. She wasn't wearing the sling now, and she flexed her fingers experimentally. Deciding she could manage if she took a little extra care, she reached for the brownie mix.

Coddling her sprained arm presented a challenge, but half an hour later she drew the hot pan out of the oven with a sense of satisfaction. The tantalizing aroma of fresh-baked brownies filled the small kitchen. Lying on the wood floor with his favorite squeaky toy, Oscar lifted his head to sniff.

"Forget it," Stacy told him with a smile. "Dogs and chocolate don't mix. But you'll get your own treat when I have mine."

She glanced out the kitchen window again. Jake, she noted,

hadn't moved since the last time she'd looked out. His head was tilted back now, and she wondered if he'd fallen asleep.

It was a perfect afternoon for outside dozing, still warm but with a nice breeze to keep the air comfortable. His chair was shaded from the afternoon sun by the large trees surrounding his cabin, so he was in little danger of sunburn. Judging from his tan, he spent quite a bit of time outdoors, which made her wonder again what he did for a living.

It was only as she stacked brownies neatly on a plate that she acknowledged she had intended all along to take some to him. Ever since they parted yesterday, she'd felt vaguely guilty about her brusqueness to him after he'd been so kind to free her from the log. The exertion had obviously been uncomfortable for him, and she should have been more grateful. It had been unfair of her to take her recent frustrations out on him when it was apparent that he had problems of his own.

Picking up the sling, she slipped it over her head and nestled her aching arm in it, grateful for the renewed support. Oscar perked up again when she picked up his leash. He hopped around at her feet until she bent to clip it to his collar. He loved his walks, loved being outside, even though it inevitably led to a thorough brushing of his long, silky hair afterward.

"We're going to stop for a visit next door," she said, slipping her good wrist through the loop in his leash to free her hand for the plate of brownies. "Be polite, you hear?"

He made a sound that resembled a snort, and tugged her toward the door. Wondering if she was letting her Southern manners lead her into a big mistake—which wouldn't be a first for her—Stacy followed.

JAKE WASN'T ASLEEP. He was watching a couple of squirrels playing tag. He'd been observing them long enough that he could tell them apart now, and he had named them Duke and Butch. He didn't have a clue if they were male or female, but they looked like Duke and Butch to him.

Duke was the bigger one. Faster, too. But Butch had stamina. Didn't have to stop and rest as often as Duke.

Jake wondered what would happen if they were pitted against each other in a long-distance race. Would Duke know to bide his time, save his superior speed for the end, when it really counted? Or would he start out too strong and use himself up, creating an opportunity for the patient and steady Butch to dash ahead and win?

And how pathetic had his life become that he was fantasizing about racing squirrels?

A sharp bark sent Duke and Butch scampering into the treetops. Jake recognized that bark by now. Stacy must be taking Oscar for another walk. And if she fell into a hole this time, she could just darned well stay there until Oscar figured out a way to free her, he thought with a grumpiness caused by his still stinging ego.

He hadn't forgotten the way she had implied that she would have been fine without his help, even though she had offered perfunctory thanks for his assistance. Just before she had made her escape as though she couldn't wait to get far away from him.

He really wasn't accustomed to being treated that way by attractive young women. He couldn't say he liked it, he thought, glumly rubbing his still unshaven face. Apparently, he had become rather spoiled during the past few years of fame and success. He was going to have to watch out for that. He'd never wanted to become one of those conceited jerks who believed all their own press.

Staying next door to Stacy, even for a few days, was probably a character-building experience, he thought wryly. The more she ignored and rebuffed him, the better a person he would become for it.

Which made it all the more startling when she spoke to him from the far side of the deck. "I hope I'm not disturbing you."

He rose to his feet, breaking into a smile, despite his earlier resolve not to be so friendly to her. Which was yet another sign of how hungry he was for companionship, he figured. "Not at all. I'm just being lazy."

Moving up the short flight of steps onto the deck, she extended a foil-covered plate. "I don't know if you like brownies, but I made a batch this afternoon. I wanted to offer you some as a thank-you for coming to my assistance yesterday."

Pleasantly surprised, he reached for the plate. "As it happens, I love brownies. That was very thoughtful of you."

She gazed up at him. She really was tiny, no more than five feet three, compared to his own six feet. And very feminine, with her delicate features and flawless skin and silky curls. The kind of woman who made a man feel more masculine in comparison. Rather protective. A line of thought she probably wouldn't appreciate from anyone, much less a complete stranger, he reminded himself.

"I didn't want you to think I was ungrateful for your help yesterday," she said with a smile that was almost apologetic. "I was so embarrassed about getting myself into that predicament that I'm not sure I expressed my gratitude very well."

He shrugged. "As you pointed out, you'd have managed on your own eventually."

A touch of color stained her smooth cheeks at the reminder of her less-than-gracious comment. "Anyway, thank you again."

"You're welcome." He had the distinct feeling that she was planning to leave now that she'd gotten the obligatory thank-you gift out of the way. And he would be left here to eat brownies alone, with only Duke and Butch for entertainment.

To detain her just a little longer, he asked, "Can I get you anything? How about some nice cold milk? We can eat brownies. Talk, maybe."

"Oh, I—"

"Just for a little while? Brownies are always better when shared." He smiled winningly and hefted the plate she'd brought him.

She almost smiled. Encouraged, he pressed his advantage. "Look at Oscar. He'd like to stay and visit."

They both looked down at the dog, who was scratching his ear with his back paw, looking more bored than anything.

Stacy hesitated a moment longer, then lifted one shoulder. "Maybe just for a few minutes."

Pleased, Jake motioned toward a chair. "Have a seat. I'll get us some milk."

She almost said something, then stopped herself and merely nodded, moving toward the chair he had indicated.

Maybe it was pride that made him try to minimize his limp as he headed inside. He was walking better with each passing day, he assured himself. Within the next couple of weeks, he hoped to be back in good enough shape that no one would notice anything at all out of the ordinary in his gait.

He caught a glimpse of his reflection in a decorative mirror when he entered the kitchen. The sight was enough to make him wince. He needed a haircut. Badly needed a shave. No wonder Stacy still seemed wary of him. He looked like someone a mother would warn her daughters about and a father would run off with a shotgun.

Since there wasn't time to shave now, he ran a hand through his dark hair to tidy it and then took two glasses out of a cabinet. Setting them on a serving tray, he poured the milk, careful not to overfill them. On an impulse, he took out a fried ground-beef patty left over from his dinner the night before, broke half of it off, and wrapped it in a napkin. After adding a few more napkins to the tray, he lifted it carefully and carried it out the door.

Stacy was sitting at the round patio table when he returned to her, with Oscar lying at her feet, quiet for a change. Jake set the tray on the table and took a seat opposite her. "I brought Oscar half of a hamburger patty left over from last night. Is it okay to give it to him?"

She smiled and nodded. "He'll enjoy that."

Okay, treats for her dog elicited real smiles from her. He would have to remember that. "Here you go, pup," he said, tossing the meat to the deck. "Eat up."

Feathery tail wagging, Oscar sniffed the meat, then happily began to gulp it down.

"Wow," Jake said after swallowing his first big bite of brownie. "These are really good."

"They're just a boxed mix."

"They're still good."

"I'm glad you like it." She finished the one small brownie square she had accepted and washed it down with a dainty sip of milk. At their feet, Oscar had finished his own snack and was busily sniffing the deck to make sure he hadn't missed any crumbs.

Making small talk, especially with attractive women, had never been difficult for Jake. He'd been told that he could always be counted on to keep a conversation moving. So what was it about Stacy that had him sitting here like a lump, chewing brownies and trying to come up with something halfway intelligent to say?

Deciding to fall back on the obvious, he nodded toward her sling. "How did you break your arm?"

Glancing downward, she shook her head. "It isn't broken. Just a sprain. I'll probably stop wearing the sling within a day or two."

"I was in a sling myself until last week. Tore up my shoulder." Among other things that he didn't want to go into right now.

She glanced at the healing scar at his temple. "You were in an accident?"

"Yeah. Six weeks ago. But I'm almost completely recovered." At least, that was what he hoped to convince his doctor in the next couple of weeks.

"I'm glad to hear that."

Abandoning the deck sniffing, Oscar approached Jake, standing on his hind legs to plant his front paws on Jake's thigh in a blatant request for an ear scratching.

"You gave him food," Stacy murmured. "You're his new best friend."

Obligingly patting the dog, Jake studied Stacy's faint smile. She had a nice mouth. Soft and curvy. Perfect white teeth. He'd bet a full smile from her would be dazzling.

Lifting his gaze to her eyes, he thought of how striking they were. Such a light, clear gray-blue, surrounded by long, dark lashes.

He would like to hear her laugh. He'd bet her whole face lit up when she laughed, and her cool blue eyes warmed. He wondered what had happened to make her so guarded. Or was she just naturally reserved? She didn't seem to be shy, exactly. But there was definitely an invisible wall around her.

"You have a nice place," he said, nodding toward her cabin.

"It belongs to my brother, actually. He comes here almost every weekend during the summer, and fairly often in fall and winter."

"I see."

A brief silence fell between them, and then Stacy made an attempt to keep the awkward conversation going. "Do you own this cabin?"

"No. It belongs to a friend of mine. He's letting me use it until I've recuperated enough to get back to work."

"What do you do?" she asked, lifting her glass to take another sip of milk.

So she really didn't recognize him. He hadn't been sure until now. Not entirely unusual—some people just didn't follow NASCAR. But because he was usually surrounded by friends and associates from within the sport, it had been a long time since he'd met anyone who had no clue who he was.

It was sort of refreshing, actually. Especially now, after his season had ended so heartbreakingly.

"I'm a driver," he said, leaving her to make of that what she would.

She nodded. "My best friend's husband drives a truck. Are you on the road all the time, like he is?"

He really should correct her misconstruction of what he did. But he found that he wasn't quite ready to deal with that. Instead, he answered honestly, "Yes. I travel a lot in my work."

"Do you enjoy it?"

"I love it," he answered simply. He lived for it, he could have added. Racing was in his heart, his blood, every breath he took. But maybe that would sound just a bit too dramatic, he thought wryly.

"What do *you* do?" he asked, instead.

"I'm a freelance editor for a small publishing company. Mostly nonfiction—biographies and history and a few self-help books."

"Now, that sounds interesting. Being freelance, I suppose you can set your own hours?"

"For the most part, though obviously I have to meet the publisher's deadlines."

"So you're taking a little vacation this week?"

She gave a small shrug. "Like you, I'm recuperating here, even though I brought some work with me."

"How did you hurt your arm?" he asked, hoping he wasn't getting too personal, considering how private a person she seemed to be.

She gazed down into her glass of milk. "I fell."

He got the distinct feeling that she was telling the truth—but not all of the truth. And because it was exactly what he'd done when she asked about his job, he frowned, wondering what her real story was.

Not that it was any of his business, of course, he reminded himself.

As he had earlier, she quickly changed the subject back to him, diverting attention away from herself. "You said you were in an accident. Was it on the job?"

"No, it was a boating accident," he said, knowing his expression had gone grim. "Some fool showing off for his friends barreled without any warning into the boat I was driving. It was like he came out of nowhere. I was in the hospital for a couple of weeks. But with the exercises I've been prescribed and a little more time, I've been assured I'll recover completely, except for a few scars."

And some very painful memories.

Her eyes were somber on his face. "Were you the only one in your boat?"

He spoke a bit gruffly, finding the words difficult to say, "No. A friend was with me. He was killed in the impact."

She looked dismayed. "I'm so sorry."

"Thanks. Do you want another brownie?"

"No." Setting her half-empty glass aside, she reached for Oscar's leash. "I'd better get back to work," she said, her expression still somber. "I have another couple of chapters I want to edit today."

He nodded, relieved that she had let the subject of his accident drop. Maybe she had sensed that he didn't really want to talk about it now. "Thanks again for the brownies. I'll enjoy the rest of them while I'm here."

"You're welcome." Clutching the leash in her good hand, she turned toward the steps.

"Stacy?" he said impulsively.

She paused and looked over her shoulder. "Yes?"

Now that he'd stopped her, he wasn't sure exactly what he'd wanted to say. "Um, since your brother owns the cabin, I assume you've spent some time in these parts?"

She nodded. "I've been here many times."

"Any recommendations for something a bored out-of-state visitor can do? I'm getting a pretty severe case of cabin fever."

"There's a lot to do around here. The obvious, of course, fishing. And hiking. And if you drive into Mountain View, about a half hour from here, there's the Ozark Folk Center and Blanchard Springs Caverns and lots of quaint little shops and music shows."

"All of that sounds great. Maybe you'd like to show me around one afternoon? If you don't have anything better to do, that is."

"Oh, I—"

He held up one hand to stop her, giving her an out before she had to come up with one. "I understand if you're too busy with your work. You probably came here to get away from interruptions."

"I did," she agreed with a slight nod. "I've fallen a little behind."

"No problem," he assured her. "I can get around on my own."

She started to take another step toward the edge of the deck. And then he heard her sigh lightly. She turned back around, her face oddly rueful now. "I can probably take off a couple of hours tomorrow afternoon. If that's—"

"That would be great," he cut in with a big smile. "It will be nice to have the company. And Oscar's welcome to come, of course."

"After lunch, then? Say, one o'clock?"

"One o'clock," he repeated. "I'll be looking forward to it. And I promise to be on my very best behavior, so you won't regret spending time with a perfect stranger."

She smiled suddenly, and the way it transformed her face almost made him gulp. The change was even more dramatic— and more appealing—than he had imagined. "Are you saying you're perfect, Jake?"

"Not even close," he admitted, shaking his head with a chuckle. "But for tomorrow, I'll make an effort."

"Should be interesting," she remarked, and finally left the deck, heading toward her brother's cabin without looking back. Oscar bounded along at her feet.

"Should definitely be interesting," he murmured, watching her go.

LATER THAT EVENING, Stacy sat in the living room of her brother's cabin, a manuscript on her lap, and a cup of hot tea on the table by her side. She wasn't paying much attention to either. Her gaze was focused on a side window, through which she could just see the lights from the cabin next door. Even after several hours had passed, she was still finding it hard to believe she had agreed to go sightseeing with Jake tomorrow afternoon.

There were so many reasons she should have declined. The fact that he was pretty much a stranger to her—a "perfect stranger," as he had asserted—was primary among those reasons. She wasn't usually so trusting.

She wasn't comfortable making conversation with people she didn't know. She supposed that was a throwback to her youth, when she had always worried about how much new acquaintances knew about her family. Specifically, the scandal that had rocked her family when she was twelve.

Her most recent brush with notoriety was even more incentive for her to keep to herself this week. Maybe Jake—it occurred to her only then that she didn't know his last name—had missed the news coverage of her recent misadventure, but that didn't mean she wouldn't be recognized by someone else while they were out. And that would be awkward, to say the least.

So many reasons she should have said no. And only one why she'd said yes. It had been the bleak look in his eyes when he had told her about the accident in which he'd been injured and a friend had been killed.

He hadn't embellished the explanation, had kept his voice steady and his expression unrevealing. But she had seen the suffering in his eyes and it had reminded her of the way he had looked sitting on his deck earlier. Sad. And alone. And before she could muzzle it, her too soft heart had made her blurt out an offer to be his tour guide the next afternoon.

She shook her head in self-reprimand. When was she going to learn to stop getting involved with other people's problems?

Maybe she should consider therapy. At the very least, she should work harder at remaining detached. After all, she had come here this week to get away from other people and their requests—and darned if she hadn't already met someone who appealed to that exasperatingly tenderhearted side of her!

She doubted that Jake would appreciate being seen as the object of her pity. She'd gotten the impression that he was accustomed to taking care of himself, for the most part, despite his quip about needing a whole crew to keep him out of trouble.

After all, he had come here alone to recuperate. She doubted that a guy who looked like he did, with a smile like his, would be alone in a vacation cabin unless he wanted to be.

Apparently, he was beginning to rethink that decision. He'd looked forlorn when she had spotted him earlier, and he had invited her to have a brownie with him with almost humorous eagerness, even though she hadn't been particularly encouraging to him.

Even his suggestion that they should spend some time together sightseeing tomorrow had seemed to be motivated more by loneliness and boredom than flirtation. As if he'd have been just as likely to befriend her brother, had he been the one staying next door this week.

Instead of feeling slighted by that possibility, Stacy found it rather a relief. She had enough feminine ego to secretly hope a good-looking man like Jake found her at least somewhat attractive, but she was in no mood for a vacation flirtation. She had far too much to worry about right now without adding that complication. Even making a new friend was awkward enough, since it would eventually lead to a conversation she just didn't want to have.

But Jake had only asked her to show him around the area for an afternoon, she reminded herself. Just a few hours of pleasant companionship. A harmless diversion. It would probably be good for both of them to spend some time with another person, distracted from dwelling on the circumstances that had brought them into seclusion in the first place.

So she would go. She would be friendly and affable without encouraging anything more. He would go back to wherever he came from impressed with Arkansas hospitality, and she would have a nice afternoon to remember from her enforced vacation.

"A win-win situation," she murmured aloud to reassure herself.

Asleep on the couch beside her, Oscar snorted softly.

CHAPTER THREE

JAKE WOULDN'T HAVE BEEN particularly surprised if Stacy changed her mind about accompanying him Tuesday afternoon. She had definitely been skittish about accepting his spontaneous invitation, and he still wasn't sure what had made her change her mind. Not that he was complaining. Looking forward to the outing with Stacy had given him a reason to get out of bed this morning.

He was pleased when she came out of her house to meet him promptly at one o'clock. She looked especially nice in a pretty pink top with jeans and wedge sandals that revealed pink toenail polish. Her brown hair fell in soft curls to just brush her slender shoulders.

Once again, it occurred to him that the word *feminine* seemed to suit her perfectly.

"You look nice," he said, keeping his tone offhand since he didn't want her to think he was making advances.

"Thank you."

"Where's Oscar?"

"He's staying at home today. Since I thought you might like to go into some of the local shops and attractions, it's better if Oscar isn't with us. Don't worry," she added, "he'll be fine. There's a small fenced enclosure on the other side of my brother's cabin and a little doggie door Oscar can use to go in and out when he needs to. My brother built it for his own two dachshunds, and Oscar is very comfortable with it."

"Oscar doesn't mind being alone?"

"Not for a few hours. He has food, water and his favorite toys, and I leave a television on for noise. He seems to like country music videos."

Jake laughed. "Not what I would have expected from a prissy little Yorkie."

Stacy raised an eyebrow, and for a moment, Jake wondered if he'd offended her. But then she smiled and murmured, "I guess that teaches you about judging on appearances."

He chuckled. "I guess it does. Not wearing the sling today?"

She had been subconsciously holding her left arm bent in front of her. At his question, she slowly straightened it. "No. I didn't think I really needed it."

He wondered if the sling had made her self-conscious. "You're sure? Bad sprains are nothing to take lightly. I've had a few myself."

"A few? You seem to be the accident-prone type."

He had to laugh at that. "I've had my share."

She studied him curiously, but said merely, "I'll be fine without the sling, as long as I don't overuse the arm. It's time for me to stop wearing it anyway."

"So I guess we're ready to go, then."

Her nod looked a little less than certain.

JAKE HAD RENTED a car when he'd arrived in Arkansas. They strapped in and then he backed down the driveway. "Which way?"

She pointed, and he turned obligingly. "Where are we going?" he asked, not that he really cared as long as he was getting out of that cabin for a few hours.

"We have a couple of options, actually." She dug in the olive-green canvas bag she'd carried as a purse and pulled out a folded sheet of paper. "I wanted to make sure I didn't forget any of the local attractions, so I went online this morning."

He was amused at how seriously she'd seemed to take his request to show him around the area. He hadn't meant the suggestion quite so literally, but he was game for sightseeing. "What are our choices?"

"One of the bigger draws to this area is the caverns. Blanchard Springs Caverns. I've been through them several times, and they're quite impressive. There are guided tours on a regular basis throughout the day, anything from a fairly easy walking trail to a tougher trek through the wild part of the cave."

"As intriguing as that sounds, I'm not sure I'm up to climbing through a cave just yet," he admitted rather reluctantly. He'd gone for a short hike in the woods earlier that morning, and had been dismayed by how difficult it had been. He still had a way to go to rebuild his former stamina—which meant that he would work even harder with the free weights and other workout equipment that had been provided for him in the cabin.

Stacy nodded. "No problem. There are several other choices. The Ozark Folk Center is pretty interesting. Lots of demonstrations of old-time crafts and blacksmithing and herbal gardening. Or there's the town of Mountain View itself. Have you driven around this area at all?"

"No. I came straight from the airport, following my friend's directions. I didn't really see anything of the local area."

"The town is a popular destination in itself. Full of crafts and antique shops and music stores. There's a courthouse square where people gather from all over the area just to play instruments and sing. Old bluegrass and country and gospel songs mostly. And there's a museum of local history—or if you're interested in racing, we can drive to Batesville, which isn't very far from here. My nephew likes to visit the NASCAR museum there. It's located in a car dealership owned by a NASCAR driver who grew up in this area. I've never been, but my nephew loves it."

Jake had to make a deliberate effort to loosen his grip on the steering wheel. "You're not a NASCAR fan?" he asked lightly.

"I'm afraid the extent of my sports viewing is limited to watching Olympics coverage every couple of years. But if you'd like to see the museum, I'm certainly open to expanding my knowledge."

He supposed he should tell her exactly what he did for a living. That he not only knew who had started that particular museum, but he was actually on a friendly basis with the guy, one of his early NASCAR heroes.

For one thing, there was always the chance that he would be recognized by someone else while they were out, though he had done what he could to change his usual look. His hair was longer than he usually wore it. He was still bearded, though he'd done his best to neaten the look that morning. And he wore a plain green polo shirt with his jeans, rather than the customary team or sponsor shirts he was usually seen in. He'd brought along black-plastic-rimmed sunglasses, rather than the branded aviators he typically wore, and a hat that bore the logo of his favorite football team instead of his race team.

Combined with the lack of publicity about him being in the vicinity, he hoped his pseudo-disguise would prevent him from attracting attention from the locals. It was possible that he could get through the day in total anonymity. Which didn't give him an excuse to lie to Stacy, even through omission. And yet it was such a novel experience to spend a day with someone who didn't know him as a notable NASCAR driver that he found himself wanting to delay the revelation for just a little longer.

"I think I'd like to walk around Mountain View, if that's okay with you," he said. "Just to get a feel for the area and the people here."

She nodded in approval of his choice. "I think you'll find it interesting. Turn right at the next intersection."

Still feeling vaguely guilty that he'd let a perfect opportunity for confession slip by, he followed her instructions.

ALREADY A FEW CLUSTERS of musicians had gathered around the courthouse and in front of some of the shops in the square, though there would be quite a few more later that day, after working hours. In groups of three or four, they sat in chairs they'd brought themselves, jamming with guitars, banjos, fiddles, dulcimers, mandolins, autoharps, bass fiddles—pretty much anything portable and playable.

Some sang along with the old songs and hymns, but mostly they just played, no sheet music in sight, no one asking for money or expecting applause. They were there simply for the joy of making music together.

Though business wasn't as brisk as it was on weekends or during summer-vacation times, there were a few tourists in town on this beautiful fall afternoon. Most were older couples without children, since it was a school day. They were already gathering in their own chairs to listen to the music, moving from one spot to another to better sample the range of free entertainment. Several enjoyed ice cream cones or lemonades purchased from a stand tucked into an easily accessible corner of the square.

"It's like stepping back in time," Jake murmured, looking around in appreciation.

"Well, almost," Stacy responded wryly as an enormous SUV with intrusively modern music booming through the windows cruised through the square. The musicians ignored the distraction, though some of the tourists frowned and muttered disapproval of the discourtesy.

Jake paused in front of a large store specializing in hand-forged ironworks. His attention focused on an intricately designed bench, he said, "This place looks interesting."

"I love this shop," she confessed. "There's an amazing wrought-iron sleigh bed here that I would buy in a minute, if I could afford it. And if my apartment was big enough to hold it. My brother has some of their tables in his cabin. I've bought a few candleholders and other decorative items."

"Mind if we go in?"

"No, of course not."

She was intrigued to see that Jake seemed genuinely interested in the iron furniture. Bypassing the knickknacks and candleholders, he went straight to the big things—glass-topped tables, an iron-and-glass wet bar. A display of cushioned iron benches similar to the one he had seen outside held his interest for a while, until he was drawn to a tall baker's rack with an intricate pattern of leaves and acorns worked into the back.

Apparently realizing that his interest in the merchandise amused her, he gave her a lopsided grin. "I'm slowly furnishing my house back in North Carolina," he said. "I get easily distracted by furniture and stuff these days."

"Did you just buy your house?"

"I had it built, starting two years ago. Finished it last winter. Most of the rooms are still empty, because I haven't had time to concentrate on it lately. My friends tell me I should hire someone to take care of that stuff, and I may, eventually, but I sort of like being involved in choosing things."

Several points in that explanation left her even more confused by Jake than she had been before. She assumed he was close to her own age of twenty-eight—around thirty, give or take a couple of years. Most of the single guys she knew of that age in Little Rock lived in apartments.

One of her friends had bought a modest home for the investment value, and had then let his mother and girlfriend decorate it. His only contribution to the decor had been a large-screen TV, a massaging recliner with built-in speakers and cup holders, and a state-of-the-art gaming system. She couldn't imagine him showing any interest in wrought-iron baker's racks.

Something else that had caught her attention about Jake's comments was his casual mention of "most of the rooms." Just how big was his new home? Either he had come into a tidy inheritance, or he made a darned good salary as a truck driver. He hadn't blinked an eye at the rather steep prices marked on the items he'd seemed to like most.

Reminding herself that his finances were absolutely none of her business, she asked instead, "Do these wrought-iron pieces fit in with your decorating plan?"

He laughed at that. "You make it sound as if I *have* a decorating plan. I don't know one style from another. Have no idea what the current trends are. I just know what I like. And I really like these benches," he added, nodding toward the display that kept drawing him back. "I can see one of those at the foot of my bed, where I could sit to put on my shoes."

"I'm sure they'll ship one of the benches to North Carolina."

He nodded. "I'll consider that while I'm in the area."

"How long are you planning to stay?" she asked, moving into the next display area.

Following, he shrugged. "A week. Maybe two. Depends on when I'm ready to get back to work. How about you?"

"Nick—my brother—said I could stay as long as I want. And since I can work anywhere, I thought I'd stay until I get bored. Maybe another week." She hoped that would be enough time for the unwelcome attention to die down, letting her return home in relative anonymity.

He paused. "This is the one, isn't it? The bed you've been admiring."

Because there were several sleigh beds in the large showroom, in addition to four-poster, canopy-style and other types of frames and headboards, it surprised her that he had chosen exactly the one she had lusted after. "Yes, that's it. How did you know?"

"It just looks like you, I guess."

She wouldn't have thought he'd gotten a strong enough impression of her yet to make that kind of connection.

"It's a great bed. I can see why you like it so much."

It occurred to her suddenly that they were both standing there picturing her in that bed. Clearing her throat, she turned away. "Yes, well, it's about the size of the entire bedroom in my apartment, so I guess I'll have to pass for a while longer. Did you see these fireplace tools? They're great, aren't they?"

"Yeah. Great." But he looked over his shoulder again at the bed as they moved away.

IT WAS a charming little town, full of intriguing shops, friendly people and music. Music on every corner. Jake could almost feel the tension easing from his shoulders as he and Stacy made their way slowly around the square.

They went into every shop, and while some of the merchandise was too hokey-touristy for his taste, he spotted several more upscale items that would look right at home in his spacious, but ultimately comfortable house on Lake Norman. The iron bench. A set of iron fireplace tools and a matching screen. A walnut sideboard and an old trunk he found in an antique store. Hand-turned cherry salad bowls in a crafts guild shop.

Deciding he would come back to town another time to purchase and arrange shipping, he made a mental note of the items he wanted. He didn't want to buy then for several reasons. He wasn't really an impulse shopper, so waiting a couple of days would give him a chance to decide if he really wanted those things.

Making shipping arrangements would involve giving his name and address to the salesclerks, who might realize who he was. And he didn't want to risk looking as if he were flaunting his wealth in front of Stacy, who had candidly admitted that she couldn't afford the bed she coveted.

And speaking of Stacy...

He smiled as he studied her rapt attention to a display of fragrant soy candles in pretty glass jars. The town was working its magic on her, too. She had relaxed considerably during the past couple of hours, smiling more often, talking more easily, even laughing a couple of times at his lame attempts at jokes. As he had predicted, her laughter was musical. Infectious. Very appealing.

On a whimsical impulse, he stopped at a row of machines that dispensed bubble gum and cheap toys for quarters. Plugging two quarters into one of the machines, he grinned in surprise when his "prize" turned out to be a plastic race car. A purple plastic race car, to be precise.

Had to be fate, he figured, turning to offer the car to Stacy. "For you," he said. "A souvenir."

Smiling a bit quizzically, she took the car and slipped it in her pocket. "Thank you. I'll remember you every time I look at it."

He laughed. "Yeah, I figure you will."

He changed the subject before she could ask what he meant by that.

They found a restored 1900-era soda fountain tucked into a pharmacy a block west of the square, and of course Jake couldn't let that opportunity slip by. He and Stacy found two stools side by side at the polished marble counter. They faced a bevel-edged mirror with leaded-glass cabinets on either side and three stained-glass pendant lights in front. He studied a menu that advertised "milk shakes, malts, ice cream sodas, banana splits, sundaes and phosphates."

"What sounds good to you?" he asked Stacy.

She wrinkled her nose in a wry expression. "Are you kidding? It's ice cream. It all sounds good."

It took him a moment to remember what they'd been talking about. Dragging his gaze away from her smile, he forced his attention back to the menu. "I'm thinking about trying that banana split."

"I'll have a milk shake," she murmured. "Now I just have to choose a flavor. Chocolate? Strawberry? Or pineapple?"

By the time the green-aproned teenager behind the counter approached them for their orders, Stacy had made up her mind. She requested a strawberry shake. Jake ordered a banana split and a fountain cola. He would work off the calories later, he figured. This was the first afternoon of indulgence he had enjoyed since his accident. He was going to make the most of it.

"Here y'all go," the perky young woman chirped as she set their treats in front of them. She was, perhaps, eighteen or nineteen, barely out of high school, Stacy judged. "You need anything else?"

"No, we're fine, thanks," Jake assured her.

The girl looked at him for a moment, and he felt the muscles in the back of his neck go tense. "You look kind of familiar," she said. "Have you been in here before?"

"No, this is my first time."

Still frowning a little, she looked at Stacy. "Actually, you look familiar, too."

"I've been here several times before," Stacy replied easily. "This is a favorite vacation area for my family."

"I guess that's it," the girl murmured. And then, to Jake's relief, she was summoned by another customer, becoming too busy with work to dwell on why Jake's appearance rang a mental bell for her.

He looked down at his generously sized banana split—three large scoops of ice cream flanked by slices of banana, covered with chocolate, strawberries and pineapple and topped with whipped cream, nuts and three maraschino cherries. "I think she's given me enough for two people here."

Stacy studied her own supersized milk shake with whipped cream and a cherry towering precariously above the soda-fountain glass. "Tell me about it."

He picked up his spoon. "Looks like we have our work cut out for us. Dive in."

Chuckling, she took a first sip of her shake, murmuring her appreciation of the taste. Something about that little purr made him gulp his first bite of banana split, almost choking on a chunk of strawberry. He reached quickly for his cola, telling himself to pay attention to his dessert and try not to focus so much on his attractive companion.

AFTER VISITING the old grist mill and a music shop filled with handcrafted and vintage instruments—none of which either of them played—they returned to the car. Stacy noticed that Jake's limp had become more pronounced after so much walking, but she didn't comment. She figured he was ready to go back to the cabin and rest.

Climbing behind the steering wheel, he set down the box of pecan fudge he'd been unable to resist buying at a candy store. "You're sure you don't want a piece of this fudge?"

She groaned and rested a hand on her tummy. "After that enormous milk shake, I don't think I'll be hungry again for the rest of the day."

"Can't say I'm hungry right now, either. But that fudge just smelled too good to resist. I'll enjoy it for a snack tomorrow."

She snapped her seat belt and settled comfortably into her seat. "I've had a very nice time this afternoon."

"It's not quite over yet," he reminded her. "We're still going to visit that dulcimer shop and the old general store you told me about, aren't we? Unless you're getting tired?"

"No, I'm not tired." She had thought he'd forgotten about those two places. Was he really so reluctant to go back to his cabin? He must have badly needed a diversion from his unhappy memories. "Turn left at the next intersection."

Jake seemed as intrigued by the dulcimer store as he had been by the other places they had visited. He examined every item in the place—mostly handcrafted dulcimers, of course, but also some other craft items—and then he watched a skilled craftsman actually making a dulcimer. He asked questions, complimented the workmanship, even played a few notes himself with friendly assistance from the store owner.

How was an obviously straight man like Jake still single? She smiled to herself as she watched him chatting with the older man. Good-looking, charming, personable—and he even liked shopping. For furniture, no less.

"Stacy, try this," he encouraged her, turning to her with a smile. "It's called a *kalimba*. It's really easy to play."

She looked obligingly at the instrument he was holding. Mounted on an oval cedar board about six-and-a-half inches long, eight thin strips of metal, one for each note in the octave, resonated when plucked with the thumbs. Much like the mechanism of a music box, she realized, listening as he followed a numbered music sheet to pluck out a slow version of "Twinkle, Twinkle, Little Star."

She clapped politely when he finished. "Bravo."

His grin was just a little sheepish, but he turned toward the cash register. "I think I'll buy it. It's the only instrument I've seen this afternoon that I might have a chance of learning how to play."

She had to laugh. She didn't bother to tell him that she'd been tempted on several occasions to buy an instrument—any instrument—after a trip to this area. There was just something so appealing about watching the musicians gather in the square, old friends and newcomers alike welcomed into the impromptu sessions.

She knew the local music traditions dated back to a much simpler time when people had gathered for music and dancing as their primary form of socializing. Lacking television and computers and video games, they had entertained themselves with the old tunes, passing the skills down to their children.

So many things in the area evoked those old days, including the two-story, white-framed general store to which she directed Jake next. Antique wagons and vehicles sat outside, along with an old gas pump and several vintage tin signs. Benches, rockers and pickle barrels lined the full-length, gingerbread-trimmed wooden porch.

Walking into the store was like stepping into the early part of the previous century. Bottled colas arranged in hinged-top chests, brightly colored candy sticks presented in big glass jars. Moon pies and country-cured hams were displayed for sale along with a dizzying selection of merchandise. Reproductions of antique toys were popular items, along with tins, cookbooks, candles, jellies and honey, gifts and—true to the surroundings—vintage instruments.

Antiques and flea market items were for sale in the back of

the store, and logo-bearing collectibles were displayed everywhere. The green-and-yellow trademark of a famous tractor
maker and distinctive red-and-white designs advertising a brand
of cola appeared on plaques, plates, aprons, clocks, tea towels,
tote bags and too many other items for her to identify at a quick
glance.

His face alight with a grin, Jake looked up from a barrel filled
with colorful marbles for sale by the scoopful. "You were right,"
he told her. "This is a cool store. Takes me back to when I was
a kid in rural North Carolina. There were still a couple of places
like this back in the hills then, though I'm sure most of them are
long gone."

Rural North Carolina. It was the first mention he had made of
his childhood. "I thought you would like this place. Everyone
does."

"If I weren't still full from that banana split, I'd be into the
candy display," he admitted. "I haven't seen some of those
flavors in years."

He certainly had a sweet tooth, she thought, glancing at his
slim waist. It was a wonder he stayed in such good shape. "Is
there any food you don't like?"

He had a jar of blackberry jam in his hand and had that look
in his eyes that told her it would probably be going back to the
cabin with him, along with his fudge and his *kalimba*. "Actually,
I hate curry," he said absentmindedly. "And English peas. And I
have to be careful with onions, because eating too many triggers
headaches."

"You suffer from migraines?"

He shrugged, set the blackberry jam back on the shelf and
picked up a jar of peach preserves. "Yeah, sometimes. I've got
a few allergies that cause them, though not very often."

She watched as he exchanged the preserves for the jam again, apparently making a decision. "I have migraines sometimes myself. Mine seem to be more weather and stress related."

He looked at her and smiled. "See? Something else we have in common."

"Ice cream and migraines. Obviously, we were separated at birth."

That made him laugh, and the sound warmed her. As hard as she had tried not to, she was starting to like Jake very much.

Maybe she should find out his last name soon, she thought in bemusement. She was learning so many other trivial facts about him that it seemed odd she didn't even know his full name. She tried to remember if he had ever mentioned it. Maybe he had introduced himself by his complete name and she simply hadn't bothered to remember since she hadn't expected to spend any time with him. But, no—she distinctly recalled him saying only his first name. Just as she had given only her first name in return.

"We haven't seen the stuff in that corner," she said, nodding toward the back of the store. From where she stood, she could see that the merchandise there seemed to focus on NASCAR. Even she, who knew almost nothing about the sport, recognized the black-and-white-checkered pattern, and the prominent display of the car number of a late, beloved racing icon.

It looked as though there were some die-cast cars and other memorabilia for sale, but apparently Jake wasn't interested in racing knickknacks. He took one look in that direction, then turned toward the cash register with his jar of blackberry jam. "I think I'm ready to check out. Would you like a soda or anything?"

"No, I'm fine, thank you."

While Jake paid for his purchase, she examined a revolving rack of postcards close to the door. She heard him chatting congenially with the garrulous man behind the register, and she marveled at how easy it was for Jake to make casual conversation with strangers. She was terrible at small talk, her mind going frustratingly blank when it was her turn to speak. Her usual pattern was simply to smile and nod a lot.

"You know," the other man said to Jake as he bagged the jam, "you look kind of familiar to me. Have you been in before?"

"Nope," Jake responded lightly as he handed over cash to pay for his purchase. "First time. Probably won't be my last, though. I might have to come back for some of that hot sauce over there."

"It's good stuff. You should try it," the shopkeeper urged, easily diverted.

"I'll do that. You have a good evening, now." Tipping his baseball cap, Jake carried his purchase toward Stacy, who opened the door as he approached.

"Do you hear that a lot?" she asked as they belted themselves into the car.

He turned the key to start the engine. "What's that?"

"Two or three times today someone has commented that you look familiar."

"Oh, that." He shrugged as he drove out of the parking lot. "Yeah, I get that sometimes. Guess I have one of those faces."

"One of those faces," to her, meant average. Generic. She wouldn't have put Jake in that category at all, she mused, studying his profile. Even beneath his short, dark beard, his strong bone structure was evident, as were the dimples that flashed with his bright smiles. The dark glasses he wore now hid his eyes, but they were definitely memorable. Dark, gleaming, just slightly devilish when he grinned.

It was a face that any camera would love, she decided—and she could almost picture him smiling up at her from a glossy magazine page. Actually, the image was so clear that she frowned. Was it possible…?

"So, what do people do around here in the evenings?" he asked, changing the subject.

"There are several good restaurants. At least half a dozen musical shows in various venues. A drive-in theater. Or, of course, the music on the square. People sit around until all hours sipping sodas or lemonade or hot drinks, gossiping and listening to the musicians. Sometimes they join in and sing the old songs."

"That sounds relaxing."

"It is. My brother and I both enjoy it. My fourteen-year-old nephew, of course, is bored out of his mind. He brings his MP3 player and a handheld video game system."

Jake chuckled. "I guess most fourteen-year-old boys aren't into listening to bluegrass under the stars."

Not many thirty-year-old men were into such passive activities, either, she mused. But Jake seemed different from so many of the men her age she knew. She was still having trouble picturing him as a truck driver. She supposed she was guilty of stereotyping, but he was just…well, different.

"I suppose you need to get back to Oscar," he said, just a hint of reluctance in his tone.

"Yes, I should. He's been alone for several hours now."

"Poor pup's probably getting lonely."

"I'm sure he is."

"You said there's a drive-in theater in town?"

"Yes. One of the few remaining in the country, I believe. The films begin whenever it gets dark through the summertime, until the nights get too chilly. Another week or two—into early October, I think."

"I haven't been to a drive-in movie since I was a little kid, still in pajamas with feet in them. Maybe you'd like to check it out with me one evening? Oscar can come, too."

She bit her lower lip, trying to decide how to answer. She hadn't expected him to try to prolong their time together. Was he having that much fun with her? Or was he that reluctant to be alone again?

"Actually, Oscar doesn't do well at the drive-in," she said finally. "People in surrounding cars don't appreciate him barking at everyone who walks by."

"Then maybe he could stay home again for a few hours one evening this week? Maybe Thursday?"

"I'm sure he'd be okay for a few hours Thursday evening."

"Is that a yes?"

"Sure. Why not?"

Jake flashed her a grin that made her glad she'd made an effort—and then made her wonder if she was making a mistake to spend so much time with him. Just the way she reacted to that gleaming smile, with a little thrill of excitement and a rush of warmth to her cheeks, was enough to make her question her decision to accept his invitation.

CHAPTER FOUR

STACY HAD JUST COME IN from a long, brisk walk with Oscar early that evening when her cell phone rang. For a moment, she thought it might be Jake, and her pulse jumped a little. They had exchanged cell numbers when they'd separated, just in case anything came up. And then she chided herself for being an idiot. She'd only parted from the guy two hours ago, for heaven's sake.

Noting her best friend's number on the caller ID, she opened the phone. "Hi, Mindy."

"Tired of your lonesome hidey-hole yet?"

"Not just yet, no."

"Really? I'd be going crazy there all by myself with nothing to do but work."

"I'm not all by myself."

"The dog doesn't count."

"Don't tell Oscar that. He would be highly insulted."

"People, Stace. You need to see people."

"I have nothing against people—in general. It's reporters I don't want to see."

"You can't blame them for being intrigued by your story. The guy was a foot taller than you, outweighed you by seventy-five pounds and had a gun to your head. And you still managed to disarm him and kick his knee so hard he's still walking on crutches. People find that interesting."

"Okay. Maybe," Stacy conceded reluctantly. "I could understand the initial news reports, even a couple of feature items afterward. But it just kept going. Everywhere I went, it was all anyone wanted to talk about. The local reporters kept begging me to go on the morning shows and reenact the whole ordeal."

She shuddered at the idea.

"This morning one of the local shows had a couple of Junior Leaguers demonstrate how to make place-card holders out of apples. I mean, seriously, does anyone really use place cards anymore? And how hard is it to cut a slice in an apple and stick in a card? We gotta have step-by-step instructions?"

Sensing that her friend was about to go off on one of her infamous diatribes, Stacy murmured, "Uh, Mindy—"

"Right. My point is, local morning shows are notoriously desperate for anything to fill airtime for a couple of hours every day—as are the national morning shows, for that matter. I know you got called by a couple of them, too. You were just the latest feature fodder. Just keep turning them down, and they'll move on soon enough."

"That's my plan. I figured if I lie low here for a few more days, they'll forget all about me."

"Better stay a bit longer, then. Alvetti's being arraigned Tuesday, and that's likely to get it started all over again."

Stacy groaned. "Just what I need."

"So, do you at least have someone to talk to there? Any nice neighbors on vacation?"

Hesitating, Stacy tried to decide how completely to answer that question. "Actually, there is a nice man staying in the cabin next door," she said finally.

"A nice man?" Mindy jumped on that description like a duck on a June bug, as Stacy's grandmother would have said. "Single guy?"

"Yes." At least, she assumed Jake was single. She hadn't actually asked, but he wouldn't be here recuperating alone if he had someone in his life, would he?

"How old is he? Is he good-looking?"

"He's around our age, and yes, he's nice looking." Which, of course, was a major understatement, but if she were to tell Mindy exactly how attractive Jake was, her overreactive friend might read too much into the description.

"And he's there by himself?"

"Coincidentally, he was in an accident recently and he came here to rest and recuperate until he can get back to work."

"What does he do?"

"He's a truck driver."

"Like my Paul," Mindy exclaimed. "I wonder if they know each other."

"I doubt it. He's from North Carolina. The cabin belongs to a friend of his who usually rents it out to vacationers and fishermen."

"Sounds like you've talked to him a bit."

"Some. We drove into Mountain View for a couple of hours today. He's never been to this area before, so I showed him around the square."

"Really." There was a great deal of speculation in the one word.

"And we, um, sort of have a date Thursday night. Well, not a date, actually—we're going to the drive-in. Just for something to do."

"Stacy. That's a date." Mindy sounded as though she was trying not to laugh.

"Well, technically. Maybe. What I meant was, it isn't a romantic thing. We're just being friendly. Neighborly. He's going back to North Carolina in a week or so, and I'll be coming back to Little Rock, so it's not like there's a future in it."

"Oh, I don't know. Truck drivers can settle anywhere, you know. Plenty of work around here for them. For that matter, free-lance editors can work anywhere, though I'd have to protest loudly if he tried to take my best friend too far away."

Stacy sighed loudly. "Put away the bags of rice, will you, Min? Jeez, I just met the guy."

"Well, yeah, but you never know. Something could develop."

Mindy had been trying to fix Stacy up for the past three years, ever since Mindy had married Paul. But this was going too far—planning a long-term relationship between Stacy and a man she'd met only two days before. A man Mindy hadn't even met herself. For all she knew, he could be a creep with a capital *C!* Of course, Mindy trusted Stacy to know a creep when she met one, but still…

"We're just killing time together until we can get back to our regular lives, okay?" she said flatly. "For all I know, he could leave tomorrow, and I'd hardly even notice. So don't get all excited. And please don't mention him to anyone—especially Nick, if you should run into him. Nick's been overprotective ever since the incident at the courthouse."

"Can you blame him? I've been feeling the same way. Every time I think about how easily we could have lost you that afternoon…" Mindy's shudder carried clearly through the phone lines.

"I love you, too," Stacy said with a smile.

"Yeah, yeah. You're just trying to distract me from asking more about Mr. Next Door."

"Okay, you caught me."

"Fine. You don't want to talk about him. I get it. So, have a good time with him. And be careful—just in case he's not as nice as he seems. But look who I'm talking to," she added with a laugh. "He gets out of line, you'll just kneecap him."

"Don't you start," Stacy warned.

"I won't. Call me later in the week, okay? I'm going to want details."

"I will," Stacy promised before disconnecting. Not that she expected there would be any details to pass along, she mused, moving to fill Oscar's food bowl. As she had assured Mindy, she and Jake were simply going to see a movie as a way to kill a couple of hours. Nothing in the least romantic was implied.

Which didn't at all explain why she'd been unable to resist telling her best friend about her impending date with the good-looking guy next door, a tiny, unnerving voice inside her pointed out.

STACY DIDN'T KNOW if she would see Jake Wednesday, but he hailed her as soon as she went outside for a walk with Oscar that afternoon. Jake was already on the hiking path that led into the woods, just about to start climbing the hill as she approached.

"Hi," he said.

"Hi, yourself. How's your leg feeling today? You didn't overdo it yesterday, I hope."

Smiling, he shook his head. "I was pretty tired last night," he admitted, "but I took a couple of ibuprofen and crashed in front of the TV, and this morning it felt a lot better. I thought a hike would be nice today. Weather's perfect, isn't it?"

"Yes, it's very nice," she said. "I'm glad it's not too warm."

"Would you like to join me for a walk?"

"Oscar and I would be pleased to join you."

Jake's smile deepened, and she gruffly, silently ordered her racing pulse to behave itself.

Oscar, for whom half a hamburger patty had forged a lifelong friendship, was delighted to have Jake along for their walk. He bounced at Jake's feet until Jake obliged by reaching down to scratch his ears, and then the dog was off, straining at the end of his leash to investigate every interesting sight, sound and smell.

Stacy and Jake followed at a more leisurely pace, watching him indulgently. They talked about Oscar for a few minutes, Stacy telling Jake how she'd come to own the Yorkie, and sharing a few amusing stories about his puppy antics.

Laughing, Jake was reminded of a dog a friend had once owned, a mutt named Doofus, who, Jake insisted, had been the dumbest dog that ever walked the planet. He backed up that claim with several stories that had Stacy laughing until tears filled her eyes.

"I think you're right," she agreed after several of those anecdotes. "Doofus was the dumbest dog ever. If all those stories are true, of course. Are you sure you haven't exaggerated just a little?"

Looking overly innocent, Jake raised a hand. "I swear it's all true. I haven't even told you all the stupid things he did, just a sampling. It was a wonder he lived to a ripe old age. I like to think he's still bumbling around somewhere, having a wonderful time and giving everyone around him nervous palpitations."

"Maybe he is. Pets are a real blessing, aren't they?"

"I've never really owned one myself. My mom and I never settled any place with a yard for a pet to run in. And now I travel so much that it doesn't seem like it would be fair to the pet. Someday, though, I'd like to have a dog. Or maybe a cat."

She couldn't imagine never having a pet. She and her brother had owned several during their childhood, including a lazy cat that had let Stacy hold him and cry into his fur during the roughest times of her youth.

They talked a while about the different types of pets people they knew owned, from dogs and cats to birds and lizards. Stacy even knew someone who had a pet pig that thought it was a person, and she entertained Jake with a few stories about the pig.

And then they were back at where the path diverged to their separate cabins, and the pleasant walk was at an end.

"That was nice," Jake said, looking reluctant to part with her.

"Would you like some fresh lemonade?" she heard herself asking without consciously intending to do so. "I have a pitcher in my refrigerator."

His eyes brightened. "I'd like that, if it isn't too much trouble."

"No trouble at all," she assured him, telling herself that sharing one glass of lemonade and a few more minutes of conversation couldn't cause any problems.

The one glass turned into two. They drank the second while they played Monopoly. She couldn't remember how the subject came up, but it turned out they both loved that particular game, and were both fiercely competitive at it.

Stacy chose the dog token, and Jake the race car, and the game was on. It lasted a long time, as Monopoly often did, and by the time it ended, Jake was nearly bankrupt.

"You won," he said, sounding surprised, and making her wonder if he wasn't used to being beaten.

"I told you I was good at it," she said, putting her piles of brightly colored money back into the box.

He took the defeat well, though he did warn her that if they ever had another chance to play, he wouldn't go so easy on her.

She smiled, and then noticed how late it had gotten while they'd played. It seemed only polite to invite him to stay for dinner. "I was playing on making a chicken quesadilla for myself," she said. "I have plenty of ingredients for us both."

"That sounds great. Is there anything I can do to help?"

Telling him he could chop the salad while she prepared the ingredients for their quesadillas, she ushered him into the kitchen. Another hour or so together was no big deal, she assured herself. They were just being neighborly.

At least, that was what she tried very hard to believe.

Jake left just over an hour later. He paused as she showed him to the door, and for just a moment she thought he might be thinking about kissing her good-night. But then he simply thanked her again for the lemonade and the dinner, told her he'd like a rematch at Monopoly sometime and let himself out.

Locking the door, Stacy assured herself that she was greatly relieved he hadn't tried to kiss her. That would have been awkward and uncomfortable, she decided, especially considering that they had already agreed to go to the drive-in together. She was glad he was keeping their interactions friendly and platonic, just a couple of casual friends spending time together to stave off boredom.

That was all she wanted, after all, she told herself. At least until she got to know him better, to make sure he wasn't the love-'em-and-leave-'em kind. She'd had enough dealings with that type to last the rest of her life.

WHAT JAKE HAD BEEN dreading finally happened at the drive-in theater. Fortunately, Stacy wasn't there to witness it.

"Oh, my gosh. You're—you're Jake Hinson."

Jake winced, then managed to smile at the red-faced teen on the other side of the concessions counter. "Hi. How you doing?"

The boy's eyes were as big as saucers. "You're him, ain't you?"

Grateful that he had come for snacks at a time when few other people were around, Jake lowered his voice to say, "Yeah, but do me a favor, will you, buddy? Keep it between us for now? I'd really like to watch the rest of the movie."

"Oh, yeah. Folks find out you're here, they'll start bugging you for autographs and stuff, right?"

Jake nodded. "Right. I'm trying to be sort of incognito for now."

The boy looked around with exaggerated stealth, his voice a dramatic stage whisper when he said, "You're, like, my favorite driver *ever,* man. I thought for sure you were going to win the NASCAR NEXTEL Cup championship this year, you know? So, how you doing? You getting better?"

"I'm doing great," Jake assured him. "I plan to be back behind the wheel for the last few races this season. And next year, I'm going to start working toward that championship title again."

"You'll get it, Jake. You can *drive,* dude."

"Thanks. What's your name?"

"I'm J-Joey," the kid stammered. "Joey Baker."

"Tell you what, Joey. Write down your name and address for me, and when I get back home, I'll send you some team stuff. My way of thanking you for helping me out tonight."

"No sh—really? Oh, man, that would be so freaking cool. And could you sign something? You know, to prove I met you?"

"You bet." Jake scrawled his name and a quick message on a napkin, handed it to the boy, then pocketed the scrap of paper Joey gave him in return. Picking up the cardboard tray of snacks he'd ordered, he said, "I owe you, Joey. Thanks a lot."

Beaming, Joey nodded, folding the autographed napkin as if it were made of the finest spun glass. "Thank *you,* Jake. I'll be watching for that stuff."

"Give it two or three weeks. I'm not sure when I'll get back home, exactly, but I promise I won't forget."

Looking confident that his hero would follow through on that promise, Joey turned reluctantly to his next customer, a woman with two small children who were beginning to whine for their treats. Because Joey still looked flushed and excited, Jake hoped the boy would be able to resist bragging about the meeting at least until the movie ended. As it was, it was going to be harder for Jake to spend time in town unrecognized if word got out that he was in the area.

"That took a while," Stacy commented when he climbed back into the car a few moments later. "Was there a long line?"

"No." He handed her the soda and small popcorn she had requested, keeping a soda and hot dog for himself. "I got to talking to the kid behind the counter and lost track of time. I'm sorry I was gone so long."

"That's okay. You didn't miss much. Thank you for the popcorn and drink."

"You're welcome." He looked through the windshield at the large outdoor screen on which a clichéd but moderately entertaining action-adventure film was playing, the sound relayed through the car's radio speakers.

The movie was a big enough draw that there were quite a few other vehicles around them—cars, pickup trucks, minivans. Some viewers had brought lawn chairs, while others sat in the back of their trucks. Many munched on concessions, or food they had brought from home. Fortunately, it was a pleasantly cool evening, and there were few mosquitoes to mar the pleasure.

Children dashed among the vehicles, and quite a bit of noise came through the open windows of Jake's rental car, but it didn't really matter. It wasn't as if the movie required close attention.

The outside distractions didn't have much to do with Jake's inability to concentrate on what little plot there was. His eyes kept turning in Stacy's direction, studying her delicate profile in the flickering light. He watched as she lifted her soda from the drink holder with her left hand, then winced and set it quickly back down.

"Is your arm hurting?"

She glanced at him with a slight shake of her head. "It's fine," she said—as he suspected she would have even if it was killing her. "Just a little sore. I've used it more today than I have in a while. I did some housecleaning and laundry."

"I hope you haven't overdone it."

She wrinkled her nose. "I was thinking the same thing about you earlier," she admitted. "I noticed you were limping a bit more than before when you came back from the concession stand."

He nodded to acknowledge the touché. "I worked out more today than I have since the accident. My leg's a little tired, but I think the exercise was good for me."

"Same for me."

He cleared his throat. "Stacy, about that trip to the concessions stand—"

A burst of sound from the speakers cut off the impulsive confession. They both turned their attention to the screen, where the beleaguered hero was engaged in a battle for his life. Maybe it was a good thing he'd been interrupted, he thought. This probably wasn't the time for a serious talk.

"You were saying?" Stacy prodded a few moments later.

He smiled and shook his head. "Never mind."

There would be plenty of time to tell her later, he assured himself. When the opportunity was right.

"THAT WAS an interesting experience," Jake said as he left the drive-in theater lot and turned in the direction of the cabins.

"Yes. The movie wasn't great, but it's always fun to go to the drive-in," Stacy agreed. "My brother and my nephew and I have been there together a couple of times."

"What does your nephew think about that? Does he enjoy the drive-in more than the music on the square?"

"He used to when he was little. But not for the past couple of years. He says it's 'lame.'"

"Those teenagers in the pickup truck beside us didn't seem to think so."

Stacy cleared her throat as she remembered the rather obvious groping that had been going on in the truck. "Yes, well, I don't think they'd have enjoyed the experience quite so much had their parents been around."

"You talk about your brother and your nephew, but I haven't heard you mention your sister-in-law."

"That's because she's not in the picture," Stacy replied with a slight shrug. "She divorced Nick five years ago. Three years later, she sent my nephew, Andrew, to live with his father. She claimed she couldn't handle him anymore, but the truth was, Andrew was interfering with her social life."

And then she stopped herself with a shake of her head. "I don't mean to sound judgmental. My brother and sister-in-law were only nineteen when Andrew was born. Very young for such a responsibility."

"Actually, their story sounds a bit too familiar," Jake replied somberly. "I was raised by a young single parent myself. In my case, it was my mother who took the responsibility when my father decided that parenthood was too demanding. He took off when I was little more than a toddler."

"Do you have any brothers or sisters?"

"No. It was just me and my mom. She died when I was a senior in high school. An anaphylactic reaction to a bee sting. She was at home by herself when it happened and she waited too late to call for assistance. By the time the EMTs arrived, there was nothing to be done."

Stacy's heart ached in response to the tragic tale. It seemed her impression that Jake was very much alone had been more accurate than she'd known. He had certainly had his share of heartache in his short lifetime. "I'm sorry."

"Thanks. I just wished she had lived long enough to…well, anyway. We haven't talked much about our families. Are your parents still living?"

"My mother is. She married a very nice retiree three years ago and they're doing what she's always dreamed of doing. Traveling around the world. They've been to ten different countries since they married. She's having a ball." And no one deserved it more, after the hell her first husband had put her through, Stacy thought, though she had no intention of discussing that now.

"Good for her." Jake braked for an intersection, waiting until a long motor home passed before making a left turn. "You and your brother are close?"

"Yes. We supported each other through some difficult times. And I've tried to help him with Andrew." Which hadn't been an easy task, since Andrew had become a rebellious and withdrawn teenager.

"Your brother is older than you, I take it."

"Five years older. He's thirty-three."

"I always wanted a brother. But I've been fortunate. I have a lot of really good friends in my business. One, especially, is almost like a brother to me. His name's Wade. Great guy. He's getting married in January, and I'm going to be his best man."

The pride in the announcement made her smile. "Do you like his fiancée?"

"Very much."

"There aren't a lot of weddings in January."

"Yes, well, it's one of the few months Wade has free. Um, Stacy, about—"

"Look out!"

Jake spotted the speeding truck at the same moment Stacy cried out. Weaving over the yellow lines, the old vehicle was coming right toward them, headlights aimed blindingly through their windshield. Stacy braced herself for the impending crash.

CHAPTER FIVE

HAD THERE BEEN other cars in the intersection, there would have been a terrible wreck. As it was, Jake missed a head-on collision only by the narrowest margin.

His skillful handling of the car got them out of harm's way and back in their lane almost before Stacy realized they had avoided disaster. She was jolted in her seat, the seat belt tightening across her, but she sensed in relief that Jake was in complete control of the vehicle.

"Are you okay?" he asked, pulling over to the narrow shoulder and already reaching for his cell phone.

She had to swallow hard before answering. "Yes, I'm fine. I'm just very glad I wasn't driving."

He turned on his phone. She'd noticed he wore it clipped to his belt, and she had assumed he kept it on to receive calls. Apparently, he hadn't wanted to take any calls this evening.

"I need to report a drunk driver in a red pickup truck," he said into the phone a moment later. He then proceeded to give the details of location, model and approximate make of the pickup, and even a partial description of the driver, a heavyset, balding Caucasian male.

Stacy was amazed that he had gotten all those details in the split seconds while he was avoiding a wreck. Even with nothing else to do but hold on, she hadn't had the presence of mind to notice any of the details, not that she'd seen much in the darkness outside their own vehicle.

Call concluded, Jake slipped the phone back into its holder and put the car into gear. "I hope they catch him before he hurts someone."

"So do I." Her pulse rate was still elevated from the near miss. "I think that's as close as I've ever come to being in a car crash."

"Really?"

His response had an odd twist to it. Almost ironic. "You've been in an accident before?" she asked.

"Yeah."

No details, but again his tone seemed to carry hidden meaning. "I guess it's a hazard of your job."

"You could say that."

He parked the car in the driveway of his borrowed cabin. "You're sure you're okay? That was a pretty hard jolt you took when I slammed on the brakes."

"I'm fine. You handled it masterfully."

Without responding to the praise, he reached for the door handle. "I'll walk you to your door."

"Oh, that's not necessary."

"I'll walk you."

She knew that tone. It was the one she always referred to as "stubborn-man mode" when she heard it from her brother. It was almost always accompanied by "overprotective-male syndrome." After years of practice with her brother, she had gotten pretty good at putting her foot down when she chose to. But it just didn't seem worth the effort over something this trivial. She didn't argue any further when Jake fell into step beside her.

Security night-watcher lights gave soft illumination to their path. A very light breeze ruffled the tree leaves around them, creating a soothing, intimate sound. Had they been on a real date, she would have considered this stroll a romantic end to the evening.

She reminded herself firmly that there was no romance involved here. Jake had given no evidence that he regarded her as anything more than a new friend. He had been a perfect gentleman at the drive-in. Exactly as she wanted, she assured herself with a bit too much fervency. As for herself...well, a trucker from North Carolina didn't seem a likely match, since everyone knew how difficult long-distance courtships could become.

Courtship. The old-fashioned word made her feel oddly wistful. If Jake *had* been from this area, and if he had shown special interest in her, and if he hadn't been the charming, good-looking vagabond he seemed to be, then she might have allowed herself to hope something might develop. He seemed so nice. So easy to be with, and to talk to, which was a relatively new experience for her when it came to someone she had known such a short time.

She wanted love and family as much as any other average woman. She had been subject to occasional moments of envy when she was around her happily married or seriously involved friends. But she had also seen the devastation left in the wake of affairs gone wrong, and she didn't need any more heartbreak in her life.

"Beautiful night, isn't it?"

Jake's quiet comment broke the silence between them, causing her to look up at him. Moonlight did very nice things to his already handsome face, creating soft shadows beneath his chiseled cheekbones and gleaming in his dark eyes. If ever she'd met anyone who could almost tempt her into a reckless vacation fling, this would be the guy. Good thing she had such well-developed willpower when it came to that sort of thing.

"I was just thinking how nice an evening it is," she said, stepping onto the front porch of her cabin.

He chuckled. "Great minds, I guess."

A motion-activated light came on as they approached the front door, and both of them blinked in the sudden brightness. She heard Oscar barking inside, eager to welcome her back.

"Thank you for going to the movie with me tonight," he said, leaning one shoulder against the wall beside the door. "I can't tell you how good it felt to get out again for a while."

"I'm happy to have provided a diversion," she answered lightly.

"It was more than that," he assured her. "I enjoy being with you. I think you and I have quite a few things in common."

Her smile felt a bit strained. "Now, how could you know that after only a few days?"

Nodding with mock gravity, he replied, "You know, you're right. It would take more than a few days to tell for certain. So, how do you feel about spending more time together? Maybe discussing our tastes in books, music and television as a means of comparison?"

She hesitated, trying to read between the lines of the light-hearted invitation. *Was* she just a convenient diversion for him— or was it more than that? Was he hoping for that vacation fling she'd thought about only moments before—or was he interested in finding out if they could be compatible for something more? Or was she way overthinking the whole thing? She tended to do that on occasion.

"Stacy?"

He must wonder why she was taking so long to answer a simple question. "Sure. Why not?"

Once again he gave her a smile that made her equally glad she had said yes and wary of her almost visceral reactions to him. "Great. There are a lot of things about you I'd like to learn. And a few things I should tell you about myself."

She would decide later exactly how much she would share with him about herself. As for the things he wanted to tell her...well, she would deal with those when she heard them.

"I'd better get inside," she said, sticking her key in the lock. "Oscar's starting to sound impatient."

She wondered if she only imagined reluctance in his nod. "I'll see you tomorrow, then?"

"Yes. Good night, Jake. Sleep well."

His smile was a little melancholy. "Maybe tonight I will."

He touched her cheek before he moved away. Just a fleeting brush, but enough to cause her pulse rate to leap.

She stood just inside the partially opened door and watched him walk away. He was dragging his injured leg just slightly after the day's exertions, but he held his shoulders straight. His head higher. He looked more tired than sad now, which was a big improvement over a few days ago.

Realizing that she was standing there with one hand covering her cheek as if to hold on to the warmth of his touch, a foolish smile playing on her lips, she dropped her arm and abruptly closed the door.

Oscar stood on his back legs beside her, front paws pumping as he tried to get her attention. Feeling like a complete idiot, she reached down to pick him up, cradling him in her arms as she turned away from the door.

WADE CALLED again Friday morning. "You sound chipper this morning," he said after Jake answered the phone. "Feeling better?"

"Yeah. Workout went well this morning. I can really tell I'm getting my strength back."

"That's good to hear. So, how come you've been keeping your phone turned off? And why aren't you returning Pam's calls? She's going nuts here."

Jake sighed. "Tell her I'm sorry. I just haven't been in the mood to deal with PR stuff. She keeps asking when I'll be back, when I'll be ready to talk to the media again, when I want to start the promo stuff again—and, well, I just don't know how to answer her. I'll be back in a week or two. I'll talk to the press after I've been cleared to drive again, so I'll have definitive plans in place. And I'll start making personal appearances again at the same time. I've told her all of that, but she gets pushy sometimes."

"It's her job to be pushy. And yours to be available to your sponsors and fans," Wade reminded him, always the crew chief even when he had called as a friend.

Grimacing, Jake agreed. "I'll come back in full-press mode, I promise. You and Pam will see my ugly mug everywhere you look."

Wade chuckled. "It'll be difficult, but somehow we'll survive that."

And then his tone grew serious again. "If it makes you feel better, Woody asked me to tell you to take all the time you need. He knows you're impatient to get back in the car, but he wants to make sure you're ready. He said your ride is waiting for you whenever you decide to climb back into it."

Jake didn't need to be reminded that he drove for what he considered the greatest team in the sport, Woodrow Racing. The team owner, Ernest "Woody" Woodrow, was as passionate about racing as anyone Jake had ever met. Gruff, obsessive, demanding, he was rabidly loyal to his employees, and he expected them to be loyal in return. As almost all of them were. Hundreds of them, working in the offices, the shops, the garages and the pits of the four cars he ran on the NASCAR NEXTEL Cup circuit.

As for Jake, he would pretty much cut off his arm if Woody

asked him to. Woody had given him a shot at a lifelong dream when Jake was still young and untried. He intended to give Woody a gift in return—the championship trophy that Woody had come close to claiming several times, but had never quite been able to cinch.

"How's the rookie holding up?" It wasn't necessary for Jake to be more specific, even though there were technically two rookies on the Woodrow Racing NASCAR NEXTEL Cup team this weekend. Scott Rivers was driving his first full season in one of the Woodrow cars, but Jake was only interested for now in the rookie temporarily manning the Number 82 car. Jake's car.

"We'll see at qualifying today. He's been pretty jittery this week, but then he and Woody had a talk over coffee—you know that thing Woody does. Pete came back with a new attitude. Had that look in his eyes I've seen in yours a few times. The one that says he's not letting any obstacle prevent him from getting what he wants—a full-time ride."

"I remember how that felt."

"You should. It wasn't that long ago. You've still got a lot of racing left in you, Jake. *We've* got a lot of races ahead. Don't let this one setback get you down."

"You know me. The Bounce-Back Kid. Tell Pete I've got faith in him for qualifying well, okay?"

"I'll do it. That'll mean a lot to him, coming from you."

It was perhaps the most touchy-feely conversation Jake had ever shared with his crew chief, and it was beginning to make both of them uncomfortable. "Say hey to everyone for me, okay?" he said more lightly. "And tell Pam I'll call her Monday."

"She'll hold you to that. You going to be watching qualifying on TV?"

"That depends. There's a very pretty lady in the cabin next door. I've been spending some time with her. Given a choice between doing something fun with her or watching someone else driving my car, guess which one I'm going to choose?"

Wade didn't laugh out loud very often, but he did then. "So *that's* why you're suddenly in a better mood. I should have known that even alone in the rural hills of Arkansas, you'd end up with a 'very pretty lady' right next door."

"They don't call me 'Lucky' for nothing."

"Who calls you Lucky?"

"It was a figure of speech, Ice. Work with me, okay?"

"Yeah, well, just don't let your hormones distract you from your exercises and stuff, you hear? Pete's a good kid with a solid future ahead of him—but I'm ready to be back in Victory Lane."

No surprise there, Jake thought as he disconnected the call a few moments later. Like everyone else who worked for Woodrow, Wade was satisfied only with a win—and then only for a few days, until it was time to start getting ready for the next race.

He wondered what had made him tell his friend about Stacy. He wasn't one to talk about the women he dated. Not that he had dated Stacy, exactly. Which didn't mean he wasn't interested. Because he was. For the first time since his accident, he found himself thinking about romance.

Okay, so maybe his thoughts about Stacy weren't quite that lofty, but he genuinely liked her in addition to being increasingly attracted to her. He couldn't even say why exactly. It wasn't as if she had been completely forthcoming with him. And that apparently innate reserve of hers made it difficult to get to know her quickly.

So maybe it was the puzzle that intrigued him. The challenge. Maybe once he got to know her better some of the fascination would wear off. It was possible, he reminded himself. He regretted to say that he'd shown a rather short attention span in his past affairs. When it came down to a woman or a race car, he had always chosen the latter, which hadn't led to lasting relationships.

But maybe it would be different with Stacy. From what little he had seen, she seemed like the steady, settled, home-and-family type, unlike a lot of the women he met in the racing circuit. She knew nothing of NASCAR, so he didn't have to worry that she was more interested in his fame and money than in himself. She had a career of her own—even better, a portable career—so maybe she wouldn't expect a degree of attention he couldn't promise.

Maybe Stacy was exactly what she appeared to be. And maybe this initial attraction could blossom into a great deal more. Maybe he had found what Wade had with Lisa, and Ronnie with Katie, and Mike with Andrea, and all his other happily committed racing friends—even though this was hardly the ideal time to find it.

Or maybe he was just getting carried away because of his boredom and restlessness, he told himself, firmly applying the brakes to his speeding imagination.

"WHAT'S YOUR favorite color?"

"Green."

"Favorite dessert?"

"Ice cream."

"Favorite sport?"

"Figure skating."

Jake frowned. "That's not a sport."

Dipping her spoon into a warm dish of peach cobbler topped with ice cream, Stacy replied, "Of course it's a sport. Those skaters are serious athletes."

"The men wear tights."

"Can *you* leap straight into the air off a slippery surface and spin four times before you touch down again? And land on one thin blade without falling on your butt?"

"Well…no," he admitted, amused by the image.

"There you go, then. What's *your* favorite color?"

"Purple."

Her eyebrows rose, as if the answer surprised her. "Most men say blue."

"I'm not most men."

"Mmm," she murmured, and took a sip of her coffee, leaving him to wonder exactly what that sound had meant.

"Besides," he added, setting down his own cup, "I have a reason to like purple."

Which would have been a good lead-in to his explanation of what he really did for a living, had she asked what that reason was. Which she didn't. She simply moved on, imitating him. "Favorite dessert?"

"Right now it's peach cobbler," he said with appreciation of the big bite he had just swallowed.

"Favorite sport?"

"Stock car racing."

And once again she continued without giving him a chance to elaborate. "Favorite kind of music?" she asked, improvising now.

"Country. Yours?"

"I guess it's called soft rock."

"Favorite group?"

"Matchbox twenty. Yours?"

Enjoying the quick back-and-forth and the humorous way she mimicked his questioning, he replied, "Brooks and Dunn. Favorite type of movie?"

"Action-adventure. With a romance. How about you?"

"I like lots of movies. The type you mentioned. Sci-fi. Spy films. Comedies. The occasional horror film. No historical dramas."

"More men in tights, right?"

He grinned. "Exactly."

They'd been together several hours that day, taking a leisurely walk through the woods with Oscar, then leaving him behind to dine together at a restaurant that advertised "the world's finest country cookin'." Jake wouldn't go quite that far, but the food was good. The company was better.

She set down her spoon and touched her napkin delicately to the corners of her mouth. "You've been asking me questions all afternoon. Do you feel like you're getting to know me now?"

Smiling, he propped his chin on one fist and studied her across the table. "I've learned some details. Likes and dislikes, that sort of thing. But in some ways, you're still a mystery to me."

She shook her head with a self-deprecating wrinkle of her nose. "There's not really that much more to know."

"Let me sum up what I've learned." He was having a good time, he realized. The best time he'd had in more than a month. Maybe longer. All because he'd met a woman he genuinely liked and felt comfortable with. A woman he wanted to get to know quite a bit better.

She spread her hands. "Go ahead."

Ticking off the points on his fingers, he began, "You were born and raised in central Arkansas, attended public schools, left the state to earn a degree in English lit in Chicago, taught high school there for a couple of years, then came back to Arkansas to work for a friend who owns a small but moderately profitable publishing company.

"You have one older brother, Nick, who's a computer genius

and a single father. Your nephew is fourteen and his name is Andrew. Your father died several years ago and your mother is married now to a man who is showing her the world. She calls you every three or four days just to tell you how happy she is and to make sure you're getting along well without her. Your best friend is married to a trucker, you live in a small apartment in Little Rock, you're beautiful and you've been freelance editing for just over a year."

"You have a good memory," she said, seemingly impressed by the trivial details he had remembered. "That's all exactly—"

And then the compliment he'd slipped into the list hit her and her cheeks warmed. "I mean, *most* of that is exactly right."

He gave her a look of exaggerated innocence. "What did I get wrong?"

"I'd like some more coffee," she said, looking around for their server.

It amused him that his teasing but true flattery had flustered her. Either she hadn't been flirted with in a while—in which case, she must be surrounded by morons back in Little Rock—or he'd been a little too buddy-buddy with her so far. In his attempt to set her at ease and reassure her that she was safe hanging out with him, he may have neglected to convey that he found her attractive. *Very* attractive.

After both their coffee cups had been refilled and they were alone again, he decided to press the issue a bit further. Take a test run, so to speak, and see how she responded. "What I *don't* know is why a talented, competent, beautiful young woman is staying alone in her brother's cabin this week."

"I told you. I hurt my arm and I came up here to recuperate and catch up on some work."

And she said all of that while staring almost fiercely into her coffee cup to avoid meeting his eyes.

He had been convinced from the start that there was something Stacy wasn't telling him. That there was more to her being here than she had revealed to him. Of course, he was in no position to criticize, since he'd been doing much the same thing to her.

"Listen, Stacy," he began, deciding it was past time to remedy at least half of that situation. "There's something I need to—"

"Oh, my gosh." The exclamation cut into Jake's words as a well-rounded bottle blonde in stretchy clothes and flip-flops practically skidded to a stop beside the table. "I know who you are!"

He swallowed a groan. So much for carefully choosing his words. Pasting on his patented greeting-the-fans smile, he turned toward the woman—only to find her staring openmouthed at...

Stacy.

"You're Anastasia Carter, aren't you?" the woman demanded. "I saw you interviewed on TV. And your picture was in the *Democrat-Gazette*. I cut it out and mailed it to my niece. She takes karate. Or judo or something. I can never keep them straight."

Jake turned his gaze slowly to Stacy, who seemed to be struggling to hold on to a polite smile.

"You *are* Anastasia Carter, aren't you?" the woman insisted.

Stacy nodded reluctantly. "Yes. But, really, I—"

"That was amazing what you did. I mean, like, the bravest thing I ever heard about. I'd have been screaming my head off, totally useless, but you were just so cool and calm and you knew exactly what to do. Weren't you scared at all?"

"Of course I was afraid."

Afraid? Jake frowned. What on earth were they talking about?

"I mean, he had a gun to your head. And he'd already shot one guy, so you had to know just how much danger you were in. But you still kept yourself together enough to use your karate stuff—"

"Tae kwon do," Stacy murmured.

"Yeah, whatever. Anyway, it's no wonder the press fell in love with you. You being such a little bitty thing and all. And him being so big. And then there's…well, you know. Who your dad was and all."

Stacy's jaw was so tight now that Jake imagined he could almost hear her teeth grinding together. "Yes, well, it's all over now. I'd just like to put the entire ordeal behind me. I'm sure you understand."

The woman nodded vigorously. "I don't blame you for that. Anyway, I just wanted to stop by and tell you how much I admire what you did. You were a real inspiration for women everywhere, you know?"

"Thank you." Stacy reached for her coffee cup, raising it to her lips with both hands, a polite but not so subtle signal that the conversation was at an end.

The woman took the hint. She moved away from the table, giving Jake only a fleeting glance as she passed. "How you doing?" she murmured absently, her attention still focused on Stacy.

Shaking his head in bemusement, Jake turned back to his dinner companion—who was becoming more intriguing with each moment he spent with her.

STACY HAD TO GIVE Jake points for patience. Even though he had practically bristled with curiosity ever since the encounter at the restaurant, he hadn't asked one question during the brief drive to the cabins. He had obviously sensed that she hadn't wanted to talk about the incident with the woman who had stopped at their table, so perhaps he assumed she would be no more willing to discuss it with him.

As much as she appreciated his discretion, she had already decided to tell him everything. It wasn't that big a deal, she assured herself. She wasn't really trying to hide anything; she'd just been reluctant to bring up a subject that would very likely become awkward and uncomfortable. Could even change the way he looked at her, even though she was still exactly who she had presented herself to be.

"Would you like to come in for coffee?" she asked him when he walked her to her door. "Decaf, of course. Or herb tea, if you prefer. I'll try to explain what the woman in the restaurant was talking about, if you're interested in hearing it."

"Of course I'm interested," he admitted with a rueful smile. "To be honest, it's been driving me crazy. You have to admit that some of the things she said were…intriguing."

"She made more of a deal of it than it really is." Stacy opened the front door to her brother's cabin, locked it, then reached down to scoop up Oscar, who was yapping and leaping around her feet to welcome her home. Snuggling him against her face, she headed toward the kitchen.

"Which would you prefer?" she asked over her shoulder. "Decaf coffee or herbal tea?"

"Whatever you're having. I like it all."

"Have a seat. I'll be right back."

Setting Oscar on his feet, she smiled when he dashed straight to Jake for an ear rub. She figured the two would be fine while she boiled water for tea and organized her thoughts about how she would explain why the woman in the restaurant had recognized her.

CHAPTER SIX

JAKE AND OSCAR WERE playing when she returned a short while later with two fragrant, steaming mugs of apple-chamomile tea. Jake had found Oscar's fire-hydrant chew toy and was tossing it to various corners of the room. Each time it landed with a shrill squeak, Oscar jumped on it with all four feet, mock-growling and shaking it between his teeth until he carried it victoriously back to Jake. And then they started all over again.

"He'll do that for hours, you know," she said, setting one of the mugs on the coffee table in front of the couch where Jake sat.

"Doesn't he ever get tired?"

She settled in a chair near his end of the sofa. "Yes. But chances are, you'll wear out first."

He chuckled. "Chances are, you're right."

Picking up his tea, he let Oscar keep the toy the next time. After a moment, Oscar accepted that the game was over and leaped up to curl beside Jake on the couch, officially designating Jake one of his new best buddies.

"So," Jake said after taking a few cautious sips of his hot tea, "someone had a gun to your head."

He said it as if those words had been stuck in his mind ever since he'd heard them.

"He wasn't exactly holding the gun to my head," she said.

"He was just sort of waving it around. While he had an arm around my neck."

"Friend of yours?" he asked, his tone a little too bland.

She smiled fleetingly. "Hardly. More like me being in the wrong place at the wrong time."

"And where was that wrong place, exactly?"

"At a courthouse in Little Rock. I'd gone there to fight a traffic ticket—"

His eyebrows shot up as if that surprised him, but he didn't interrupt.

"I was ticketed for speeding, even though I wasn't," she added, growing indignant just at the memory. "There were several white cars on the road at the time, and I'm quite sure the officer pulled me over by accident after clocking someone else with his radar gun. Then he was too pigheaded to admit he'd made a mistake, so he insisted on ticketing me."

"And you went to court to fight it."

"Of course. I wasn't going to pay if I didn't deserve it."

Looking a bit bemused, he nodded. "Okay, go on. The man with the gun?"

"He was in the courthouse for another reason. He was going to be taken straight from there to jail. Somehow he grabbed an officer's gun and broke away. I happened to be in his way when he tried to escape and he grabbed me from behind. He planned to hold me hostage and make everyone stay back so he wouldn't hurt me or anyone else, and it was working. The officers started backing away."

"You must have been terrified."

"It happened so fast I didn't have time to panic. I just knew he was out of control and that I'd have to do something immediately before the situation got out of hand."

"What did you do?" he asked, his tea forgotten now as he

leaned forward with his elbows on his knees and his gaze focused intently on her face.

"I jerked his arm downward to keep the gun pointed at the floor, and then I landed a solid kick on the side of his knee. It tore his ACL, causing him to collapse."

"Tae kwon do," he murmured, referring again to the conversation at the restaurant.

She nodded. "Just over three years ago, I won a month of free lessons from a charity raffle. I'd never really won anything before, so I decided to try it out. I enjoyed it so much I kept going to classes."

"You've been testing for belts?"

"Yes."

"So what's your rank?"

"I'm a first-degree black belt."

It surprised her when he laughed.

"You find that amusing?"

He shook his head. "Just surprising. I'm sure I'm not the first to be startled to learn that you have a black belt in tae kwon do."

She knew her petite size gave the initial impression that she was delicate. Maybe a bit fragile. "You aren't the first," she admitted.

"The woman at the restaurant said your attacker was much larger than you."

"Over six feet. But the knee is a vulnerable spot for a person of any size. That's why so many big, strong football players suffer knee injuries. An ACL tear can put an end to a season. A bad-enough knee injury can end a career."

He nodded soberly. "So you took his knee out. Then what happened?"

"Two officers rushed Alvetti, the guy who'd grabbed me, disarmed him and cuffed him. That's when I hurt my arm. I was wearing heels, and when one of the cops shoved me out of the way, he threw me off balance so that I couldn't catch myself. He didn't mean to be so rough, he was just trying to get me out of harm's way. Alvetti was taken away by ambulance."

"And you?"

"Also left by ambulance," she admitted reluctantly. "I kept telling everyone I didn't need that, but they all insisted. By the time I'd been treated for the arm sprain and released, the press descended on the hospital. They made a big deal out of photographing me leaving with the sling on my arm. They turned it into a David-and-Goliath story and embroidered the details to make it sound much more dramatic than it was. And because it was a slow news week, the national press picked up the story. I wasn't sure whether you'd seen it when we met."

"No. But I haven't been watching the news a lot lately."

"That's what I guessed."

"The woman at the restaurant said Alvetti had already shot one man," Jake said, suddenly remembering.

She nodded. "He shot the officer whose gun he'd taken. Fortunately, the injury wasn't life threatening."

"Did you know he'd shot someone when he grabbed you?"

"Yes. He was yelling something about having shot one cop and not being afraid to shoot more people."

"And you still kept your cool. I agree with the woman earlier. That's very heroic."

She felt her cheeks warm. "I acted on impulse, using the moves I've been practicing for three years. I wasn't trying to be a hero—I just wanted to get away from him."

"Maybe you weren't trying to be a hero, but I suspect your quick thinking kept the situation from becoming much worse. You may very well have saved lives."

"That's what the press kept saying. But there were several

officers on the scene. I'm sure they would have regained control quickly even if I hadn't been involved."

"I take it you don't enjoy being in the spotlight."

She tried not to shudder, but she was only partially successful. "No. I don't enjoy it."

"And that's why you came here alone. To get away from the press?"

She nodded. "They were driving me crazy. The phone kept ringing with people asking to interview me. They wanted me to go back down to the courthouse and pose on the steps—and to be sure and wear my sling, by the way. They wanted me to demonstrate tae kwon do moves on morning TV shows. And they wanted to know…"

"To know what?" he asked quietly.

She shook her head abruptly, deciding she had told him enough. "Can I get you anything else?" she asked, rising to her feet. "More tea? A cookie or something?"

"I've had dessert," he reminded her.

"Right. Well, now you know why I'm here. Why I've been avoiding attention until it all blows over and someone else does something that makes the press salivate."

"You don't have a high opinion of the press."

"I have reason not to." Carrying her empty teacup toward the kitchen, she said over her shoulder, "Now you know. No big mystery. I kicked a guy in the knee and came here to recuperate from the fall I took in the process. That's pretty much the most exciting thing that's ever happened to me. All in all, I'm pretty ordinary."

"Somehow I doubt that."

She hadn't realized he'd followed her until he spoke from the kitchen doorway. After setting her cup in the dishwasher, she turned to take his and add it to the rack.

He didn't move out of her way when she walked toward the doorway. She came to a stop a few steps away from him. "Are you waiting for a password?" she asked pointedly.

Smiling down at her, he shook his head. "I was hoping you'd finish your sentence."

"Which sentence?"

"The press wanted to know…?"

She sighed. "They wanted to know if Harley Carter's daughter could generate as many juicy headlines as *he* did fifteen years ago."

JAKE HAD BROUGHT a laptop computer with him to Arkansas, though he'd hardly turned it on while he'd been there. He sat in front of it late Friday night, staring blankly at the NASCAR screen saver flashing on the screen.

Though it had been several hours since he had parted from her, he was still trying to process the things Stacy had told him about herself. The black belt. The unexpected streak of defiance in fighting a traffic ticket she hadn't thought she deserved. The terrifying incident at the courthouse. The ensuing media frenzy.

Just the thought of her being held at the mercy of a desperate gunman made his blood chill. Despite her training, that situation could have easily turned tragic. She had been extremely fortunate not to have been injured more badly than she was.

He was dismayed, and then rather concerned, by the way his chest clenched in response to the thought that he might never have met her.

He focused on the computer again. It would be so easy to type in the name Harley Carter and see what popped up. A little digging, and he would have a few more answers about the rather mysterious young woman in the cabin next door. Probably wouldn't even be very difficult, if her father had made headlines fifteen years ago.

But something kept him from typing in that name. It wasn't only consideration for her privacy, though that was certainly part of his hesitation. But there was also a part of him that wanted the answers to come from her, not from a computer. He would like to know that he had earned her trust enough for her to tell him about herself.

He was not unaware of the irony that there was still so much he hadn't told her about himself. It wasn't really an excuse that he'd started to tell her several times and had been interrupted. He was well aware that he'd had plenty of deliberately missed opportunities to open up to her.

He could completely understand why she had been reluctant to talk about her recent brush with fame. She had been tired of the questions and the gawking, being treated like a victim and a heroine, both of which made her uncomfortable. She must have been relieved to spend time with someone who had no idea what she'd gone through, just as he had enjoyed being with someone who knew him only as Jake, and not Jake Hinson, NASCAR star.

The difference was, he thought, that it wasn't so much a matter of trust on his part. For him, it had been the novelty of anonymity. But for her, there was a lot more to it. She would have to trust before she revealed more of herself. And he realized now that he wanted to know *everything* about her. And he wanted her to be the one to tell him.

He closed the computer.

She had rushed him out of her cabin almost immediately after she'd revealed her father's name. Politely, for the most part. Claiming weariness, she had walked him to the door without explaining what she'd meant about her father making headlines.

He had wanted to kiss her good-night. Pausing in the doorway, his gaze on her lips, he had wanted so badly to kiss her that he could almost taste her. She would taste of apple-chamomile tea, he'd mused. Touched with her own natural sweetness.

The strength of that sudden rush of desire had taken him aback. She hadn't had to push him out the door. He'd darned near bolted. And now here he sat, alone in his borrowed cabin in the middle of the night, thinking about her—and nervously wondering if he was falling for her.

He had known her less than a week. He had just learned her last name. As far as he knew, she still didn't know his. So there was no logical reason to think he was developing strong feelings for her. Lasting feelings.

He was just bored, he assured himself. A little lonely. She was attractive. Likable. Combined with the unanswered questions about her, it was only natural that he would be so intrigued by her. For now.

For some reason, he found himself thinking about his friend and teammate, Ronnie Short. Ronnie had been signing autographs at a car dealership when a little boy had spilled a Sno-Kone on him. The boy's cute, flustered, red-haired aunt, a kindergarten teacher named Katie, had apologized profusely and tried to clean his shirt with her hands. He claimed to have fallen in love with her before the ice melted. They had married less than a year later and were now anticipating their first child.

Love at first sight, Ronnie had called it, though many of his teammates had expressed doubt that such a thing existed. But it was hard to argue with how happy Ronnie and Katie were together, how strong the bond was between them.

Jake had envied them, but he'd never expected anything like that to happen to him. He'd figured when he was ready to settle down, he would start looking around for a suitable mate. Date a few qualified candidates. Interview them, in a way. Find someone who knew his business, accepted the demands of his job, fit in well with the other racing wives.

He had never even considered the possibility that he could be blindsided by feelings for someone who had no clue who he was. Someone who had a great deal of baggage of her own. Someone who had come along at absolutely the worst time in his life, career-wise.

So there was no need to get too carried away here, he cautioned himself. This was just a…well, he couldn't even call it a fling, since he hadn't even kissed her. Yet.

In a week, maybe two, he'd be headed back to North Carolina, ready to throw himself into whatever remained of the season. He wouldn't have time to think about anything except getting back in the forefront of his sport and preparing for next year's restart. Stacy probably wouldn't even cross his mind, except in passing, maybe. Probably.

He rubbed his chin, aware that he was trying just a little too hard to convince himself.

OSCAR WANTED to go out early Saturday morning. Maybe he was tired of watching Stacy pace aimlessly through the cabin, which she had been doing since dawn. After a very restless night, she'd finally given up on sleep. She had been wandering through the cabin ever since.

Apparently deciding she might as well put all that energy to use taking him for a walk, Oscar stood by the door and yapped until she finally gave in and clipped his leash to his collar. It was barely eight o'clock when they stepped outside, and the ground still glistened with dew in the shade. Oscar immediately started sniffing the ground, his tail wagging as he took in the scents of a fresh, new morning.

Stacy wore a short-sleeved, scoop-neck, purple T-shirt with blue jeans and sneakers. The faintest of breezes brushed her bare arms, but it was warm enough that she didn't even shiver. Though it was clear now, gathering clouds in the west warned her that rain was headed this way later that morning. It would be a good day to close herself into the cabin and concentrate on work.

She had bundled her dark hair into a loose ponytail, the curly ends of which tickled her nape as it swung with her steps. She wore no makeup, just a thin layer of moisturizer with sunscreen. She wasn't concerned about her appearance. Chances were, she wouldn't run into anyone—and if she did, she wasn't trying to impress him. Whoever it might be.

She glanced at Jake's cabin as she stepped onto the path into the woods. Seeing no signs of activity, she assumed he was still in bed. No reason for him to be up this early on his vacation.

Memories of the evening before flitted through her mind as she and Oscar made their way leisurely through the trees. She and Jake had been having such a good time before that woman stopped by their table. Sharing their likes and dislikes, getting to know each other, flirting a little. Just like a real date. The type with the potential to lead somewhere.

The woman's intrusion—well-intentioned as it might have been—had changed Stacy's mood. It wasn't just the reminder of the incident in the courthouse that had brought her mood down. Rather it had been the inevitable connection to the reason she was so publicity shy in the first place. Which had led to some painful memories of several past disappointments and disillusionments, most having to do with charming and ultimately untrustworthy men. Two of whom she had loved deeply before they shattered her heart.

She had spent most of the night reminding herself that there was no reason to worry about Jake breaking what was left of her heart. They barely knew each other, after all.

Even if he was every bit as nice and honorable as he seemed to be, their time together would be fleeting. She wouldn't have to worry about his reaction to her family history because there was really no good reason to tell him. All in all, it was simply better if they left their relationship exactly where it was now—friendly, casual, superficial.

Temporary.

Maybe it would be best if she avoided seeing him today, she mused, tugging slightly at Oscar's leash to keep him moving when he stopped to paw at a soft patch of ground. Things had gotten uncomfortably personal last night. It was time to put some safe distance between them again.

When her walk with Oscar ended, she would close herself into the cabin and concentrate on work. If Jake should knock at the door, she would politely tell him she had a lot to do and needed time alone to do it. She was sure he would take the hint.

Pushing a low-hanging branch out of her way, she edged around a large boulder toward a pretty little creek she had found on previous outings. She had discovered a grassy nook in a curve of the creek with a flat boulder that made a perfect spot to sit and watch the water flow by.

She certainly hadn't expected to find Jake sitting on her rock.

His head was down, his face hidden in his hands. As she came closer, she saw that both his hair and the back of his gray T-shirt were damp with sweat, despite the mild temperature.

"Jake?" she said quietly, concerned by the slump of his shoulders.

He straightened immediately, turning his head to look at her. His smile was strained, and did not lighten his dark eyes. "Good morning. You're out early."

Oscar bounded toward him, ears perked for attention. Jake reached down to scratch the dog's head, causing the feathery tail to beat blissfully.

Following her pet, Stacy studied the hollows beneath Jake's eyes. "You're out early, too. Are you okay?"

He shrugged and spoke lightly. "Oh, sure. I've been hiking the path. I just stopped for a rest."

He had pushed himself too hard, she concluded, lowering herself to sit on another large rock near his. She could see signs of pain around the corners of his mouth. And his thoughts, when she had interrupted him, had not been happy ones.

He wore a pair of charcoal-gray running shorts with his lighter gray T-shirt and an expensive pair of running shoes. Her gaze drifted downward to his sturdy, well-shaped legs—then lingered on the scars that marred his left calf. "You had surgery on that leg?"

He nodded, glancing downward at the evidence of his injuries. "Yeah. I had a pretty deep cut down my leg. Lost a lot of blood from that and some other wounds. Apparently my friends were told that my condition was serious when I was taken into surgery. Scared them pretty badly, they said."

He hadn't talked much about his accident. It must have shaken him very badly to come so close to losing his life. "You were fortunate to have recovered so quickly."

"It doesn't feel quick," he muttered, watching Oscar now, who was happily exploring at the farthest reaches of his leash. "I've missed seven weeks of my life."

"Seven weeks doesn't seem so long to pay considering how bad it could have been."

"Seven weeks is a lifetime in my line of work," he murmured. And then he shook his head. "But you're right, of course. I'm sitting here feeling sorry for myself when I should be counting my blessings. After all, my friend lost his life in the accident. And I'm sulking because I had a few injuries."

"Were you close to him?"

Jake hesitated a moment before answering. "We weren't close, exactly. We knew each other a long time, from junior high school days. Saw each other a couple of times a year. I'm on the road a lot, and he traveled quite a bit in his job, too. He was divorced, had a couple of boys that he didn't see as often as he would have liked. We got together every once in a while just to fish and catch up and remember the scrapes we got into when we were kids."

"You'll miss him."

Jake sighed heavily. "Yeah. I will. I don't have many connections to my past. No family or anything. Eric was one of my last ties to my childhood."

"I'm so sorry."

He pushed a hand through his damp hair, leaving it spiked around his face in a manner that was too appealing for her peace of mind. "Like I said, I was just indulging in a bout of self-pity. Weekends are the hardest days for me, but it's time for me to stop brooding and get back to recuperating."

She wondered if the accident had happened on a weekend, but she didn't ask. He didn't want to dwell on the details, and she couldn't blame him for that. "Have you had breakfast?"

He shook his head. "Not yet."

"Neither have I. Do you like waffles?"

She didn't know what had prompted her to ask that question, considering that she had just vowed to spend the day avoiding him. She suspected her tender heart was leading her into trouble again. Yet when she saw the way his expression lightened, she couldn't really be sorry.

"Who doesn't like waffles?"

"Why don't I make breakfast for us while you clean up?" she suggested, using her right arm to boost herself to her feet. Her sprained left arm was still somewhat sore, but much better than it had been. Compared to Jake's ordeal, she had no reason at all to complain, she reminded herself.

They would still go their separate ways soon enough. She would still have to be careful about starting to care too much for him when the risks to her heart were so high. But in the meantime, she could be a friend to him, help him through a rough spot in his life.

Following her lead, he stood, wincing only a little when he put his weight on his left leg. She wondered how long he had been pushing himself that morning before she'd found him. She hoped he realized that there came a point of diminishing returns when it came to regaining strength through exercise.

She reached out to steady him when he seemed about to stumble, but he caught himself quickly, giving her a wry smile. They stood only a foot or so apart, their gazes locking—and holding.

Seeing that they were preparing to leave, Oscar bounded toward them, yipping excitedly and dashing around their feet. The result was that they all became entangled in the long, baby-blue leash. Trying to step out of the loop, Stacy reached out with her right hand, resting it against Jake's chest for balance. In return, he gripped her forearm with his left hand. Both of them were laughing…

And then they weren't.

Standing so close together that his suddenly accelerated breath brushed her cheek, they stared at each other. Jake's smile faded. His heart beat firmly, rapidly beneath her palm. His fingers were so warm on her bare forearm that she could almost imagine he was leaving a handprint there.

It had happened so fast that it caught her unaware. She had

been trying to ignore her attraction to him, and had told herself that he saw her as no more than the nice girl next door. Nothing more to it at all, she had believed.

She might have been mistaken.

Lost in the gleam of his dark eyes, she stood motionless as he lowered his head slowly toward hers. Her lips parted on their own volition. She held her breath, waiting for the first touch of his mouth to hers.

Oscar barked again, tugging at the shortened leash. Jake paused, his lips barely an inch from hers.

"Sorry," he murmured. "I almost got carried away."

"Did you?" Her voice was slightly hoarse. She cleared her throat before asking, "How so?"

The corners of his mouth tilted into a rueful smile. "I almost kissed you."

"That would have been..." Fabulous. Amazing. Life changing. "...a mistake."

"Yeah. Maybe."

Maybe? She cleared her throat again. "Well, obviously. I mean, you and I—we're just..."

"Just?" He still hadn't put any more distance between them.

"Acquaintances."

He lifted his right hand to stroke her cheek with his fingertips. "Maybe a little more than that."

"Friends," she amended. "New friends."

"Better," he agreed. "So what's a kiss between friends?"

"Well..."

"Just a friendly kiss," he added, a rakish twinkle appearing in his eyes now. "A thank-you for being so nice to me."

She supposed one kiss wouldn't be too dangerous. Just a casual kiss. She could accept it as a gesture of appreciation from someone whose spirits she had lifted by being a friend.

And besides, a little voice inside her whispered, she would love to know what it was like to kiss Jake. Just for curiosity, of course.

She tilted her face upward.

CHAPTER SEVEN

WITH A SMILE of satisfaction, Jake swooped, his mouth covering hers before she had a chance to change her mind. Not that she would have.

His lips were firm. Warm. His short beard was surprisingly soft against her face. She had thought it would feel rough.

The hand she had rested against his chest crept upward, pausing at his shoulder and then moving around to slide into the back of his thick, shaggy hair. Taking that as permission, he wrapped her more closely in his arms, so that her body was flattened against his.

Even though he was so much taller than Stacy, she didn't feel overwhelmed by him. He held her just snugly enough to make her feel cradled. Safe. And yet, excited. Aroused.

It seemed as though she had been mistaken again, she mused as she felt her thoughts begin to turn hazy. One kiss from Jake could, indeed, be dangerous. Could very well lead to wanting more. Much more.

Breathing harder now, Jake finally lifted his head. Spots of warm color touched his cheeks above the beard, evidence that he had been as affected by the kiss as she had.

"I have a confession to make," he murmured without releasing her.

She moistened her still-sensitive lips. "What is it?"

"I've wanted to kiss you since I found you trapped beneath that log."

Her heart jumped, but she kept her tone even. "Have you?"

"Yes. I didn't say anything because I didn't want to scare you away. Me being a stranger and all."

"A *perfect* stranger, you said."

His grin endearingly lopsided, he nodded. "That is what I said, isn't it? So maybe I'm not perfect—but I'm not such a bad guy, either."

She believed him. He wasn't a bad guy at all. In fact, he was a very nice man with a warm smile, a kind heart, a friendly personality and an infectious sense of humor. Not to mention a great body. Nice eyes. A blinding smile. And the ability to empty her mind of everything but him with only a "friendly" little kiss.

Oscar tugged impatiently at his leash. Somewhat reluctantly, Stacy pulled herself out of Jake's arms, untangled the leash and took a couple of steps backward. Jake didn't try to detain her.

"I'll start breakfast," she said, turning toward the cabins.

Jake nodded. "I'll clean up quickly. All of a sudden, I'm ravenous."

FINGERING his freshly shaved jaw, Jake approached Stacy's door with the odd feeling that he should be carrying flowers or something. But maybe that would have been too much. He didn't want to completely scare her off. He had taken a big enough step by kissing her.

Maybe it had been the wrong time for a first kiss. He'd been sweaty and grubby, and she'd found him in a grim, self-pitying mood. But then she had seemed to be at ease with him for a change, both of them laughing at her dog's antics. Kissing her had been irresistible, even though he'd risked making her retreat from him again, go back to the careful, wary way she had treated him when they'd first met.

It had been a great kiss. And not only had she not pulled away, but she had actually cooperated. Kissed him in return. He could still feel the way her hand had burrowed into his hair, a memory that still made his pulse trip. He couldn't be sorry he had finally kissed her, though perhaps he could have set the scene better.

Kissing her had settled a few issues for him. For one thing, he no longer tried to convince himself that his interest in her was based merely on boredom. There was a lot more to it than that.

He wasn't quite ready to call it love—but neither would he deny that it had the potential to develop into just that.

She opened the door when he knocked. Her eyes widened when she saw his clean-shaved face. "You look different."

He smiled. "Good or bad?"

"Good," she decided, studying him with her head tilted and a slightly quizzical look on her face.

Was she thinking he looked a bit familiar now? Wondering if she had seen him somewhere before? Even though she didn't follow NASCAR, it was quite likely that she had seen one of his magazine or TV ads. And his face had been on a box of cereal just the previous month. Maybe she'd seen him at her breakfast table before and just hadn't realized it yet.

Before this day ended, she was going to know exactly who he was, he promised himself. But first—breakfast.

She held a cup of coffee in her hand, which she handed him as he entered. If her smile was self-conscious or displayed any regret of their kiss, he couldn't tell when he searched her face.

"Thanks," he said, lifting the cup toward his lips. "I needed this."

"I figured you would by now. Sit down, I'll get your waffles."

Taking a seat at the kitchen table, he watched as she poured batter into one of those flip-over waffle makers. It looked pretty easy to use, he decided. Maybe he should buy one for his house back in North Carolina. Not that he was there for breakfast all that often.

He wondered how she would feel about living on the road every weekend. Should it ever progress to that stage between them, of course.

"These smell great," he said when she set his plate in front of him and turned back to the waffle maker to start her own.

She nodded toward the center of the table. "I wasn't sure what you liked on them, so I set out syrup, honey and powdered sugar. Help yourself. Would you like some orange juice?"

"No, just coffee for now, thanks." He drizzled maple syrup on his waffles, then waited for her to join him a few moments later before picking up his fork and digging in. She had cooked bacon to go with the meal; she set the platter in the center of the table as she took her chair. Jake helped himself to a couple of crispy slices.

Maybe they both needed to talk about lighter subjects during breakfast, ignoring for now the reasons they were there, the injuries and losses they had suffered, any plans for the future. They talked, instead, about movies, a subject they both enjoyed. Which films they considered their favorites, which ones had given them nightmares as kids, which they considered guilty pleasures and some they'd considered a waste of two hours of their time.

Jake was rather surprised by the number of times they agreed, though they had a spirited debate about which was the best *Lethal Weapon* film—he said the first, she preferred the third, but they both disliked the second. And about whether a certain classic movie villain lost much of his effectiveness after a prequel revealed he'd once been a cute little boy called "Ani."

Jake said it didn't make the character any less ominous; she said it had completely changed her way of viewing the guy. Laughing, they agreed to disagree.

He loved watching her laugh. Her whole face lit up, her gray-blue eyes warmed and crinkled in the corners, her mouth curved so sweetly that he ached to taste her again. Desire hit him like a punch as he realized that he could sit with her for hours without getting bored. Just talking to her. Watching her laugh.

Her cell phone rang just as they were loading their dishes into the dishwasher. She glanced at the screen, then wrinkled her nose. "Sorry. It's my friend Mindy. I should probably take it or she'll worry that something is wrong."

"Go ahead. I'll go into the living room and catch up on the news."

Nodding, she lifted the small phone to her ear. "Hi, Mindy."

Jake didn't actually try to eavesdrop on her conversation with her friend. But the cabin was small, and she had to raise her voice occasionally to overcome static in the connection. Even though he had tuned the TV to CNN, he couldn't help but overhear a few things.

"I was just chatting with my neighbor," she said. "Yes, he's very nice. No, I can't—how's Paul?"

Smiling, Jake realized that her friend was prying, and that Stacy didn't want to talk about him while he was there to overhear.

A few moments later, he heard her gasp in indignation. "What?" she asked, her voice rising sharply. "Why did she call you? I hope you told her where she could go... Yeah, that's exactly where I would have suggested. Can you believe the nerve? I swear, if I never see another camera pointed in my direction, I'll be perfectly happy."

Jake winced.

"I swear, Mindy, I'm going to live so deep in the shadows from now on that no reporter will ever find a word to write about me," she continued crossly. "I'm never agreeing to another interview. I'm never getting involved with another fame-hound, so I'm warning you, if you go and get famous or something, I'll have to stop being your friend."

Even though she sounded as though she was teasing a bit at the end, there was a note of truth in Stacy's tone that made Jake's heart sink.

There was no way she could be involved with him and avoid the spotlight. No way she could spend the rest of her life avoiding cameras and interviews.

This should teach him to let his heart get ahead of itself, he thought glumly. He'd been fantasizing about a future with Stacy even before he revealed to her who he was. She had told him how she felt about the press, but he hadn't seen how serious she was. Hadn't wanted to see.

She came into the room shaking her head. "Can you believe it? A woman Mindy and I went to high school with called her today, hounding her to talk me into an interview. Lynn's a reporter now for a local newspaper and she wants an in-depth story on me. How I feel about the past, whether I've used tae kwon do as an escape for my 'emotional pain.'"

She made a face, as if the words tasted sour on her tongue. "Mindy and I haven't seen Lynn in years, but all of a sudden she's a 'dear friend.' What a crock."

"I suppose she's just doing her job," Jake suggested cautiously. "Guess she figured the worst that could happen was that you would say no."

Scowling, she shook her head. "I still think she crossed the line when she called Mindy. And when she was so blatant about wanting to use what she knows about my past."

Reminded that he still knew very little about her past himself, Jake kept quiet.

Stacy sighed and plopped onto the couch. "I suppose I should tell you, my father was a politician who had a habit of making headlines for all the wrong reasons. He ran for everything from mayor of a small town to county sheriff and state senate. Every time he got elected to anything—and it's unreal how often he charmed people into voting for him—it always ended up in some sort of scandal. Money. Women. Abuse of power. He was always in the newspapers for something outrageous he'd said or done, and reporters followed us all the time while I was growing up. It was humiliating."

Not at all the sort of background he would have imagined for her. "What was he like as a father?"

"Absentee. He was rarely home, and when he was, he was always on the phone or closed into his home office with his cronies. He remembered his kids only when he needed us to pose for campaign photos depicting him as the loving family man."

Strike two, he thought with a hard swallow. She probably had an aversion to men who worked long hours and had little time for traditional family activities. She probably wouldn't want to hear that there were ways to compensate for those job demands, not perfect solutions, but definitely workable.

Before he could think of what to say, she shook her head impatiently. "Sorry. I didn't mean to dump all that on you. I mean, you didn't have a father in the home at all."

"I can understand your aversion to the press," he conceded, "but it sounds as if your father did his part to egg them on."

"My father loved being in the spotlight," she agreed. "On his terms, of course. It made him furious when the media reported things he didn't want known."

"And your mother?"

"My mother was dazzled by him for a long time. By the time the enchantment wore off, she had two kids and a lot of shared debt. And she was raised to believe that divorce was unacceptable."

"So she stuck with him."

"Yes. She, Nick and I spent a lot of time at home together, sort of closed off from the rest of the world. Then, when I was twelve, my father made his final headline. He dropped dead of a heart attack in a courtroom where he was facing charges of mail fraud and money laundering.

"Come to think of it, courthouses have never been very kind to my family," she added thoughtfully.

He supposed she'd meant that as a joke. A way to lighten the conversation. He offered a weak smile in response.

"You know what? I don't want to talk about this anymore," she said suddenly, pushing herself to her feet. "I don't even want to think about the past or the press or anyone who has anything to do with either. Do you want to watch a movie? It's starting to rain outside, so it isn't as if there's anything else to do. My brother has, like, a thousand DVDs here."

Not the time to tell her about his very public career, he decided. "Sure," he said. "Let's watch a movie. What are you in the mood for?"

THEY CHOSE A FILM with lots of action, plenty of funny lines, and a dash of romance. Just the kind of mindless entertainment Stacy liked best. She had seen this one before, so she didn't have to concentrate that hard—which made it even better.

Jake started the DVD in a funny mood. Sort of distracted. Maybe he was thinking about the things she had told him about her past. Or maybe he had his own problems on his mind. But the movie soon worked its magic on him, too, and he began to relax. Laugh. Enjoy.

They sat at opposite ends of the couch when the movie started. Halfway into it, they were sitting close together, making room for Oscar, who curled up to sleep at Stacy's other side. By the time the film was almost over, Jake's arm was around her shoulders and she reclined comfortably against his chest. And what had been a lousy day had turned heavenly.

Maybe it didn't matter to him, she thought, staring at the screen now without really seeing the action there. Maybe her father's dubious fame was immaterial to a truck driver from North Carolina, unlike the aspiring CEO she had dated in Chicago.

She and Greg had been college sweethearts, and she'd thought they would be together forever. And then he had done a little research on her family history. And had decided that Harley Carter's daughter was not the best match for a man on the rise in the cutthroat corporate world.

That was when she had moved back to Arkansas. Back to a quiet life of working at home and spending her free time with a few close friends and her brother and nephew. It might have seemed odd to some that she had come back to a state where so many people remembered her father, knew all about her family. But she'd figured that at least here she wouldn't have to tell the story to every new person she met.

Of course, that applied only to people who had actually lived in the state while her father was alive, and remembered his escapades, she thought, glancing up at Jake.

He looked so different without the scruffy beard. She'd thought he was good-looking before, but now—wow. She'd nearly swallowed her tongue when she'd opened the door to him.

He glanced down at her with a questioning smile. "What?"

"Nothing." She looked at the television screen, realizing that the movie was nearing the conclusion. She rather hated to see it end, and it wasn't because she was enjoying the plot that much.

The rain was still pouring outside when Jake pressed the stop button on the remote control a few minutes later. A brisk wind blew the drops against the windows in a steady rat-a-tat, making it sound very appealing to stay inside for the afternoon.

"Do you need to work today?" Jake asked, glancing without enthusiasm toward the rain-lashed window. "If so, I can go back to my own cabin and watch TV or something."

She couldn't help but smile. He probably thought he was being considerate making the offer to leave, but he couldn't have been more obvious in his reluctance to do so.

"Why don't we hang out here for a while?" she suggested instead. "I'm pretty much caught up with work for today. Nick keeps plenty of rainy-day activities stocked here. Board games, like the Monopoly set we played the other day, video games, that sort of thing."

Jake's smile broadened. "That sounds great. I've been eyeing that video game system, actually. I have the same one in my—at home."

She noted the slight stammer, but paid little attention to it. "My nephew is addicted, of course. He has two or three game systems at home, but Nick only allows this one here. And he doesn't let Andrew play more than a couple of hours a day, though that's a constant battle."

"I'm sure it is. So, are you any good? At video games, I mean."

She lifted an eyebrow. "I can hold my own with some of them. Some of the others are entirely too complicated for me."

"Then I'll let you pick what we play. I like them all."

"I warn you, I'm pretty good at the golf game."

He chuckled. "That's not my strongest one. You'll probably stomp me."

"I'll certainly try," she agreed, grinning up at him.

His arm twitched spasmodically around her shoulders and his

smile faded as he gazed down at her. Their faces were close together, their bodies cozily aligned. And suddenly it was very warm in the room.

Jake reached up to brush back a stray curl that had escaped her loose ponytail. His fingers lingered on her cheek, curving to cup her face. "You have the most amazing eyes," he murmured. "Such a clear gray-blue. Like the sky on an autumn morning. I guess you hear that all the time."

"Uh…" She cleared her throat. "No, not really."

"Then you've been around some very unobservant people."

"Or maybe you're just more full of blarney than most." The retort might have been more effective had her voice not been quite so breathless.

He laughed softly, a low, seductive chuckle that slid right down her spine. "Maybe you're right. But I really do think you have beautiful eyes."

"Thank you." She wasn't very good at flirtation. Should she tell him that his eyes were beautiful, too? Because they were.

He didn't give her a chance to say anything at all. His lips brushed hers, lightly at first. Testingly. And even that was enough to empty her mind.

He must have read willingness in her response. Rather than drawing away, he deepened the kiss, tilting his head for a better angle. She put her arms around his neck and parted her lips for him.

THIS KISS WAS explosive. Amazing. And just a little bit terrifying, because she couldn't imagine ever being kissed so perfectly by anyone else. Would she spend the rest of her life remembering this moment? Comparing every future embrace to this one and finding them lacking, because they wouldn't come from Jake?

That thought gave her the strength to draw back, breaking off the kiss. Jake's arms tightened just a moment, but he released her without further protest. Though his features were tight with arousal, he managed a smile. "Too fast?"

"Much too fast," she agreed a bit hoarsely, and pushed herself to her feet. "I'll go refill our glasses with more iced tea. You choose a video game."

He sighed in resignation. "Yes, ma'am."

Her knees a bit rubbery, Stacy walked into the kitchen, where the first thing she did was open the refrigerator and let the cool air rush over her.

She heard Jake's cell phone ring just as she pulled the tea pitcher off the refrigerator shelf. Adding fresh ice to the glasses they'd sipped from during the movie, she took her time pouring the tea and adding slices of lemon to give him a chance to complete his call in privacy. Yet he was still talking when she carried the two glasses to the doorway.

"I'll call you tomorrow, Pam, I promise," he was saying. "I just need a little more time."

That brought her to an abrupt stop. Pam?

"I know I've been avoiding you," he added, sounding apologetic. "I just didn't know what to say. I wasn't ready to make any commitments until after I talk to the doctor."

Commitments. Stacy swallowed, wondering just what she had interrupted.

"So do you forgive me?" he asked in his teasing, ultracharming voice, making Stacy's fingers tighten fiercely around the glasses. "Okay, sweetheart, I'll call you in the morning. 'Bye, now."

Suddenly aware that she had been eavesdropping, Stacy flushed. "Um, here's your tea. Are you hungry yet? I can make sandwiches."

"No, not yet, thanks." He rose to take his glass, searching her face as if to gauge how much she'd overheard. "That was my assistant," he said lightly. "She handles all my scheduling."

She'd never heard of a truck driver needing an assistant, but what did she know? Besides, it was none of her business whom he'd been talking to. Or what his relationship with the other woman involved.

"I'm sure your friends are anxious to have you back soon," she commented, taking a seat at the far end of the sofa, so that Oscar would be sitting between her and Jake.

"Yeah, I guess."

"You must miss them, too."

"I'll enjoy seeing them again—but I haven't been missing them so much since I met you."

Lifting her glass to her lips, she didn't answer. She had teasingly accused him earlier of being full of blarney. She couldn't help wondering now just how accurate that accusation had been. Was he a compulsive flirt? Were easy endearments and fabulous kisses things he passed out a bit too generously?

Had she read too much into what had been happening between them?

He handed her a video game controller. "Let's see if you're as good at this golf game as you claim to be."

Playing video games seemed like a safe enough way to pass the afternoon. Setting down her tea glass, she gripped her controller. "Okay. You're on."

THEY PLAYED for over an hour, and then broke for lunch. By then Stacy was smiling again, flushed with success at beating him at golf. Twice. He got his revenge by winning every other game they played. She didn't seem to mind, apparently content with her golf championship.

Jake wasn't sure how much she'd overheard of his conversation with Pam. He had been honest with her about Pam's role in his life—but he wasn't entirely certain she had believed him. Had there been a hint of jealousy in her eyes? Would it be too shallow of him to be a little pleased if there had been?

He'd have to level with her soon, of course. He had to admit that it would have been easier before she'd gone off on her animosity toward the press—and pretty much anyone who lived in the spotlight.

She went into the kitchen to make sandwiches for lunch, declining his offer to help. Oscar tagged along at her heels, probably hoping for scraps. Jake took advantage of the opportunity to switch the television to the coverage of qualifying, checking to see how his teammates were doing. With just a few cars left to qualify, Ronnie Short was in third. Not bad. If he could keep running well, Ronnie could very well be one of the front-runners for the cup.

Rookie Scott Rivers was sixth, and Mike Overstreet ninth. Three of the four Woodrow drivers in the top ten. Woody would be pleased. Unfortunately, the Number 82 car with temporary driver Pete Sloan at the wheel was way down in the field.

Though he was one of the most promising drivers in the NASCAR Busch Series, twenty-year-old Pete was still having trouble finding his rhythm in NASCAR NEXTEL Cup racing. It had to be killing him to be messing up his chance at showing what he could do—and Jake had no doubt that Pete could handle top-level racing eventually. It was simply a matter of gaining experience and confidence.

Something clattered in the kitchen, and he heard Stacy mutter a curse. Grinning, he turned off the television, stood and walked to the door, and he realized that he was hardly limping at all now.

He was getting better. It wouldn't be long at all before he was back on the track. He wondered if Stacy would still be in his life then, or if she would have decided that she had no interest in a man who lived in a fast-moving fishbowl.

"Problems in here?" he asked from the doorway.

She was down on her knees, wiping up what appeared to be a splatter of mayonnaise. "Dropped the container," she admitted, making a face.

"I like mustard better anyway," he said.

"*Now* you tell me."

Chuckling, he pulled out a chair at the table, forgetting about the television.

Stacy rose to her feet, still shaking her head at her clumsiness. "I guess I'm still distracted by Mindy's call. Still furious with our so-called old friend. I'll try to put it out of my head now. I just keep reminding myself that the spotlight will have to seek out someone else soon, and that by the time I return home, I'll be happily anonymous again. That makes me feel a lot better."

Jake's smile slid right off his face. He had planned to tell Stacy everything about himself over lunch, but maybe this wasn't the right time after all. Not while she was still so worked up about the reporter's call.

He could tell her later, he assured himself. After she'd calmed down a bit. And after he figured out a way to convince her that being in a fishbowl wasn't such a bad way to live if the incentives were strong enough.

She walked him to the door after lunch. Knowing she had work she wanted to get to that afternoon, he didn't try to linger, nor did she try to detain him.

It had stopped raining. He hadn't even noticed until he opened the front door. The sky was still low and gray, and puddles of water were scattered between the cabins, but at least he wouldn't get wet going back to his place.

Glancing at Stacy, he said, "Thanks for the breakfast. And the lunch. You really made my day better."

"I'm glad."

"I'd like to see you tomorrow."

She moistened her lips, then nodded. "I'd like that, too."

He knew he shouldn't kiss her again until he leveled with her. But when it came to Stacy, he was learning that his willpower was weak. He contented himself with a quick brush of lips, knowing that brief taste would still be enough to torment him through the night.

"We'll talk tomorrow," he promised her—and himself.

Her smile was just a bit strained, as if somehow she had some premonition that talk wasn't going to be an easy one.

CHAPTER EIGHT

STACY WAS PACING again Sunday afternoon, and this time Oscar seemed resigned that there was little he could do to distract her. He sat in a corner gnawing on a rawhide chew, looking up only occasionally to see if she had come to her senses yet.

She was afraid he might have to wait a while for that.

Jake had left not long after lunch the day before, claiming he was giving her time to work and that he had a few things to do himself. He had seemed very distracted after she'd told him about her family history. Maybe the sordidness had bothered him more than he had let on.

After all, she reminded herself, Jake was a very private person. He, too, had chosen to recuperate in solitude. He had probably been appalled at the thought of being surrounded by reporters and photographers hoping to find out something interesting about Harley Carter's daughter. She couldn't blame him for that.

But at least it was out in the open, she told herself, trying to find something positive in the situation as she plopped onto the couch. He knew exactly who she was now. If he was interested in getting to know her better, then she was certainly willing to spend more time with him. Cautiously, of course.

And if he wasn't interested...well, she hadn't really expected anything to come of this anyway, she assured herself. The hollow feeling inside her that accompanied that thought made her scowl and reach for the television remote in an attempt to distract herself from any further thoughts of Jake.

A NASCAR race came onto the screen. Colorful cars roared around a track while names and numbers scrolled across the top of the screen and faceless announcers kept up a lively commentary.

Great, she thought with a sigh. Even the television was conspiring to make her think of Jake, automatically tuning in to his favorite sport. She reached again for the remote, thinking maybe she would find an old movie or an interesting biography or something that had nothing whatever to do with…

A knock on the door made her catch her lower lip between her teeth. So much for not thinking about him. She had no doubt that he was the one on the other side of the door.

Turning off the television, she rose and crossed the room, Oscar bouncing at her feet.

She'd guessed correctly, of course. Jake stood on the doorstep, his expression somber. "May I come in?"

"Of course." She moved out of the way, then closed the door behind him when he entered. Watching as he bent to greet Oscar, she asked, "Can I get you anything to drink? Tea or coffee?"

"No, I'm fine, thank you."

He straightened and pushed a hand through his hair as though bracing himself for something. She held her breath, wondering what he was trying to work up the nerve to say.

After a moment, he gave her a wry smile and said, "You know, I think I would like a glass of tea, if it isn't too much trouble."

He was stalling. From what, she didn't know, but she was willing to go along. Judging from the look in his eyes, she wasn't sure she was in any hurry to hear what he had to say.

He followed her into the kitchen and watched while she filled two tumblers with ice cubes and tea, adding slices of lemon from a bowl in the fridge. "Can I get you anything to go with it?" she asked. "A snack of some sort?"

"No, thanks. This is good."

He looked down at the glass as if he wasn't sure what to do with it now. Whatever he had come to say, it was apparently difficult for him to get started—which made her even more nervous.

He cleared his throat. "Um, Stacy, there's something we need to talk about."

No good conversation had ever begun with those particular words, she decided on the spot. Figuring they might as well get it over with, she set her untasted tea on the counter and squared her shoulders. "What is it?"

"It's about my job."

That surprised her a little, but she nodded. "Go on."

"I know you think—"

Whatever he was going to say was interrupted when they both heard the front door open in the other room and a man's voice call out, "Hey, Stace? You here?"

Jake's eyes narrowed.

"My brother," she told him, turning toward the kitchen doorway, unsure whether she was relieved or frustrated by the interruption. "I forgot he'd said he might drive up this afternoon."

"Oh." He glanced at the kitchen doorway as though considering whether he should make a fast escape, but then he followed her toward the living room.

Nick stood in the center of the room, his pleasantly homely face a bit tense around the corners of his mouth. She identified the source of his stress when she saw that Andrew had already thrown himself on the couch and reached for the television remote, his sullen expression telling Stacy that he and his father had been arguing again.

Her brother and nephew looked so much alike, their coloring almost identical. Yet Nick wore his medium brown hair in a professionally short cut that befitted his career as a bank executive. Andrew's was perpetually long and shaggy, almost hiding his eyes, which were the same blue-gray as his father's and his aunt's. Nick dressed in businessman's casual khakis and polo shirt, while Andrew's costume of choice was baggy hoodies and ripped jeans.

Shaking his head in annoyance at his son's sullenness, Nick held out a canvas bag to Stacy. "I see you've quit wearing your sling. I guess the arm really is feeling better, as you assured me on the phone? I brought your mail and your newspapers. And you had a package from your…"

He lost his train of thought when he spotted Jake behind her. "Oh. Sorry. I didn't know you had company."

Setting the bag aside, Stacy said, "Jake, this is my brother, Nick Carter, and my nephew, Andrew. Guys, I'd like you to meet—"

"Oh, my gosh." Tossing a hank of hair out of his eyes, Andrew lunged to his feet. His mouth hung open as he gaped at Jake, making him look somewhat less intelligent than he really was, Stacy thought ruefully. "You're…you're…"

Both Stacy and Nick stared at the boy, perplexed by his uncharacteristic behavior.

"Andrew, what on earth—?" Nick began, only to be interrupted again when Jake stepped toward Andrew with his right hand extended.

"Nice to meet you, Andrew. I'm Jake."

"Jake Hinson," Andrew breathed, making the name sound almost sacred.

"Yes. Jake Hinson."

STACY TURNED to Nick, expecting him to still be as bewildered as she was. But now he, too, was looking at Jake with a startled expression. "You're Jake Hinson? *The* Jake Hinson?"

"Nice to meet you, Nick," Jake said, offering his hand again.

"What are you doing in Arkansas, Jake?" Andrew demanded, crowding closer. "How come you aren't *there?*"

"You know why he isn't there," Nick chided his son. "You knew about his accident—we talked about it. We were real sorry to hear about that, Jake. I hope you're doing well."

Stacy couldn't stand it any longer. "How on earth do you know about Jake's accident?" she asked them both. "And where is 'there'?"

Nick and Andrew stared at her now, disbelief written on their eerily similar faces.

"There," Andrew repeated, motioning toward the television. "The race."

"Everybody who follows NASCAR even casually heard about Jake's accident," Nick added. "I'd have thought even you would have heard."

"I don't follow NASCAR even casually," she reminded them slowly. And all of a sudden so much of what Jake had told her made perfect sense.

"You're a driver," she said, turning to him.

Apology in his eyes, he nodded. "I told you I was."

And he had known all along that she had misunderstood what that meant.

"So you hang out with Scott Rivers, right?" Andrew asked, brushing off his aunt's incomprehensible ignorance. "What's he like?"

Jake smiled wryly. "He's as crazy as you think he is. Great kid. Almost as good behind the wheel as I am."

Andrew laughed. He actually laughed, Stacy thought in

shock. She couldn't even remember the last time she'd heard her nephew laugh right out loud. "You're good," he conceded. "But Rivers is seriously cool."

"Last time I saw Scott he was putting a rubber mouse in Mike Overstreet's motor home. Overstreet's got a real thing about mice. Freaks out every time he sees one."

Andrew laughed again. "That sounds like the wild Scott Rivers I see on TV. What did Overstreet do when he saw the mouse?"

"He freaked," Jake replied, grinning. "Screamed like a little girl. His fiancée had to prove to him that the mouse was rubber before he'd go back in the RV. Overstreet's an iron man on the track, but when it comes to furry rodents, he's a real wuss."

"Did he ever find out it was Scott who put it there?"

"Oh, yeah. He found out. Last I heard, he was still plotting the perfect revenge."

"Sounds like you guys have a great time," Andrew said wistfully.

"Yeah," Jake answered simply. "We do."

Realizing that they were still standing in the middle of the living room, Stacy roused from her shock long enough to say, "Maybe we should all sit down. Andrew, do you want a soda and some cookies?"

The teen didn't even glance her way. "Yeah, thanks. You want to watch the race, Jake?"

Giving Stacy a quick, rueful glance, Jake shrugged. "Sure. Why not?"

"I'll help you get the drinks, sis," Nick offered as Jake and Andrew sat on the couch.

Knowing she was in for questions, Stacy nodded and accompanied her brother to the kitchen.

WATCHING THE RACE with the unabashed fan of another driver was an…interesting experience, Jake decided a while later. Andrew Carter seemed to have no doubt that "his" driver was the real star of NASCAR, even though Scott Rivers was only finishing his first year in the NASCAR NEXTEL Cup Series. Of course, it had been a fairly successful first year. The rookie had two wins and eight top-five finishes under his belt. He was pretty much a shoo-in for rookie of the year.

At least Andrew's hero was on the Woodrow Racing team, he thought. Could have been worse. Andrew could be cheering on one of Jake's fiercest rivals.

After being in the kitchen for a significant time, during which he imagined Nick grilled Stacy about her acquaintance with Jake, the brother and sister joined him and Andrew to watch the rest of the race. They brought sodas, cookies and popcorn with them, and Andrew dug in, his eyes never leaving the screen. Oscar bounced from person to person, begging for attention and treats, receiving more of the former than the latter, at Stacy's insistence.

It was obvious that Stacy had never watched a race before. She confessed that, other than knowing that the first car over the line at the end was the winner, she knew absolutely nothing about the sport.

Seemingly embarrassed by her ignorance in front of a racing insider—and maybe showing off his own knowledge a little— Andrew gruffly tried to educate her.

Jake assumed that Stacy had explained as best she could to her brother about how she and Jake had become friendly. Nick studied him with curiosity and some wariness, as Jake might have expected from a protective older brother. Andrew seemed to simply accept Jake's presence, excited to meet his racing hero's teammate, and thrilled to be viewing a race with someone who could tell him interesting behind-the-scenes anecdotes.

Jake couldn't help watching Stacy during the race. He

couldn't really read her expression when she happened to glance his way. Was she angry? Hurt? Disappointed? Impressed? No, not that. Whatever emotions her bland smiles were hiding, being starstruck was not one of them.

"That's my teammate in the lead," he told her when Andrew gave him a chance to speak. "Ronnie Short. Great guy. He and his wife, Katie, are expecting their first child soon."

"Your teammate?" she asked, obviously uncertain what that entailed.

He nodded. "We both drive for the same owner, Woodrow Racing. Woody runs four cars in the NASCAR NEXTEL Cup Series. Ronnie, me, Mike Overstreet and the rookie, your nephew's favorite, Scott Rivers. Look, there's my car on the screen now. The purple-and-silver Number 82?"

Focusing on the car he'd pointed out, she nodded. "I see it. Who's driving it today?"

"Pete Sloan. He's just a kid, but he's been doing real well in the NASCAR Busch Series. He's had some trouble since he's been filling in for me, mostly because he just wasn't quite ready to move up to the top level of racing. He needed another year or two in the Busch Series. But he's good—he'll get another chance to prove himself."

"They drive so close together," she fretted at one point. Sitting in a chair with Oscar in her lap, she frowned at the screen. "How can they possibly keep up with where everyone else is around them?"

"That's what the spotter's for," Andrew said before Jake could speak. "The spotter talks to the driver all the time through his headset and tells him where the other cars are. Isn't that right, Jake?"

He nodded. "Arnie, my spotter, has been with me since the beginning. I trust him completely. Trust is crucial between drivers and spotters, because our peripheral vision is so limited in the cars that the only way we know how to avoid a crash sometimes is by having our spotters tell us."

As if on cue, someone hit the wall, then slid down the track right into a tightly grouped pack of cars. Tires smoked, brakes squealed and cars went spinning across the track, into the grass, into each other. Jake winced as Scott Rivers slammed into another car, having nowhere else to go.

"Oh, crap!" Andrew exclaimed in dismay. "That Number 56 car just took out all those other guys from nothing but pure stupidity. He should have known there wasn't room for him to pass on the outside in Turn 3."

"You're right, it was a reckless move," Jake agreed, assessing the situation on-screen. "He got too impatient. The rookies are bad at that. For that matter, some of the veterans make pretty stupid mistakes at times. I've made a few myself."

"I bet Scott's pissed."

"Quite likely."

"Watch your mouth, Andrew," Nick said wearily, as though he'd said it entirely too many times before.

"Are they all right?" Stacy asked, looking at the wreckage in consternation.

"Everyone's fine," Jake assured her. "It wasn't that bad a wreck."

"Not that bad?" she asked, staring at him as though he were crazy. "Look at those cars."

"Those cars are made to absorb the impact and protect the driver, who's strapped into a seat built specifically for him. NASCAR has dedicated a great deal of time and resources toward ensuring driver safety, and their efforts have paid off. See how all the drivers involved have put their window nets down? That's a signal that they're okay. Look, most of them are either driving toward the pits or getting out of their cars on their own. It just takes a couple of minutes to unfasten all the safety equipment they're required to wear."

"But there's an ambulance."

"They'll take a couple of them to the infield care center just to make sure they're okay, but it's only a formality. See, everyone's out now. No one's hurt, but a few are mad—including the guy that caused the wreck in the first place."

"His own fault," Andrew insisted, still disgruntled that Rivers's car was so badly damaged that he'd be lucky to get back out on the track in it at all.

"Yeah. He'll either apologize for being stupid—or he'll find someone else to blame," Jake predicted with a slight smile. "Just wait until the trackside reporter gets to him to ask him what happened."

"Aren't you ever afraid out there?" Stacy asked, still looking as if she couldn't imagine why anyone would want to participate in such a sport.

"No," he answered simply, and with complete sincerity. "I'm always too focused on doing my job. I trust my team to give me a good car, and my spotter to keep me aware of what's going on around me on the track. For the most part, I trust the other drivers, though there's always someone who gets excited and makes a bonehead move during a race. I've been taken out more often than I like to remember by someone else's mistake—just like Scott was this time."

"That must be frustrating."

"Oh, yeah. Somebody just about always ends a race mad at somebody."

"What happens then?"

He smiled and shrugged. "You get over it. Next week, you

might be the one to do something stupid and ruin someone's day."

She shook her head and looked back at the screen.

With the race under caution, the network took advantage of the opportunity to go to commercials. And shouldn't he have expected, he thought in resignation, that the first one up was one of his own?

His smiling face came on-screen as he assured the viewers that he trusted nothing but Vaughan Tools in his own garage. Pulling back, the camera revealed that he wore his splashy purple-and-silver uniform, his helmet tucked beneath one arm, a large wrench in his other hand. He tossed the wrench aside, put on his helmet, snapped down the smoked face shield—and then the camera pulled back farther to reveal him climbing onto a kid's-style bicycle, which he proceeded to pedal out of the garage set in which the ad had been filmed.

It was supposed to have been funny. Now he wondered if it was just sort of silly.

Trying not to grimace, he glanced at his companions. Andrew grinned at him in awe, while Nick studied him rather cautiously. Once again, Stacy's expression was hard to read, but she didn't look particularly happy.

Four hours later Jake was genuinely pleased when Ronnie won the race. He smiled when the camera panned to an elated Katie, so pregnant and proud of her soul mate.

Even Andrew seemed satisfied with the race's end. "Short's an okay guy," he said. "If Rivers couldn't win, I guess it's okay that Short did."

"Yeah, well, it would have been even better if I'd won," Jake grumbled, only half joking.

"You'll be back, man," Andrew said, displaying his new loyalty. "No doubt."

Jake smiled. "Thanks, kid."

"So, Jake," Nick said, turning off the TV, "how long do you plan to be here in the state?"

He'd obviously been biding his time until the race ended. Feeling a bit as though he were facing a suspicious father, Jake replied lightly, "I have a doctor's appointment early next week. If he gives me the clearance I'm expecting, I'll be back in the car for the Saturday-night race in Charlotte the following weekend."

Stacy gave him another sharp look.

Andrew immediately jumped back into the conversation with another spate of questions. While they were talking, Stacy got up quietly and went into the kitchen to prepare a simple early dinner of spaghetti, breadsticks and salad.

Racing, and Jake's role in it, continued to be the main topic of conversation while they ate, even though he tried a few times to change the subject by asking questions about Nick's work and Andrew's school. Andrew was having none of it. He wanted to talk racing, and since his older relatives seemed pleased that he was talking at all, Jake cooperated patiently.

As soon as they had finished eating, Nick brought the interlude to an end. "We'd better get on the road, Andy. You've got school in the morning."

The boy's expression took on a rebellious cast that Jake suspected his family recognized all too well. "I'm not ready to go yet."

"Yeah, well, you didn't want to come in the first place, remember? I told you we were just making a quick trip to check on your aunt, and we've been here long enough."

"So I'll skip school tomorrow. Big deal."

"You aren't skipping school." Nick sounded weary.

"It's not like it matters." Andrew looked to Jake for support.

"All he talks about is school and homework and going to college and stuff like that. How it's important that I'm in ninth grade so I need to keep my grades up for college so I'll get a good job. If I wanted to work on a pit crew or in a race shop or something, I wouldn't even have to go to college, right? You and Scott didn't, I bet."

"No," Jake admitted. "I didn't go to college. Scott went for a couple of years, but then he dropped out to pursue driving full-time. I can't speak for him, but I can tell you that I'll always feel like I missed out on something there.

"As for the other team members, more and more of them are obtaining degrees these days. Engineering, automotive technology, marketing—there are a lot of degrees represented in the sport. NASCAR is a big business, you know, filled with qualified professionals. If you're really interested in a career there, you'd do well to keep your grades up and get as much training as you can to give yourself an edge against all the others who want in on the action."

Andrew's frown said he wasn't happy with Jake's answer, but Nick seemed to approve. "See? It isn't just me. Now, give your aunt a hug and let's get on the road."

Andrew grudgingly climbed to his feet without further argument, skinny shoulders slumping.

Taking pity on the kid, Jake offered, "How about if I send you some stuff when I get back home? You know, T-shirts. Hats. That sort of thing. I'm sure Scott will sign some stuff for you if I twist his arm."

Since he had already promised a package to the kid at the drive-in, he figured one more delivery wouldn't be so difficult to arrange.

Andrew brightened. "Really?"

"I promise."

"And you can tell your friends at school tomorrow about spending time with Jake today," Stacy reminded him. "That will be fun, won't it?"

He started to nod, then frowned. "They won't believe me."

"They will if you have pictures." Nick took his cell phone out of its holder. "I just happen to have a camera here. We'll print one on Stacy's printer, and Jake can sign it for you before we leave. If that's okay with you, Jake."

If there was one thing he was used to, it was being photographed with fans. "Sure. No problem."

He only hoped Andrew showing the photo around the school wouldn't somehow end up with the press on the door of his cabin, he thought as he stood with one hand on the boy's shoulder and smiled for the camera-phone.

Ten minutes later, a signed copy-paper rendition of the snapshot was clutched carefully in Andrew's hand and father and son were standing at the door.

"Nice to meet you, Jake," Nick said. "And, uh, thanks," he added with a glance at Andrew.

"No prob. It was a pleasure to meet you both."

"So, you want to walk out with us?" Nick asked a bit too casually.

"I, um—" He glanced at Stacy, who stood silently nearby, her arms crossed in front of her.

"Jake isn't leaving just yet, Nick," she said after a slight pause. "He and I have some things to talk about."

Suppressing a wince at her tone, Jake wondered if he should make his escape with Nick and Andrew after all.

CHAPTER NINE

THE CABIN WAS very still after Nick and Andrew left. Even Oscar was quiet for once, sitting on the floor and looking from Stacy to Jake as if he somehow sensed that something had changed between them.

Stacy tried to think of something to say to break the silence, but it seemed that all she could do was stare at Jake. Her mind filled with the memory of the way he had looked in that television commercial. The face that had become so familiar to her had been framed on-screen, the mouth she had kissed hours earlier smiling at the camera and smoothly promoting some tool company.

His hair had been shorter on-screen, more stylish. He'd worn a bright purple garment cover with sponsor patches rather than the jeans and Ts she'd become accustomed to seeing on him. He had looked polished and professional and completely at ease on camera—but there had been no mistaking that it was the same man who was even now looking back at her with a somber expression.

He finally spoke, and when he did, he used the same words he'd used earlier. "I told you I was a driver."

She planted her hands on her hips, her annoyance with him returning. "You knew very well I thought you meant you drove a truck."

"Well, yeah," he admitted. "I tried to tell you the truth a couple of times, but we were interrupted and..."

His voice trailed off, as if he knew exactly how weak that excuse sounded to her.

"You could have told me at any time."

He sighed. "I know. I'm sorry."

She'd held things back from him, too, she realized with a slight wince. But she *had* told him, eventually. "So your last name is Hinson. You never even told me that."

"I wasn't keeping it a secret. I guess I just didn't realize that I hadn't given you my full name."

"I probably wouldn't have recognized it anyway," she admitted, hearing the stilted tone of her own voice. "Since I don't follow racing, I don't know anything about you."

"You know a great deal about me," he corrected her, frowning. "Everything I told you was true. I just didn't elaborate about my job."

"A fairly important omission."

"I know," he said again. "I just..."

Again, his voice faded.

He just—what? Hadn't trusted her? Had he thought she was the kind of woman who would pursue a famous man for the money and attention? Had he been concerned that she would notify the press or beg for free tickets and/or merchandise for family or friends? If any of that was true, he hadn't gotten to know her at all during the past week.

"It was nice being just Jake for a few days," he said after a pause. "It's been a while since I've had that freedom."

She thought of the time they had spent in town, surrounded by other people. "I'm surprised no one else recognized you."

"As you pointed out, several people said I looked familiar. And the boy at the drive-in theater concession stand knew me

Play the Lucky Hearts Game

and get...

2 FREE BOOKS and
2 FREE MYSTERY GIFTS...
YOURS to KEEP!

Yes! I have scratched off the silver card. Please send me my *2 FREE BOOKS* and *2 FREE mystery GIFTS*. I understand that I am under no obligation to purchase any books as explained on the back of this card.

Scratch Here!

then look below to see what your cards get you... 2 Free Books & 2 Free Mystery Gifts!

335 SDL ENU9

235 SDL ENNX

FIRST NAME

LAST NAME

ADDRESS

APT.#

CITY

STATE/PROV.

ZIP/POSTAL CODE

(S-SEO-08/07)

Twenty-one gets you
2 FREE BOOKS and
2 FREE MYSTERY GIFTS!

Twenty gets you
2 FREE BOOKS!

Nineteen gets you
1 FREE BOOK!

TRY AGAIN!

The Silhouette Reader Service™ — Here's how it works:

Accepting your 2 free books and 2 free gifts places you under no obligation to buy anything. You may keep the books and gifts and return the shipping statement marked "cancel". If you do not cancel, about a month later we'll send you 6 additional books and bill you just $4.24 each in the U.S. or $4.99 each in Canada, plus 25¢ shipping & handling per book and applicable taxes if any.* That's the complete price and — compared to cover prices of $4.99 each in the U.S. and $5.99 each in Canada — it's quite a bargain! You may cancel at any time, but if you choose to continue, every month we'll send you 6 more books which you may either purchase at the discount price or return to us and cancel your subscription.

*Terms and prices subject to change without notice. Sales tax applicable in N.Y. Canadian residents will be charged applicable provincial taxes and GST. Credit or debit balances in a customer's account(s) may be offset by any other outstanding balance owed by or to the customer. Please allow 4 to 6 weeks for delivery. Offer available while quantities last.

If offer card is missing write to: The Silhouette Reader Service, 3010 Walden Ave., P.O. Box 1867, Buffalo, NY 14240-1867

BUSINESS REPLY MAIL
FIRST-CLASS MAIL   PERMIT NO. 717   BUFFALO, NY

POSTAGE WILL BE PAID BY ADDRESSEE

SILHOUETTE READER SERVICE
3010 WALDEN AVE
PO BOX 1867
BUFFALO NY 14240-9952

NO POSTAGE
NECESSARY
IF MAILED
IN THE
UNITED STATES

immediately. That's why I was gone for so long—he wanted to talk."

She remembered asking him if there had been a long line. He hadn't lied to her then, either, she saw now. He'd told her he'd gotten into a conversation with the kid behind the counter. He'd simply neglected to mention what the conversation had been about.

She remembered other things now. The way he'd acted when she had mentioned the NASCAR museum in Batesville. The way he'd avoided the NASCAR merchandise at the old general store. The things he had said that just hadn't seemed to fit the career of a truck driver.

No, he had never lied to her. He'd just withheld the details. Which was exactly what she had done to him in the beginning. Because she had been tired of talking about her ordeal. Jake had probably felt the same way.

Still, he could have told her before he had kissed her senseless. Made her start daydreaming about a future she knew now could never be.

"I was going to tell you today," he said, pushing his hands into his pockets and looking penitent. "I had just gotten started when your brother and your nephew showed up. I'm sorry you had to find out the way you did, with no warning."

Keeping her face unrevealing—at least, she hoped so—she replied, "You certainly had no obligation to tell me anything."

"I *wanted* to tell you," he said with a shake of his head. "I want you to know me, everything about me. Things can't go any further between us until we have it all out in the open."

That made her eyebrows rise sharply. "Um, things?"

His smile was wry. "I'm not expressing myself very well, but I think you know what I mean. I think you and I have made a real connection. I don't want to say goodbye to you in a few days and then never see you again."

She bit her lip.

After a moment, Jake cleared his throat. "Maybe I'm misinterpreting a few things? We *have* made a connection, haven't we?"

"We hardly know each other."

He frowned. "I'd like to think we've gotten to know each other pretty well, considering."

Considering that she hadn't known what he did for a living? That she hadn't even known his last name?

She pasted on a bright, fake smile intended to conceal her unreasonable disappointment that he wasn't the simple truck driver he had portrayed himself to be. "Andrew was so excited to meet you. He'll be a real hero at his school tomorrow, showing off that autographed picture of you and him."

Jake's scowl deepened. "Now you know why I didn't want to tell you," he muttered. "All of a sudden, you're treating me differently."

"I don't know what you mean."

"You just talked about my autograph, for crying out loud."

"I'm sorry, is that not the way it's done? I've never really met a racing star before."

He muttered something she didn't ask him to repeat, then took a step toward her. "Stacy—"

She held up both hands. "I don't—"

He moved closer, until her hands rested on his chest. He slid his hands around her waist, his eyes locked with hers. "I'm the same person you knew this morning," he murmured. "And I think I can prove that nothing has really changed between us."

He lowered his mouth to hers. And even though she told herself she should push him away, she simply closed her eyes and tilted her head back for him.

THE KISS LASTED quite a long time. By the time it ended, Stacy's knees were shaky, and she was clinging to Jake's shirt for support rather than to hold him at bay.

He rested his forehead against hers. His voice was almost hoarse when he said, "You aren't going to try again to tell me we haven't connected, are you?"

"I have to admit there's an…attraction," she conceded quietly.

"I think it's more than that. Or it can be, if we give it a chance."

She shook her head against his. "It wouldn't work. I live in Little Rock, you live in North Carolina, when you aren't at a race track or en route to one."

"I'm here for another few days, and so are you," he reminded her. "I don't want to start over, exactly, because the past week has been great and there's little I would change about it. But couldn't we just go on from here, knowing there aren't any more secrets between us?"

He lifted his head then. "Um, there aren't any more secrets, are there? You aren't married, or engaged or anything like that?"

"No. Are you?"

He smiled. "No. So, are you going to kick me out? Or can we still be friends?"

"I guess there's no reason to avoid each other while we're both here."

His mouth twisted. "I was hoping for a *little* more enthusiasm, but I'll take what I can get."

Now that she'd agreed to spend more time with him, she wasn't sure exactly what to do. "Would you like some coffee?" she asked, falling automatically back into hostess mode.

He nodded. "That sounds good."

They sat across the kitchen table with coffee cups in front of them while Stacy searched her mind for something else to say.

"Ask me anything you want," Jake encouraged, as if sensing

her dilemma. "I told you, I'm not hiding anything from you now."

She knew so little about racing that she hardly knew what to ask him next about his real life. "I heard you and Andrew talking about the championship. You said your friend Ronnie is in contention for that honor?"

Jake nodded rather glumly. "It's all based on points accumulated during the season. Only the drivers in the top ten spots compete for the NASCAR NEXTEL Cup championship during the final ten races. I was in the third spot when I had to pull out."

"So you would have been competing for the championship."

He gave her a sudden, cocky smile. "I'd have *won* the championship."

She sensed that his bravado was intended to hide bitter disappointment. And yet, she also believed she was seeing the face that racing hero Jake Hinson displayed for his public. The man she had met—sad, lonely, battered, but still sweet and charming—was completely different, and she wondered now if she had created an image in her mind of someone who didn't even exist.

"I'm sorry your season was cut short," she said.

His attitude changed, giving her another glimpse of the man she had seen sitting sad and alone on the deck of his cabin. "I can't really complain," he said quietly. "I was a lot luckier than Eric. He had kids, you know. Two boys."

And that was what kept eating at him more than the loss of his racing season, she realized. He wondered why a single man with no family had been spared over the father of two.

She had read enough about survivor's guilt to recognize it in Jake's tone. "You were lucky," she agreed. "But there was nothing you could have done to change the outcome of the accident. You told me the other driver crashed into your boat without any warning. There's no way to know why you survived and your friend didn't."

He sighed and pushed a hand through his hair. "I've spent a lot of hours replaying what I remember of the crash in my mind. Wondering if I shouldn't have seen the other boat sooner, if I could have reacted faster. But it always comes back to the fact that I was caught completely unaware. Before I knew what was happening, I was underwater and blood and debris were everywhere. Some people nearby saw what happened and pulled me out before I drowned. By the time they got to Eric, it was too late."

She shivered at the thought of how close he had come to dying in that accident. She'd have heard on the news that a popular young race car driver had been killed in a boating accident, and she would have thought it was sad. But without having known him, she wouldn't have realized just what a loss it would have been.

She couldn't even imagine now never having met him. And that made her even more worried about continuing this friendship...or whatever it was that had developed during the past week.

"Is making television commercials a part of every driver's job?" she asked to draw his attention away from the tragedy—and her own thoughts away from the complications between Jake and her.

He grimaced at the reminder of the rather silly ad. "Most of us do various things to promote our sponsors. TV and print ads, personal appearances, that sort of thing. As my crew chief says, if the sponsor ain't happy, ain't nobody happy."

"It sounds as though you stay very busy."

He nodded. "I work a minimum of six days a week for ten months a year. During the other two months the schedule is somewhat less hectic, but still pretty full. And I'm on the road for at least thirty-six weekends a year."

Dazed by that schedule, she could only say, "Wow."

"It makes it a challenge to maintain a relationship with anyone," he added, studying her face as he spoke. "But you've heard me talk about my friends who have managed to work it out."

She swallowed. Was there a reason he was suddenly talking about relationships?

"It must be a very exciting life," she said, hating the slight primness she heard in her own tone. She had a bad habit of speaking that way when she found herself in an awkward situation.

"It's *my* life," he said, moving a hand in a matter-of-fact gesture. "Racing is all I've wanted to do since I was fifteen years old and started hanging around a dirt track just to have something to do while my mother was busy with one of her jobs. I met an old guy who'd been working in various pit crews since the early days of stock car racing, and he sort of took me under his wing. Introduced me to some people who helped me get jobs in the shops and garages.

"One thing led to another and I met Woody Woodrow, who gave me a chance in the Craftsman Truck Series. The next year, I filled in a couple of times in the NASCAR Busch Series. I did well enough that Woody offered me a full-time Busch ride. Four years ago, he moved me into the NASCAR NEXTEL Cup Series when one of his longtime drivers retired."

"Are you sure you'll be ready to race again in less than two weeks?"

"I'll be fine. I've been doing my exercises, and they get easier all the time. I'll drive in that Saturday-night race I mentioned, and then the final five races after that one. I'm out of the Chase, but I can still get back out there and try to get a few more wins this season."

The sudden silence in the room when he finished speaking was jarring. Stacy could almost hear her own heartbeat as she toyed with her coffee cup.

"You're still processing all of this, aren't you?" Jake asked after a few minutes.

His wording amused her enough that her smile felt almost normal. "I suppose you could say that."

"It's just a job, Stacy."

She leveled a look at him. "Granted, I don't know much about NASCAR, but even I know it's more than just a job."

He sighed and nodded to acknowledge her point. "Okay, it's more than a job. But I'm still the same person."

He kept saying that. But the man she had met—or *thought* she'd met—had not been a famous race car driver.

"Actually, I have some work I still need to do this evening," she said, glancing pointedly at the package her brother had brought to her.

Though he looked a bit disappointed, he stood obligingly, apparently realizing she needed to be alone for a while to think about what she had learned that afternoon. To completely readjust her thinking about him.

At the door, he asked, "I'll see you tomorrow?"

"Perhaps."

He didn't look particularly pleased by the noncommittal response, but again, he didn't try to argue with her. "You have my cell number," he reminded her. "Call if you need anything."

She nodded. "I'll see you later, Jake."

"Yes. You will." Smiling, he leaned down his head to brush her lips with his on the way out, as had become his habit.

Just enough to leave her wanting more—as all those teasing kisses before had done.

STACY KNEW the moment she saw Jake's face the next morning that something was wrong. She had just opened her door in response to his knock, and the grimness in his expression struck her immediately. "What is it?"

"May I come in?"

She moved out of the way. Watching as he bent to pat Oscar, she closed the door. "What is it, Jake?"

He sighed and straightened. "I have to leave."

She blinked. "You just got here."

"No, that isn't what I meant. I have to leave Arkansas. Go back to North Carolina."

"Oh." Her stomach clenched. "When?"

"A private jet is picking me up at the airport in less than two hours."

"Two hours," she repeated slowly. "Is there an emergency?"

"Not exactly. It's a sponsor thing. A major contract deal has come through that I need to be involved with. It's a good thing for my team," he added. "A great opportunity, actually. Woody's been working on this deal for quite a while, and he's ecstatic about it."

"Then I guess congratulations are in order." She forced a smile. "I'm happy for your team."

"Thanks. I can't say much about the details yet, I'm afraid. They'll announce it later this week and I'll have to be involved with some media promotion. I tried to convince Pam to let me stay here a few more days and come back when it's all a done deal, but Woody and the sponsor insisted I need to be there this afternoon."

"'If the sponsor ain't happy, ain't nobody happy,'" she murmured, remembering his crew chief's quote.

Jake nodded, his smile not reaching his eyes. "That's the bottom line."

"Well." She crossed her arms and tucked her hands, suddenly self-conscious. "I've certainly enjoyed knowing you these past few days. I'll be watching for you on my television from now on."

Jake frowned, his fists planted on his hips. "You sound as if you're saying goodbye."

"Isn't that why you came over? To tell me goodbye?"

"No. Well, I came to tell you I'm leaving, but not to say goodbye. Not permanently, anyway." He moved toward her, setting his hands on her shoulders. "I'll call you, okay?"

"Call anytime," she replied. "I'll enjoy hearing from you."

She figured he would call a few times—and then he would get back into the frantic schedule of his real life. The calls would come less frequently, and then they would stop altogether. And she wouldn't be greatly disappointed, she promised herself, because she would be completely prepared for that outcome.

Jake was beginning to look annoyed. "Why are you talking that way? Like we're just a couple of passing acquaintances who'll probably never see each other again?"

Because the description sounded very much like what she had just been thinking, she simply looked at him.

He studied her face through narrowed eyes. "Is that what you want? Do you want me to go away and never see you again?"

The very thought made her chest hurt. But what else could they do? They lived in different states, literally. In different worlds, figuratively. "I said I would love to hear from you sometime."

"But you don't think I'll call," he finished grimly.

"I know you have a very busy schedule."

"You think I'll forget about you?"

She moistened her lips. "I'm saying I would understand if you're too busy to call."

He let out a gusty breath, and since they were still standing so close together, the warm breeze brushed her cheek, and ruffled the tiny hairs that curled around her face. "I'll call you."

"All right." She swallowed. "You'd better be on your way, hadn't you? You still have to make the drive to Batesville."

"Yeah," he said reluctantly. "I guess I'd better…but I hate to leave. You and I had so much more to talk about."

"I hope you have a safe flight home. And I hope the doctor gives you the news you want to hear later."

"He will." Jake sounded confident. "I'll be racing in Charlotte."

"Then I hope you win."

Leaving his left hand on her shoulder, he raised his right to brush her hair back from her cheek. "Maybe you'll be watching?"

A tiny shiver ran through her in response to the slight caress. "Maybe I will," she said huskily.

He lowered his head to brush his mouth over hers. Once. Twice. And then a third time. Each kiss a bit longer. More avid.

Jake lifted his head, looked down at her for a moment, then gathered her closer to crush her mouth beneath his. Her arms locked around his neck, she went up on tiptoes to give her better access to his mouth.

For a full week, these emotions had been building, through conversations and laughter and the light, teasing kisses they had shared thus far. Now, for the first time, they allowed passion to flare between them. She struggled to keep from being swept completely away by it, and she felt her heart breaking a little at the realization that the first time would very probably be the last.

Jake was breathing hard by the time he raised his head. Emotions darkened his eyes and carved deep lines around his mouth. His voice was gravelly when he said, "Now I *really* don't want to go."

She drew herself slowly out of his arms. "But you have to. Goodbye, Jake."

Shaking his head stubbornly, he said, "I'm not saying that. I'll call you later, okay?"

She nodded and reached for the doorknob. She needed to see him out quickly, while she could do so with some measure of dignity.

He paused long enough to give Oscar a farewell ear scratch. "See you around, buddy. Take good care of your friend here."

Oscar wagged his tail and did his best to lick Jake's entire face.

With one last pat, Jake straightened and moved toward the door, his eyes locked with Stacy's. He touched her cheek when he reached her.

"I'll call you," he said firmly, as if he repeated it enough she would finally believe him.

She nodded, unable to find the voice to say anything more. After only a momentary pause, he moved past her and walked outside, striding toward his cabin without looking back.

He was walking better than he had just the week before, she noticed. Hardly limping at all. There should be no reason at all why he couldn't drive again in just under two weeks.

She closed the door and rested her forehead against it, struggling against tears. Oscar nudged her ankle with his damp nose, claiming her attention. Picking him up, she nuzzled into his long, silky hair.

"You're right," she said after a pause, when she was relatively sure her voice would be steady. "I'm being foolish. I've only known him for a week."

One week. Such a short time to feel so significant.

She'd get over it, she assured herself, carrying Oscar with her to the couch. She hadn't really allowed herself to start hoping…not too much, anyway.

As for Jake, he might think now that they had connected on an important level, that they had formed a real bond—but she was more objective. She could see that he had been lonely and lost, his life on hold, his career temporarily stalled, his friends and coworkers going along without him.

He had needed a distraction. Someone to talk to, to laugh

with, to assure him that everything was going to be all right. A little boost for his battered male ego. She had provided all of that.

Now he was going back to North Carolina. Back to high-profile stock car racing. Back to his sponsors, his fans, his teammates. His life. A life that didn't include her. And she could live with that.

But, oh, she was going to miss him, she thought, burying her face in Oscar's hair again. She was really going to miss the sweet, sad, funny truck driver who had come very close to stealing her heart.

CHAPTER TEN

JAKE THREW HIMSELF onto a leather sofa late Tuesday afternoon with a heartfelt groan. He felt a bit as though he'd been dragged around the track behind a car for a few laps.

His crew chief chuckled heartlessly. "That's what you get for spending a week lazing around in paradise."

"Lazing around? I've been working my butt off getting back into shape."

"Maybe," Wade concluded, dropping into a chair near the sofa. "You certainly are walking better. Look a lot stronger. But you apparently made time to socialize with the—how did you phrase it?—the pretty lady next door?"

The reminder of Stacy made Jake's pulse jump. Not that he'd really needed the reminder. He hadn't actually stopped thinking about her all day, even though he'd been so busy he'd barely had time to breathe.

"You'd like her," he said. "So would Lisa."

"Yeah?"

"Yeah. She's great. I hope you'll get the chance to meet her before too long."

Wade's left eyebrow rose. "You're planning to see her again?"

"Absolutely," Jake answered confidently. Then added, "If I can convince her, that is."

Situating his lanky frame more comfortably in the chair of

Jake's office at Woodrow Racing headquarters, Wade ran a hand over his functionally short pecan-brown hair and studied Jake through narrowed brown eyes. Hours in the sun had tanned his skin and carved lines around his eyes and mouth, giving him a weathered, rather stern appearance, but Jake knew how that somber expression softened with Wade's rare full smiles.

"Since when do you have to convince any woman to spend time with you?" Wade asked laconically. "They're usually lined up at your door."

"Yeah, right. But either way, Stacy's not like the others. She's…well, she's pretty special."

Wade studied him more closely. "Special how?"

"It's hard to explain. She's a tiny little thing. Five-two, maybe. Five-three. Barely over a hundred pounds. Yet she has a black belt in tae kwon do and she recently used it to take down an armed criminal twice her size." He related the story Stacy had told him.

Wade whistled when Jake finished. "That took guts."

"Yeah. And apparently Stacy didn't even think twice." He chuckled. "She's got a little dog that's just like her. A Yorkie about the size of a loaf of bread who thinks he's a Doberman pinscher. His name's Oscar."

"Hmm." Wade looked thoughtful. "Sounds like you sort of fell for her."

"No 'sort of' about it," Jake admitted. "She got under my skin pretty bad in the short time I knew her. I really want to see her again, but…"

"But?" Wade prodded after a moment.

Sighing, Jake explained, "She's a very private person. Hates the press. Doesn't like attention called to herself. Said she would hate living in a fishbowl."

Wade winced. "That doesn't bode well for you. Does she know what your life is like?"

"Not much. She didn't even know who I was until her nephew recognized me Sunday afternoon. She doesn't follow NASCAR, never heard of me."

Wade looked a little surprised, then vaguely amused. "We get so used to being among insiders and fans that we forget sometimes that not everyone out there knows who we are."

"I was thinking the same thing the other day. It was nice to be anonymous for a few days—and yet, I kind of enjoy the attention that comes with the job. I mean, I race because I love it, but I like competing in front of the big crowds, too. It feels good to know I've got fans cheering me on and tracking my career, and reporters interested in what I have to say. Sure, I'd like to have more privacy at times, but that's all a part of the fame that comes with success. It's not so bad, you know?"

Wade nodded slowly. "Dealing with the press comes more naturally to some people than others. You've always been able to keep your anger and frustrations under control in front of the cameras. To hold on to your patience when you're asked a string of stupid questions while you're trying to concentrate on other things. Not everyone can compartmentalize as well as you do. I have to work pretty hard at it myself."

"I've always accepted it as part of the job. But then, I came up in the ranks when the sport was already growing in popularity by leaps and bounds."

"Like I said, you fit in well the way things are now. The press loves you. Your fans love you. Your haters love to hate you. Because you've played it so well, anyone who's interested in dating you better accept that you live in the public eye. Your fan club's going to want details."

Jake grimaced. "Yeah. Stacy's not going to like that."

"You've only known her a week," Wade reminded him.

"How soon did you know with Lisa? The first time you met her, I mean?"

Looking just a little startled by the question, Wade replied slowly, "I knew within fifteen minutes of meeting her."

"There you go, then."

"Yeah, but it took me more than six years to convince her we belonged together."

Effectively checked, Jake could only shrug.

Wade pushed himself to his feet. "I'm going to the shop. I want to see how those adjustments on the car are coming along."

Drawn to the delicious smells of grease, paint and exhaust, Jake stood, suddenly revitalized. "I'll come with you."

IT WAS SO QUIET at the river. So peaceful. So…dull without Jake there, Stacy thought with a sigh on Wednesday afternoon. Every time she looked out her window at the empty cabin next door, she was much too keenly aware of his absence.

Funny how much she missed him. She had known him such a short time—hardly long enough to make a lasting impression in her life. And yet in some ways she felt as though she had gotten to know him quite well.

She wondered how long it would be before she could take Oscar for a walk in the woods without thinking of Jake. Or eat ice cream. Or browse through intriguing little shops in Mountain View. Or play video games with her nephew. She wondered how long she would watch for his face on her television or hear his voice when she closed her eyes.

A crush, she told herself. That was all it had been. A vacation infatuation. There hadn't been time for it to develop into anything else. And crushes, by definition, didn't last long. So all she needed was time away from him to get past it. To turn him into a pleasant memory rather than a painful ache.

She looked at the purple plastic race car in her hand. He had smiled so broadly when he'd given it to her, she remembered. She knew now that he had been amused by the irony of his quarter-machine prize. And even though he hadn't shared that reason with her then, she couldn't be annoyed with him for it. Unfortunately, she understood a bit too well why he had enjoyed getting to know her without her having prior expectations based on who he was and what he did.

Trying to put him out of her mind, she set the car aside and pulled out her laptop. She worked until her neck and back were sore and her stomach growled for food. She put out food for Oscar and made a sandwich for herself, carrying the paper plate back to the laptop. She intended to start working again as she chewed her sandwich, but she found herself typing Jake's name into the computer instead.

She nearly choked on her bread and meat when she saw that there were over twenty thousand hits. Looking at a sampling of them, she noted that there were biographies, statistics, interviews, licensed merchandise, fan clubs, even gossip sites.

One of the sites she clicked on was devoted to which of the single drivers had girlfriends. It even listed names of current and past girlfriends. Jake, the site said, had dated a few women, but none were listed as serious relationships. He was apparently considered a very eligible bachelor in racing circles.

She cringed at the thought of seeing her name on that list.

Vaguely depressed, she closed the computer. Maybe she needed to get out of the cabin for a while.

"Oscar," she said. "Come on. Let's go for a—"

Her cell phone rang before she could complete the sentence.

Jake's name appeared on her caller ID screen, and for one cowardly moment she almost didn't answer. But then she told herself to stop being ridiculous. She had told him she would be happy to hear from him.

"Hello?"

"Is it too much to hope that you miss me?"

"That depends," she replied lightly. "Who is this?"

"Funny," Jake growled. "Very funny."

"Oscar says to tell you hello."

On cue, the dog yipped, making Jake laugh. "Give him my regards in return, will you?"

"Yes, I will."

"How are you?"

"I'm fine. I've been working today. I've gotten a lot done."

"I guess it's easier to work without me there to distract you."

She bit her lip, thinking of how much she would have enjoyed that particular distraction. "How are things going there? Did you get the deal finalized?"

Jake groaned. "Yeah. They've had me running since I landed at the airport. Meeting bigwigs, shaking hands, signing autographs, posing for pictures. I'm filming a new TV ad tomorrow morning. Something Pam put together at the last minute, since I'm available this week."

Shaking her head in bemusement, she asked, "What are you advertising?"

"Jeans. Apparently all I have to do is walk around and try to make my butt look good."

That certainly wouldn't take any fancy camera tricks, she thought with a sudden mental image that almost made her mouth water. "I'll, uh, be watching for that one."

He chuckled. "I'd rather have you watching me race, to be honest."

"Any news on that front?"

"I got the doctor's appointment moved up. I'll see him

tomorrow afternoon at three. I'm expecting full clearance to race in Charlotte."

"Then I hope you'll get what you're wishing for."

"*Everything* I'm wishing for?"

Something about his deep tone made a little shiver run down her spine. She swallowed.

After a moment, she heard him sigh through the airwaves. "I've got to go," he said. "I'm doing an interview this afternoon with a reporter from a racing magazine. I can already predict the questions—how do I feel about the accident, what have I been doing with myself for the past few weeks, what do I think about my chances for next season?"

"You really don't mind talking about your personal business with strangers?"

"I tell them things I don't mind them knowing," he said, sounding as though he shrugged. "Anything private I keep to myself. It's a balancing act, but it's not so hard."

"Not for some people, maybe," she murmured, thinking of all the private things that had been written about her family against their will.

"Just takes a little practice," he assured her.

She heard a woman's voice saying his name, sounding impatient.

"All right, Pam, I'll be right there," he replied, just a hint of annoyance in his tone.

"You'd better go," she said.

"I know. I'll call you tomorrow?"

"Sure," she said brightly. "I'd love to hear how the jeans ad goes."

"Should be interesting," he agreed with a laugh. And then he sighed again. "Okay, Pam, I'm coming."

Knowing he really had to go, Stacy said, "Goodbye, Jake."

"Nope," he said. "Still not saying that. I'll talk to you tomorrow, Stacy."

He disconnected before she had a chance to reply.

Oscar yapped, nudging her leg to remind her of the walk they had been going to take when her phone rang.

Sliding her phone into its holder, she snapped the leash to Oscar's collar, her thoughts far away. Jake's refusal to say goodbye to her was wryly amusing, but she couldn't help wondering how long it would last. He was already so busy again. Already back into the life he'd led long before he had met her.

It wouldn't be long, she figured, until he found himself too busy to make telephone calls. Until he ran out of things to say to someone who couldn't even imagine what his schedule must be like. Until some new woman's name appeared on that list of single drivers' girlfriends.

Maybe, she thought as she locked the cabin door behind her on the way out, it was time for her to go back to her own life. To stop hiding and start living again. All she had to do was say no to the interviews and hold her head high when she went out in public among people who knew her history.

At least no one but her had to know about the kisses she had shared with famous NASCAR driver Jake Hinson.

"YOU'RE THE BEST, dude. You'll get 'em next year."

Jake smiled and handed the young man an autographed photograph. "Thanks, man."

A beaming grandfather with his shy grandson stepped up to the table where Jake sat signing autographs for employees of his newest secondary sponsor, Durfee Oil. "He's a big fan of yours," the older man said, nudging the boy, who looked to be six or seven years old. "Tell him, Rob."

The boy hid his face in his grandfather's side.

Chuckling, Jake signed a photograph and Jake Hinson ball cap for the duo, then reached for an eight-by-ten glossy from a young woman with long blond hair and blatantly displayed cleavage. "I can't wait to see you racing again," she purred, leaning forward a little as he scrawled his name on the photo. "You are so amazing on the track."

"I'll be back next week," Jake assured her, handing her the glossy.

She delayed taking it just long enough to make sure he looked up at her. Moistening her already damp, glittering red lips, she murmured, "I'll bet you're pretty amazing off the track, too."

He laughed, gave her a wink and turned to the next fan in line.

"Jake," one of the photographers who often accompanied him to such events muttered shortly afterward, "did you get her number?"

Stretching his cramped fingers as he walked away from the table, Jake asked absently, "Whose number?"

"The blonde. You know, the one with the nice, um, headlights? She was sending you signals even a blind guy couldn't miss."

"Oh, her. Yeah, she was good-looking, wasn't she? But no, I didn't get her number."

"No? What's the matter, Hinson? You slipping or something?"

"Just busy," Jake replied with a shrug. "You know, getting ready to finish the season."

Shouldering his bag, the photographer nodded. "Guess you do have to concentrate on racing again now, don't you? Good luck in Charlotte, okay? See you around, Jake."

"Yeah, see you, Tim."

A tall, slender redhead waited for Jake at the limo, her ever present organizer in her perfectly manicured hands. "We've got to go back to the office and look at those proofs and then you have dinner tonight with Wade, Mr. Woodrow, Mr. Vaughan and Mr. Durfee. You'll barely have time to change, but you don't want to be late. You know how Mr. Vaughan is about both punctuality and personal grooming."

Jake chuckled wryly. His main sponsor was straight out of the previous century when it came to some things. He liked neckties neatly knotted, shirts tucked into pants and shoes highly polished. Old-fashioned courtesies were important to him, and he maintained tight control of the business his grandfather had founded.

His high-profile sponsorship in the fast-moving and free-wheeling world of NASCAR racing had been an educational—and very profitable—experience for him. Jake had even seen him wearing a Vaughan Tool–Woodrow Racing polo shirt the day before.

He glanced at his watch. "I really need to work a telephone call in there sometime."

"Good luck finding time," Pam replied absently, her elegant fingers already tapping on her BlackBerry. "Maybe after dinner. Unless you want to make it now."

Because he didn't want to talk to Stacy with Pam and a driver listening in, Jake shook his head and opened the file Pam had handed him to look over for his schedule the next day.

He found his thoughts drifting back to the autograph session, and the blonde who had worked so hard to get his attention. She had been pretty, he recalled. Looked like the type who'd be a lot of fun. Outgoing, open, uninhibited. Available. And yet...

His mind filled with images of a very different woman. Slender, dark haired, reserved, somewhat guarded. Her smiles were a bit harder to coax, but well worth the effort. Her laughter less frequent, but so sweet when it came. Stacy wasn't the type he'd thought he'd fall for but, boy, had he ever. Thoughts of her continued to haunt him even almost a week after he'd last seen her.

He wanted to hear her voice. Badly enough that he reached for his phone despite the lack of privacy.

"Hi, this is Stacy," he heard a moment later. "Leave a message and I'll get back to you."

He should be more careful what he wished for, he thought ironically. He'd wanted to hear her voice, but not recorded on a message service. "Hi, it's Jake," he said. "I'm going to be tied up this afternoon and part of the evening, but I'll try calling you again later, okay?"

She had left the cabin a couple of days before and was back at her apartment in Little Rock. Having never seen her in her ordinary life, he couldn't picture her there. He had no idea where she was or whom she was seeing or why she couldn't answer her cell phone. And it bugged him, he realized, snapping his phone closed.

"That girl again?" Pam spoke without looking up from her tiny screen.

Jake slid his phone into its holder. "Yeah."

"Still talking to her every day?"

"When I can."

"Busy time for you."

"I know."

"You're spreading yourself pretty thin for the rest of the season. Especially with the new sponsor deal."

"I'm aware of that. You don't have to worry about me fulfilling my responsibilities, Pam."

She lifted a perfectly arched eyebrow. He rarely got cross with her, despite her tendency to keep him on schedule through firm insistence. After all, that was why he kept her around. As his PR rep and personal assistant, she was pretty much indispensable to him, and she knew it. The fact that he allowed his annoyance with her to show now probably told her more than he intended about his emotional turmoil when it came to Stacy.

"All right," she said mildly. "Sorry."

He shook his head. "No, I'm sorry. Didn't mean to snap."

"No problem. I'm sure it's difficult getting back into the swing after being away for a few weeks. We can put a few things off a little longer if you want, tell everyone that you need a little more time to recuperate."

"No," he said immediately. "There's no need for that. Get me back in the action, Pam. I'll find time for personal matters when I've got a few spare minutes."

"It will slow down at the end of November," she reminded him. "Maybe you'll have time during the off-season to see your new, um, friend."

"Yeah. Maybe." But that was still another six weeks away, minimum. And he really didn't want to wait that long to see Stacy again.

STACY RETURNED to her apartment the Monday night after she and Jake parted and tossed her purse on the bar that separated her living room from her kitchen. Her apartment was so small that the bar was just inside the front door. Her living room wasn't really large enough for a full-size couch, so she used a love seat and two small wingback chairs with a large ottoman for a coffee table and a couple of hinge-top, square wicker baskets for end tables.

There wasn't room for a full-size dining table, so she had tucked a tall pub table and two chairs into a corner. The pint-size kitchen held a small refrigerator, a four-burner stove with a too-small oven, a dishwasher and just enough countertop to hold her microwave. She had to keep her toaster and coffeemaker in the pantry, pulling them out only when she needed them.

Walking into the bedroom, she scooted around the end of the full-size oak bed that filled up most of the floor space and stepped into the blessedly roomy walk-in closet to strip out of her clothes and don comfortable pajamas and a robe. Her plans for the remainder of the evening included a cup of hot tea, some good music and a mystery novel.

Oscar was curled up in his doggie bed, looking as though he, too, planned a lazy evening at home. She would take him and the "poop scoop" out in the grassy commons behind her ground-floor apartment just before bedtime, but for now he looked content, she decided, moving to fill her teakettle with cold water.

There were times when she would have loved a larger apartment—especially a larger kitchen—but she had chosen instead to pick a safe neighborhood and put what little extra money she had into savings. She didn't make a lot as a freelance editor, but she paid her rent and her bills and had a little left over to stash away for the small house or condo she hoped to own eventually. A very little. At the rate she was going, she figured she ought to be a home owner about the same time she filed for Social Security.

Sighing, she carried her steaming teacup around the bar and settled on one end of the cushy love seat. She was probably going to look for another job soon. Teaching, most likely. Working her own hours at home had been nice, but she really needed to earn a bit more money. Benefits. It wasn't as if she were independently wealthy and could afford to keep coasting on a fun, but low-paying job.

Her cell phone rang and she reached for it, already knowing whose number she would see on the ID screen. Jake had called every day since he'd left Arkansas. When she couldn't take the call for some reason, he left a message and then called back later.

She wasn't sure why he kept calling, but she always enjoyed the conversations. He told her everything about his life—so much more exciting and fast paced than her own—and he always left her smiling when the calls ended. Until the smiles faded into wistfulness....

"Hello, Jake."

"Hi, gorgeous. How's your day been?"

"Routine. A couple of meetings at the office. Dinner with my friend Mindy." Who had grilled her endlessly about her brief friendship with the famous race car driver. Mindy was a casual race fan, watching with her husband when he was in town on Sunday afternoons, and she had recognized Jake's full name immediately. She'd even known a few details about him that Stacy had missed in her research.

"Sounds nice."

"It was pleasant. Andrew got the package you sent him, by the way. He was absolutely thrilled. That's the most I've seen him smile in years. Nick's having him write thank-you notes to you and Scott Rivers, but I wanted to thank you personally, too."

"It was my pleasure. I guess Andrew was pleased by the race results yesterday." He had last talked to her on Sunday morning, before the race began.

"Yes. Nick and I watched with him. We all cheered when Scott won the race. Your teammates have been very successful this season, haven't they?"

"Yeah. They have." Though Jake sounded pleased, the slightest hint of regret in his tone told her that he was too keenly aware of all he had missed during the past eight weeks.

"Pete finished well in your car," she offered, hoping to cheer him up again. "He was in the top twenty, wasn't he? Andrew told me that's a good thing for your owner."

Her ruse worked. Jake's tone was a bit brighter when he responded. "Yeah. He finished fourteenth. He'd have liked to round out his substitution with a top-ten finish, but he was satisfied with where he ended up. He'll be back in NASCAR NEXTEL Cup racing in a year or two, and he'll do fine."

"I guess you're looking forward to being back in your car Saturday night."

"Oh, yeah. We're working just about around the clock to get everything ready."

"I'll be cheering for you."

"I'd like to be able to hear that."

She laughed a little. "Sorry. I'm not sure I can cheer that loudly."

"You could if you were wearing a headset. And watching from the pit box."

Frowning, she shook her head in confusion. "I don't—"

He broke in with a slight laugh. "Sorry, I'm not being very clear. How would you like to join me here for the race this weekend? I'll fly you here, make all the arrangements for you, make sure you have a good time."

He had caught her completely off guard. They'd never even discussed the possibility of her joining him for the race, which was less than a week away.

"Oh, I—"

"I know it's short notice," he said apologetically. "I thought at first that maybe it would be best if you didn't come this weekend. I mean, I'll be pretty busy and I didn't want you to feel neglected or anything—but I would really love to have you here for my first race back."

Panic flooded her at the thought of being there in the middle of all that commotion. "I don't know, Jake. I've never been to a race before. I wouldn't know what to do. How to act."

He chuckled. "It isn't that hard. You do what you want and you act like yourself. You'll get along fine."

She remembered the Internet gossip about the women who

had accompanied drivers to various races and she almost shuddered. "I'm not sure I'm ready for that."

"Ready for what? Watching a race in person?"

"Watching a race as your guest," she corrected him.

"It's no big deal. I've had guests at the races before."

"I'm sure you have." She didn't intend to sound quite so cool. She hoped he didn't read that the wrong way.

Instead, he just laughed. "Friends, Stacy. I've had friends at the races before. Tell you what. Why don't you bring Andrew? We'll show him a great time, let him meet Scott—it will be fun."

Oh, now, that was unfair. He had to realize what a trip like that would mean to Andrew. And just how hard it would be for her to turn it down knowing that, herself. "I—"

"I miss you," he said quietly, stopping her words unspoken.

And that was even more unfair. Because she missed him, too. Entirely too much, considering how brief their time together had been.

"Andrew would be thrilled by the opportunity you're offering," she said after a rather lengthy pause.

"Then take me up on it. I want to see you, Stacy."

A little thrill went through her, but she forced herself to stay in control of her voice. "You're pretty accustomed to getting what you want, aren't you?"

"Usually," he admitted. "Not every time."

It always got to her, that little hint of sadness in his voice when he thought of his friend Eric. And she always knew.

"I'll come," she said abruptly. "Mostly for Andrew. He's never been to a race, and this would be a dream come true for him. But I would like to ask for a couple of favors."

"Which are?"

"Keep us in the background. I don't want to be paraded as one of Jake Hinson's lady friends."

"Hey, I resent that. I don't date that much—especially during race season. Who's got the time?"

Which only made it more gossip worthy when he did see someone, she thought with a frown.

"What's your other request?"

"I, um, I'm just coming as a friend, okay? I mean, that's probably all you have in mind, anyway, but I don't want anyone to think...well, you know."

"You don't want anyone to think that I'm deeply attracted to you?" he asked blandly. "That I can't stop thinking about you even when I'm crazy busy? That I wake up in the middle of the night remembering how it felt to kiss you? Okay, I'll try to keep it secret."

Her face burned by the time he finished speaking. Her heart raced like Jake's Number 82 car. "You, uh..."

"Will Andrew be able to take a day off from school Friday? If so, I can fly you here in the morning so he can watch us practice in the afternoon."

He was hardly letting her complete a sentence during this call—not that she was doing that great a job of being coherent. Struggling to clear her mind, she said, "Yes, I think we can arrange for him to have Friday off."

"Great. I'll send the plane for you early Friday morning. You and Andrew can stay in my motor home at the track to give him the full experience."

He was sending a plane? She'd thought they would fly commercial. "Where will you stay?"

"My house is less than an hour's drive from the track. I'll be fine."

"I don't know. This sounds like a very expensive trip. I mean, a private plane and—"

"Stacy. I can afford it," he told her gently. "Don't worry about that, okay?"

There were several things she could accomplish with this trip, she assured herself when they disconnected a short while later, plans in place. She could take Andrew to a race, earning herself heroine status in his life for a while, and maybe having a positive influence on the negative attitude he'd had lately. She could find out if Jake's interest in her was fleeting or really as serious as he implied. And she would discover for herself just how daunting a potential relationship with a famous NASCAR driver could be.

CHAPTER ELEVEN

"OH, MAN," Andrew breathed. "This is so freaking cool."

Stacy could barely hear him. *Loud* would have been the first adjective that came to her mind to describe her initial impression of the racetrack. *Crowded* would have been the second.

Even on the day of practice, the infield was packed with motor homes and the grassy common areas surrounding the stands were crowded with big semitrailers holding licensed merchandise. Crew members swarmed like ants around the colorful cars lined up in the garage stalls. Engines roared from every stall, making even the ground beneath her feet feel as though it vibrated with the thunderous rumble. Lined up by the garages were the team haulers, painted in every color of the rainbow, hydraulic lifts raised to provide shade for the back openings.

People bustled everywhere, insiders and spectators alike. They all seemed to know exactly where they wanted to be and what they wanted to do—unlike Stacy, who was feeling a bit overwhelmed.

Andrew also looked overwhelmed, but in a different way from his aunt. His freckled face beaming beneath the sandy hair he'd agreed to have trimmed for the trip, he tried to take in everything at once. "Oh, man, it's Scott Rivers' hauler. Parked right there by the garage. See, it's the one painted red and black with his sponsor's name, Witt Hardware. You think Scott's in there?"

J.R., the tall, painfully thin Woodrow Racing employee who had picked them up at the airport and driven them here to the track, chuckled in response to Andrew's question—which was one of about a thousand the boy had asked since arriving in North Carolina. "I imagine Scott's either in the car or in the garage. He doesn't hang around in the hauler much. Too restless."

Andrew sported a Scott Rivers T-shirt with his jeans and sneakers, but he'd donned a Jake Hinson cap, showing that his loyalty was now divided. Stacy didn't own any clothing advertising her loyalty to Jake's team, so she'd worn a dark purple, three-quarter-sleeve cotton shirt over dark, straight-leg jeans and comfortable walking shoes.

Andrew had reluctantly approved her choice, as well as the similar outfit she'd brought to wear to the race the next day. He had insisted that she at least wear team colors. Even though he'd never been to a race, he'd seemed convinced that no one at the track dressed neutrally.

"So, where's Jake?" he asked, unable to completely hide his pride at that personal connection.

"Let's go find out," J.R. said with a grin.

Wearing their official passes on lanyards around their necks, Stacy and Andrew followed J.R. toward a purple-and-silver hauler parked not far from the black-and-red one Andrew had already spotted. The Vaughan Tools logo was prominently displayed on the side of the hauler, along with Durfee Oil and smaller sponsor ads. Jake's name was written in bold script across the doors of the cab.

"Whoa," Andrew murmured as they approached the open back of the hauler, giving him a good look inside. "It's so cool."

"Come on in," J.R. encouraged them, an indulgent smile softening his craggy face. "This part's the kitchen. You see all them cookies and candy jars? Jake's got himself a sweet tooth on race days. Says the sugar fuels him."

Thinking of brownies and ice cream and peach cobbler shared when it had just been the two of them, Stacy swallowed hard.

"This here's the locker area," J.R. continued, motioning as they continued toward the other end of the hauler. "And that's where we keep the tools. The backup car's on the top level, and all the way back here is the lounge and office area."

Stacy caught just a glimpse of leather couches and wood desks and multimedia equipment—before Jake stepped forward and she couldn't see anything but him. He wore his uniform, the deep purple color setting off his tan to near perfection. He looked dashing and handsome, straight off the cover of a racing magazine. She noted peripherally that other people were in the area, but her eyes was locked so tightly with Jake's that she couldn't yet get any details, including how many others were there.

Smiling broadly, he reached out to catch her hand in his. "Stacy," he said, her name sounding somehow different when he said it. "It's good to see you again. How was your trip?"

She moistened her lips and gave herself a rousing mental slap. "It was lovely, thank you. I've never been on a private jet before. Very luxurious."

He dragged his gaze from hers with what seemed to be an effort. "Hi, Andrew. How's it going?"

"Hey, Jake," the boy replied, still trying to be cool. "This is great. Uh, thanks for inviting me."

Stacy had instructed him repeatedly to express his gratitude as soon as he saw their host. She was glad he had remembered.

"You're welcome." Still holding Stacy's hand, he turned

slightly away from her. "I'd like you both to meet my crew chief and his fiancée. Stacy and Andrew Carter, meet Lisa Woodrow and Wade McClellan."

Andrew's awe slipped through a bit when he stared at Wade. "'Ice' McClellan," he said. "Oh, man."

A nice-looking man with dark hair and narrowed dark eyes, Wade chuckled. "Just call me Wade."

His beautiful blond fiancée was studying Stacy with barely veiled curiosity. "So you're Stacy. Jake has told us all about you."

Wondering what he had said, Stacy flicked him a glance, then smiled at the other woman. "It's nice to meet you. Your name is Woodrow—you're related to the team owner?"

"Lisa is Woody's daughter," Jake explained. "She's a prosecuting attorney who has recently taken a new position in Charlotte."

"So were you two talking about race strategies?" Andrew asked Jake eagerly, acknowledging Lisa with only a glance.

"Actually, we were discussing dinner plans for tonight," Jake replied somewhat apologetically. "What would you prefer? Italian or barbecue?"

Andrew waved a hand dismissively. "Whatever. So, how's it looking for tomorrow night?"

"Well, I qualified third. Not so bad for my first race back in eight weeks."

Andrew nodded, showing he'd already known the lineup. "And Scott qualified seventh. He's come from farther behind than that to win."

Jake gave Stacy a wry smile, acknowledging that he was aware that Andrew would be not so secretly cheering for his teammate. He didn't seem to mind too badly, she noted in relief. Realizing only then that he was still holding her hand at their sides, she discreetly extricated herself and stepped closer to her nephew.

"Andrew would be pleased if either you or Scott wins," she assured Jake.

He chuckled. "Don't try to be the diplomat. I know who he's going to be supporting tomorrow night."

"It really would be cool if you win, too," Andrew said, his expression slightly anxious. Perhaps it had just occurred to him who had actually brought him here, Stacy thought in exasperation.

"I don't think the race can end in a tie," Jake replied with a laugh.

"And sorry, son, but even though the kid's our teammate, we're going to try to make sure he comes in no higher than second place," Wade added in a drawl.

"Who you calling a kid?" asked a new voice from the doorway.

Stacy looked around to see a slender, fresh-faced newcomer in a striking black-and-red uniform. Leaning against the doorway with his arms crossed over his chest, the sandy-haired young man couldn't have been much more than twenty-one, maybe twenty-two, Stacy estimated. His blue eyes glinted with mischief, and she didn't need to read his sponsor on his chest to know that this was the "crazy" driver Andrew idolized. Andrew's expression alone was enough to confirm her identification.

"Scott Rivers," Andrew whispered.

Scott stepped forward with an outstretched hand. "I heard there was someone in here I'd like to meet. That must be you."

"Really?" Andrew grinned. "I'm Andrew. Andrew Carter."

"Great to meet you, Andy. You're a fan, huh?"

"Oh, yeah. I'm your biggest fan. Well, you and Jake," Andrew added with a quick look at his bemused host.

Jake and Scott laughed, Lisa smiled, Wade snorted and Stacy shook her head in resignation. At least no one seemed offended, she decided.

"So, you want a tour? I've got some free time."

"For real?" Andrew turned to Stacy, looking down at her from the three-inch advantage he had in height. He was a bit short for his age, a sensitive subject for him, but he came by it naturally since Nick, at five feet eight, was the tallest member of the Carter family. He probably liked the fact that Scott was not much taller than Andrew was himself. "Aunt Stacy? Is it okay if I go with Scott?"

Stacy looked at Jake. He grinned and nodded. "He'll be fine with Scott. Right, Rivers?" he added with a pointed look at his young teammate.

"Sure, he will," Scott promised with an exaggeratedly innocent expression. And then on his way out, he made sure everyone heard him ask Andrew, "So, have you ever ridden on top of a moving race car, kid?"

"He's kidding," Jake assured Stacy.

"I know. I just hope Andrew won't get in the way out there."

"Don't worry about it. Scott's shown teenagers around before. Sponsors' kids, mostly. He knows how to handle them. Heck, it wasn't that long since he was one."

"You arranged this, didn't you?"

Chuckling, Jake nodded. "I figured they'd both get a kick out of it. Scott cleared about an hour for Andrew, and that's about how long I've got to show you around, if you're interested. After that, Wade and I will be pretty well tied up until dinner, but Lisa offered to entertain you and Andrew."

"I hope we won't be keeping you from anything," Stacy fretted, remembering that Lisa had a high-powered career of her own. "Andrew and I will be fine on our own if you have other things to do. He'd be perfectly content to just sit in the stands and watch practice."

"He'd probably rather watch from the top of the hauler. Or the pit box," Lisa said with a smile. "And don't worry about keeping me from anything. I've got the day off. Since Wade's going to be focusing on practice for the rest of the afternoon and completely ignoring me, I'd enjoy the company."

"I'd argue with that, if it wasn't entirely true," Wade murmured laconically. "But if it makes you feel any better, you aren't easy to ignore."

"Coming from you, that's quite a concession," she answered him fondly, patting his arm.

Stacy watched the exchange with bemusement, thinking that it must take a great deal of self-confidence for a woman to so cheerfully accept second place on race weekends.

LISA AND WADE STAYED behind in the hauler when Jake escorted Stacy out for her tour. Jake kept a hand at the small of her back, ostensibly because of the frantic activity going on around the haulers and garage area. She could feel the heat of his palm through her shirt, and it lit an answering warmth deep inside her.

"You look good in purple," he murmured, staying close enough that she could hear him over the noise of the garages and the crowds.

She smiled up at him. "Thanks. Andrew grudgingly approved my choice, though he thought I should go to a NASCAR store and buy a Jake Hinson T-shirt. I have to admit the idea of wearing your face on my clothing seemed a little strange to me."

He laughed. "There are so many suggestive responses to that statement that I think I'll just let them all pass by."

Her cheeks warmed. "Probably just as well."

He walked quickly, towing her along in his wake, pointing out features of the track as they passed them. Though she looked obligingly in the directions he indicated, she was all too aware of the attention they received themselves. People literally pointed at Jake as they recognized him, and she received looks of curiosity and envy just for being by his side.

Exchanging nods, smiles and waves with practiced ease, Jake kept walking, informing her quietly that if they stopped moving they would be swarmed by autograph seekers. As it was, he signed a few while he was on the move, accepting various items thrust out to him along with markers, scrawling his name and returning the items without ever slowing down.

She noted that his limp was almost entirely gone now, and she wondered if he was having to concentrate at all on walking naturally. She could imagine that he would hate showing any sign of weakness in front of the fans who saw him as a larger-than-life hero.

They left the spectators behind when they entered a restricted area for racing personnel motor homes. The elaborate coaches were lined up tightly, forming a relatively private haven for the drivers and their families. Stacy saw children milling around the area, running and playing under close supervision, and she imagined that the drivers' kids got to know each other pretty well, living on the road together so many weekends out of every year.

It was a strange life, she mused. Hard to imagine for someone like her, who lived so quietly and anonymously, her daily routines rarely varying.

Jake guided her to a large, chocolate-brown-and-cream motor home with several hydraulic extensions jutting out from the sides to increase its size. "This is my home away from home," he said, pressing keys on a security pad beside the door. "I don't usually bring it to this track, but I arranged to have it here for you and Andrew."

"That was very thoughtful of you."

He showed her how to work the security pad, then escorted her inside. Stacy caught her breath when she walked in. "Oh, my."

The motor home was impressive, to say the least, making her little apartment back in Little Rock look absolutely stark in comparison. Chocolate and cream formed the basic color scheme with accents in mint and cherry and chrome, making her feel as though they were standing inside a luxurious soda fountain.

The fabrics were rich and inviting, soft leather and deep plush and lots of inviting pillows. Glossy woods and shiny glass reflected the recessed lighting and the glow of a crystal chandelier.

The entire coach appeared to be controlled by remote electronics. Several flat-screen TVs were placed so that they could be seen from nearly every angle, and tiny inset speakers gave evidence of state-of-the-art surround sound. From where she stood she could see the living and dining areas, which flowed into what looked like a well-appointed galley and back to a closed door that presumably led into a bedroom.

"Jake, this is…" She couldn't even think of a word to describe the coach. "Amazing" was the one she finally settled upon.

He gave a self-deprecating shrug. "This is my home for thirty-six weekends out of the year. It's where I escape from the chaos and mentally prepare myself for the races. I figure it should be a nice place to walk into."

"Andrew's going to flip out when he sees this."

Jake nodded toward the deep leather couch. "He can sleep there. It's really comfortable. I can't count the number of naps I've taken on it. And Wade spent a few nights there when he and Lisa were courting and she stayed in his motor home for a couple of races."

Courting. The old-fashioned word intrigued her, but she pushed it aside to consider later while Jake showed her how to work everything in the motor home that she and Andrew would need during their stay.

She wished for a moment that Andrew was there with them. He was the electronics wizard in the family, and he would probably learn the workings of this complicated equipment much more quickly than she could. And then Jake opened the bedroom door, and something in his expression made her rather relieved that Andrew was safely occupied elsewhere with his racing hero.

Jake cleared his throat before saying, "This is where you'll sleep."

Standing at a safe distance from him, she quickly surveyed the almost decadently inviting-looking room with its huge bed covered in designer linens, built-in appointments, another flat-panel television and a fashionably-styled ceiling fan.

"It's nice," she said, aware of how inadequate the adjective was when it came to describing this area.

"Yeah. It's comfortable."

Another understatement, she thought, glancing at the big, deep bed. She tried not to imagine him in it, tried even harder not to picture anyone else there with him, but she wasn't entirely successful at either attempt.

She spotted her bag sitting next to Andrew's in one corner of the bedroom, and was amazed again at how efficiently Jake had arranged their visit. He'd seen to every detail, apparently—or perhaps had one of his "people" do so.

She turned toward Jake with a bright and, she hoped, unrevealing smile. "I'm sure Andrew and I will be very comfortable here this weekend. Are you sure we aren't putting you out?"

"No. As I said, my house is close enough to commute, and I

can hang out in the hauler while I'm here at the track. I'd like to take you out to the house sometime while you're here, maybe Sunday morning, just so you can see where I live during the few days a week that I'm home."

"I'd love to see it." But she wasn't sure she really was that eager. If his motor home was this elegant, what must his real home look like? And how much more evidence did she need that they were about as mismatched as a pair could be?

Suddenly aware that they were standing basically in his bedroom—at least, one of his bedrooms—she moved toward the door. "You were going to show me how to work the—"

He reached out to catch her arm when she would have passed by him. "Stacy."

His voice sounded a bit deeper than usual, giving her name that special tone that only he used. She bit her lower lip as she looked at him.

He touched her face, cupping her cheek in his palm. So many times during the past two weeks apart from him, she had remembered the habit he'd had of touching her face, the caresses as intimate as a kiss, as unique as Jake himself. She'd awoken more than once with her cheek burning as if he'd touched her in her sleep, and she knew she had dreamed of him.

"It's so good to have you here," he murmured, his tone husky. Seductive. "I've missed you."

Remembering the barely controlled pandemonium outside this haven, the crowds of people that surrounded him all the time, she wondered how he could have even noticed her absence. It was different for her. She spent so much time alone with her computer that it was only natural that she had been too keenly aware of how quiet her life was without Jake in it.

"I've…missed you, too," she replied, allowing herself that one, completely candid moment.

"Since no one is around to see…" he murmured, lowering his head to hers.

She tilted her head back and closed her eyes, falling into the kiss with a sigh of surrender. No matter how much she had pretended to him, and to herself, she couldn't think of Jake as just a friend. Not when he had only to touch her to make her forget every reason why that was all they should remain.

Her arms locked around his neck as he deepened the kiss, dragging her so tightly into his arms that she could hardly breathe, and didn't care. What would she want with oxygen when she had Jake instead?

After a very long time, he broke the kiss with a slight groan, dragging in air as if he, too, begrudged the necessity. And then he kissed her again, his hand tangling in her hair, his body hard and hungry against hers.

This wasn't the lighthearted teasing they'd done before. No tentative flirting this time. He was making it clear that he wanted her, and she reacted to that desire with a flood of sensation that almost overwhelmed her.

She was trembling when she pushed against his chest with her hands. He released her instantly, if reluctantly. "Too soon?" he asked huskily.

"Too…something," she agreed, her own voice taut.

He tried to smile, managing a credible semblance of his usual grin. "That's okay. I can be patient. For a little while longer."

Was there a slight note of warning in that addition? She narrowed her eyes.

He chuckled and ran a fingertip down her nose. "Don't bite my head off. I said I'd be good. Besides, Scott should be delivering your nephew here shortly. Doesn't really give us time to get too cozy."

Oh, heavens, she had actually forgotten all about Andrew! Her cheeks blazing, she moved a few steps farther away from Jake, thinking there must be some force field around him that caused some sort of static in her mind, keeping her from thinking clearly.

"I'm sure Andrew's having a marvelous time," she said a bit too primly. "You've outdone yourself today, between the private plane, the personal tour with his idol and this fancy motor home for us to stay in. Andrew will be your admirer for life."

Jake frowned. "You think I've been trying to impress you?"

"I don't know if you tried, but you certainly succeeded. Your life is a lot different from what we're used to back home."

"It's a lot different from what I grew up with, too," he reminded her flatly. "I told you I came from dirt-poor roots. All these trappings are just part of the job I'm in. I have the means now to provide a few luxuries for myself and my friends, but I work damned hard for it."

"I never said you didn't. Nor did I accuse you of showing off your success," she reminded him. "I just couldn't help commenting, that's all."

He didn't seem overly appeased, but he didn't argue any further. He took her, instead, into the kitchen to show her the supplies that had been stocked for her and Andrew and to give her a few more operating instructions. By the time he finished, a musical doorbell let them know that Scott and Andrew were outside.

Jake showed her how to check the security screen to make sure who was outside before opening the door. Andrew burst into the motor home as soon as Jake let him in. "Oh, wow, this is so cool. Scott, do you have one of these? Is it as sweet as this one?"

Eyeing Jake and Stacy as if to see what they'd been up to before the interruption, Scott replied, "I have a motor home. Not quite as fancy as this one, but it serves my purposes. It's not here at the track this weekend, because I prefer to stay in my own bed when we're racing at home."

"Did you have a good time, Andrew?" Stacy asked, although she already knew the answer.

His face lit up in a way that proved her right. "It was so cool! Scott took me into the garage and he let me touch his car and meet his crew chief and everything. Then we saw inside his hauler and we saw the infield care center and…and…well, we saw everything. Oh, and I met a lot more drivers. Scott knows everyone."

"I've been racing them all for the better part of the year now," Scott reminded him indulgently. "They still treat me like a rookie, just to keep me in my place, but everyone's pretty friendly in this sport. Off the track, anyway."

"Everyone was really nice to me," Andrew assured his aunt. "I can't wait to tell all the guys back home who all I shook hands with. They'll freak out."

Scott glanced at his watch. "I had a lot of fun with you, Andy, but I gotta take off now. Practice starts in an hour and I've got a lot to do until then."

Stacy nudged Andrew, who gave her an impatient look. "I'm going to," he said in a stage whisper, and then turned to Scott. "Thank you for showing me around, Scott. It was really cool."

"I'm glad you liked it. I'll be seeing you this weekend, okay? And you cheer for me in the race tomorrow—no matter how hard this guy tries to win you over to his side, okay?"

Andrew cleared his throat and shuffled his feet, making both drivers laugh and assure him that he could cheer for both of them without causing any hard feelings.

"I've got to go, too," Jake said after Scott let himself out. "Lisa will be waiting for you guys back at the hauler after you've freshened up and helped yourself to snacks, if you want them. She likes to work in the hauler office when Wade's tied up—which he almost always is when we're at a track—but she usually watches practice."

Warning them to keep their passes visible when they were in the restricted areas, he followed Scott out after giving Stacy a long look that made her face go warm again.

Fortunately, Andrew seemed oblivious to the undercurrents. He threw himself onto the couch and looked around the motor home with a blissful sigh. "Man, I could so get used to living like this."

Stacy wasn't at all sure she could say the same thing.

CHAPTER TWELVE

"YOUR NEPHEW SEEMS to be having a great time," Lisa said to Stacy later that afternoon, raising her voice to be heard over the thunderous roar of the cars rocketing around the track.

"He's in heaven," Stacy shouted back, looking fondly at Andrew, who stood by J.R. on top of the hauler, both wearing headsets to hear everything being said between Jake, his spotter and his crew chief during the practice run. Stacy had worn a headset herself for a while, but she'd pulled it off to better converse with Lisa as practice went on.

"You want to watch the rest of this, or would you like to go into the hauler for a cup of coffee?"

"The coffee sounds good to me," Stacy replied, then added, "unless you'd rather watch?"

Lisa shook her blond head, and nodded toward her fiancé, who sat beside her father, big, blustery "Woody" Woodrow, on the bright purple pit box, both watching the Number 82 car with intense concentration. "Wade will let me know how it goes."

Leaving Andrew in J.R.'s capable hands, they climbed down the ladder to the ground and entered the hauler. The relative quiet in the lounge area was a relief to Stacy's ears. She would wear the earplugs her brother had recommended to watch the race, she promised herself. Or maybe she would be offered the headset again so she could hear Jake, Arnie and Wade talking during the real event.

Lisa poured coffee for both of them, and then they settled onto the deep leather sofa. A large flat-screen television was set into the opposite wall, but they didn't bother to turn it on.

"So," Lisa began, "you're Anastasia Carter."

Stacy almost choked on the sip of coffee she had just taken. "Um, yes. Did Jake tell you that?"

Smiling, Lisa shook her head. "I'm an attorney, remember? We thrive on courthouse drama and gossip. I thought your name sounded familiar when Jake mentioned you, but when I saw you today, I realized why. You took down the guy who had grabbed an officer's gun and was trying to escape. Your picture was on all the Internet news sites."

Self-conscious now, Stacy sipped her coffee again to give herself time to think of something to say. After swallowing, she said, "I acted on instinct and used a couple of moves I'd learned in martial-arts training I take for exercise and recreation. I wasn't trying to be a hero—and I certainly never expected the media attention that followed."

"It must have been disconcerting for you."

"To say the least," she agreed wryly. "I went down to the courthouse to fight a ticket and the next thing I knew, reporters were sticking microphones in my face and calling me to ask for interviews. For someone who lives very quietly and works at home, that was hard to deal with. That's why I escaped to the river cabin where I met Jake."

Lisa laughed softly. "So while you were hiding out from publicity, you met a man whose life is lived in a spotlight."

"Exactly."

"He hinted that you weren't exactly thrilled about his career. I think I understand why."

"I have nothing against racing, of course," Stacy explained conscientiously. "I mean, I'm very impressed with what I've learned about the sport during the past couple of weeks. It's so hugely popular, and the drivers are such dedicated athletes, who work very hard for the privilege of being at the top. It's amazing how much Jake has accomplished at such a relatively young age."

Lisa looked vaguely amused by her prim little speech, making Stacy feel even more foolish.

"Okay," she said with a sigh of resignation, "it freaks me out to think of even being friends with a guy like Jake, much less...anything else. I mean, I barely know him, so it's not like we're...well...to tell you the truth, I'm not even sure why he invited us here this weekend."

As disjointed and incoherent as that was, Lisa nodded somberly. "I understand completely."

"You do?" Stacy shook her head. "I wish I did."

"I understand," Lisa repeated, "because I've been where you are, in a way."

She set her coffee cup on the table in front of the couch. "I don't know if Jake told you, but Wade and I were engaged before. Six years ago."

Stacy tried to hide her surprise. "No, he didn't mention that."

"I broke it off," Lisa admitted. "It was the hardest thing I ever did. I was crazy in love with him, but I panicked. I was young and had no career of my own, and Wade was so obsessed with racing that I was afraid of losing myself in his shadow. So, I went to law school, found a career I loved, and when we came back together earlier this year, I realized that I could be with him and still have a life of my own. We won't have a typical marriage—he's going to be on the road a lot and I won't be free to follow him around from track to track the way some of the wives do—but we'll make the most of the time we can spend together. We can make it work for us."

"I'm sure you can." It would be challenging, though, Stacy thought privately. The time on the road was only one of the sacrifices made by those in the upper echelons of NASCAR racing. And she had already figured out that they did it for love of the sport as much as any monetary compensation.

"But then again, I grew up in racing," Lisa added. "My father is a very high-profile team owner. He kept me out of the spotlight as much as he could while I was growing up, but I was still used to the attention. And Wade's a crew chief, not a driver. He's still pretty visible, but not like Jake. I can see where you would find that daunting."

"Like you, I grew up with a father who lived in the public eye—though he was more notorious than famous. I hated it. All the attention that followed the, um, incident at the courthouse reminded me of my childhood and made me remember how much I disliked meeting people who already knew who I was because of gossip and so-called news reports."

"The way I knew who you were before you and I were officially introduced," Lisa murmured, her expression apologetic.

Stacy sighed lightly and nodded. "Exactly."

"I'm afraid it's hard to date a driver in secret. Especially one as visible as Jake. He's extremely popular, you know. He has a huge fan base, made up in large part of women who know he's unattached and fantasize about his good looks and amazing smile. Any time he even looks twice at a woman, they start sizing her up, trying to figure out who she is and how serious he is about her."

"You aren't helping," Stacy muttered.

"Sorry. I figured you already know all of this."

"It isn't hard to guess," she admitted, thinking of those Internet gossip sites she had discovered.

"I can see why you'd have reservations about getting involved with a stock car driver," Lisa conceded after a moment. "But Jake's pretty special, Stacy. Everyone on the team loves him. You should have seen how they stood by him after his accident. They consider themselves his family, the only family he has."

"I can see why everyone is so fond of him. He's a very nice man. Just look at all he's done for Andrew this weekend."

Lisa smiled. "It isn't only for Andrew."

Stalling again, Stacy took another drink of her coffee. She wasn't sure she had learned anything new during this little talk with Lisa, but it had been interesting, nonetheless.

THEY ATE ITALIAN for dinner. Andrew's choice, since he wasn't very fond of barbecue. Lisa and Wade joined them, along with Ronnie and Katie Short and Ronnie's crew chief, Digger Barkley. If Andrew was disappointed that Scott had other plans that evening, he didn't let it show. To his aunt's visible relief, Andrew was on his very best behavior that evening.

Winding spaghetti around a fork, Jake listened to the conversations going on around him with a sense of great satisfaction. He'd spent the afternoon back in his car on the track, getting ready for tomorrow night's race. Practice had gone well, he felt great, almost back to peak shape again—and Stacy was sitting at the table among his best friends in the world.

He couldn't get over how very right she looked there. She and Lisa and Katie were chatting like old pals, talking about Katie's baby, Olivia, who was due in another eight weeks. As round as a pumpkin, red-haired Katie glowed with happiness and Lisa and Stacy laughed frequently as Katie prattled on about how nervous Ronnie was about the pending delivery.

Andrew was still asking questions, grilling the crew chiefs about race strategies. They answered patiently, always willing to talk to excited young fans. Ronnie concentrated on eating, putting away the carbs in preparation for the next day's exhausting schedule.

"When did people start calling you Ice?" Andrew asked Wade. "Has that always been your nickname?"

"That started when he called his first race as a fill-in crew chief for a guy who'd had an emergency appendectomy that weekend," Digger said when Wade hesitated. "The whole race started going to he—er, heck, with all kinds of tire and engine problems cropping up. A record number of cautions. Everybody getting mad at everybody else and yelling and screaming in the headsets. Ol' Ice here just stayed calm as a Popsicle, took care of the adjustments to the car and brought his driver in third after being two laps down at one point."

"He hardly ever gets rattled," Ronnie agreed, looking up from his plate. "The most I ever saw him get worked up was when Lisa took off from a track to go shopping once without telling him, back when she was having some problems with an escaped con she'd helped convict. Wade was sure something terrible had happened to her, and he really got rattled. We weren't calling him Ice that day."

"I did leave a message," Lisa murmured, shaking her head. "He just didn't get it."

"Yeah, well, you left it with J.R.," Wade replied, still looking a bit sick at the memory of how worried he'd been that day, which Jake remembered very well himself.

"He has to use his ability to stay calm every week with Jake," Digger said. Grinning at Andrew, he added, "Rumor has it that Jake gets kind of excited during a race, especially when things start going wrong. He starts yelling into his mike, and Ice has to cool him down."

Jake's gaze returned to Stacy, as it did so often. She looked his way and smiled, then turned her attention back to Lisa and Katie. Just that quick exchange left him feeling unusually warm.

As the conversations continued around him, he glanced at Ronnie and Wade, who were both so visibly content to be with the women they loved, sharing their lives and dreams. Was he letting them influence him too much? Was his envy of their happiness making him unconsciously exaggerate the way he felt about Stacy? Maybe she wasn't really as special as he'd convinced himself she was. Maybe…

She laughed at something Katie said, the sound soft and musical. His chest clenched.

Okay, maybe this was real. It wasn't as if there hadn't been plenty of other women he could have focused on. Willing, race-savvy women who were much less likely to break his heart than Stacy.

That grim thought made him frown. He'd never had his heart broken. Maybe because he'd never entrusted it to anyone who held the power to do so. But he had a feeling that Stacy could hurt him worse than he'd ever been hurt before. Losing her could be a great deal more painful than losing a shot at the championship. There would always be more race seasons. But he didn't think he would meet anyone else like Stacy.

Too soon, he reminded himself. It was too soon for him to be feeling this way.

Wade had subtly warned him earlier, after seeing him with Stacy, that Jake seemed to be getting in over his head. Even Scott had expressed doubts about Stacy's suitability for Jake. Not in so many words, of course. He'd said simply that Andrew seemed like a great kid, but his aunt was a little reserved for Scott's taste. Not quite the adjective Scott had used, but basically the same meaning.

Stacy, herself, had told him he was moving too fast, right after kissing him until he'd had a hard time remembering his own name.

Too much, too soon. Everyone seemed to believe that—except him. All he knew was that for the first time in his life he'd met a woman he could picture in his future. *All* of his future.

"You got a problem, Jake?" Wade asked, claiming his attention. "The way you're frowning, you look like someone licked the red right off your lollipop."

Andrew laughed at the saying, but everyone else looked at Jake curiously. He forced a smile, carefully avoiding Stacy's gaze.

"Just thinking about tomorrow," he lied. "Pam's going to have me running all day, from daylight until the race starts. I've got a sponsor meet-and-greet at eight in the morning—can you believe it?"

"I can believe it. I'm going to be there with you," Wade reminded him. His quizzical tone told Jake he didn't buy the explanation, but he let it go for then, to Jake's relief.

A GROUP OF FANS in town for the race recognized Jake and Ronnie as they were leaving the restaurant. They were surrounded in the parking lot, and Jake and Ronnie patiently signed autographs and fielded questions and well-wishes for the race while everyone else hung back out of the way. One of the fans realized that the two crew chiefs were also present and drew them into the impromptu autograph session.

Stacy noticed that Andrew was fascinated by the interlude, while Lisa and Katie merely looked resigned, apparently accustomed to this sort of thing.

"We're really glad you're back, Jake," one of the young men said as Jake handed him a signed sheet of paper.

"Thanks," Jake replied. "I'm glad to be back."

"You're good to go? All healed from your accident?"

"Yeah, I'm doing great. Thanks."

"Sorry about your season. But you'll get 'em next year, right?"

"You bet."

"Oh, and, uh, sorry about your friend."

Jake's voice never changed, though everyone else within hearing cringed to varying degrees. "Thanks. I appreciate that. See y'all at the track tomorrow. Good night, now."

Skillfully extricating themselves, the racing group moved on, saying good-night and climbing into different cars to go their separate ways for the evening. Jake had driven Stacy and Andrew. Andrew scooted forward on the backseat to ask Jake, "Do people do that a lot? Mob you for your autograph, I mean."

"Often enough. You get used to it. Sit back and put on your seat belt."

"I'll be okay. Do you ever get tired of signing autographs? Because I think it would be pretty cool to be famous."

"The car doesn't move until the seat belts are fastened," Jake said firmly, tapping his fingers on the steering wheel.

Andrew heaved a sigh, but settled back in the seat and snapped the restraint into place. "Now you sound like my dad."

"If that means your dad doesn't let you ride in a vehicle without using proper safety equipment, then I'll take it as a compliment."

"Nick would never let Andrew ride in a car without a seat belt," Stacy commented.

"Good for him. You talk to any driver and he'll tell you that conscientiously using our safety equipment saves our lives every week," Jake told Andrew, glancing in the rearview mirror as he drove out of the restaurant parking lot. "We don't take unnecessary risks."

"Okay, I'm wearing it already."

"Good. Make sure you always do. As for being famous, yeah,

it's cool sometimes, but there's other times when it's kind of a pain."

Stacy wondered if that comment had anything to do with her own distaste for public attention.

Passing easily through all the layers of security around the track, Jake took them straight to the motor home for the remainder of the night. He explained that he would go home himself to get some rest for the long day ahead, and advised them to do the same.

Already tired from the eventful day they'd just spent, Stacy looked forward to a few hours of quiet. And since Andrew would have access to state-of-the-art television and video game technology in the motor home, he seemed content with the plan, as well. He would never admit that he was tired, of course, but Stacy could see that he was on sensory overload. It would be good for him to get some rest before tomorrow's events.

Jake walked them to the door of the motor home, exchanging greetings with the few people they met along the way. Although noisy parties were in full swing in the area where fans' RVs were parked for the night, the area reserved for racing families was quieter, less active.

"I told Dad I'd call him tonight and tell him all about the day," Andrew said when they walked into the motor home. "I'll go into the bedroom to make the call. See you tomorrow, Jake, okay?"

"Was that a ruse to leave us alone for a few minutes?" Jake asked quizzically when the bedroom door closed firmly behind the boy.

Locking her hands in front of her, Stacy tried to smile. "Maybe he was just impatient to tell Nick all about his day."

But she wouldn't put it past him to have been leaving them alone together, either. She remembered his saying that he could get used to this life; maybe he figured he could do so through his aunt.

"Maybe," Jake said with a smile that was a little too knowing. "But it serves the same purpose. I was wondering how I was going to sneak a good-night kiss."

She lifted an eyebrow. "You didn't pay him to go in there or anything, did you?"

Feigning insult, he shook his head. "Absolutely not. But only because I didn't think of it," he added.

She shook her head with a sigh. She believed that it hadn't been his idea, but she wouldn't have put it past him, either. As she had noted earlier, Jake went after what he wanted with a single-minded determination that had served him well in his career. He needed to understand, however, that his wants weren't the only ones that counted in a relationship—not that they had a relationship, exactly. Nor would they if he couldn't accept that nonnegotiable fact.

Which, of course, was only one of the obstacles to a relationship between them.

He pushed a strand of hair off her face, smiling down at her. "Such a serious look. I would ask what you're thinking, but I figure you would tell me if you wanted me to know."

"I was wondering how long you're satisfied once you achieve one of your goals. How long before you have to go after the next objective? The next win, the next trophy, the next title?"

He seemed startled by her serious response to his whimsical question. She was a bit startled herself. The words had left her before she'd had time to think about them.

"How literally do you mean that?" he asked after a moment. "Is this really about racing?"

Maybe he was a little too perceptive. "Take it as literally as you want."

After only a momentary hesitation, he shrugged, still standing very close to her. "I'm never content with a win. Not for long, anyway. I start looking toward the next race, and then the one after that. I'm determined to win a championship title, and after I accomplish that—which I will—I'll want another one. And I'll go after it."

Well, he'd answered honestly. Maybe a bit too much so.

"And now you're wondering if I have the same philosophy toward women," he murmured.

She didn't respond. But maybe that was an answer in itself.

"No," he said flatly. "I don't."

She couldn't think of anything to say.

"You don't believe me?"

"I don't disbelieve you."

"That's not the same thing."

She was aware of that.

His hand was on her face again now, his smile bittersweet. "I'm not looking for the next conquest, Stacy. When it comes to that part of my life, I'm looking for forever."

She held her breath as he lowered his face toward hers.

"Aunt Stacy?"

She and Jake broke apart as if they had been caught doing something illegal. Clearing her throat, Stacy looked toward her nephew, who stood in the open bedroom doorway looking apologetic for the interruption. "What is it, Andrew?"

"Grandma's on the phone. She beeped in while I was talking to Dad. She said she's been trying to call you but your cell phone's turned off."

It wasn't turned off, but she had turned the ringer to silent mode so it wouldn't disrupt dinner. She had instructed Andrew to do the same with his own. She had planned to check messages later, after Jake left.

"Thank you," she said. "Tell her I'll call her back in just a minute."

"Okay." Andrew closed the door again.

The mood broken now, Jake dropped his hand. "I guess I'd better go. I'll send J.R. in the morning to collect you and Andrew. I'll be crazy busy tomorrow, so we won't have a lot of time to spend together, but I've made sure you and Andrew will get the whole race experience."

She walked with him to the door. "We'll look forward to it."

He reached out to snag the back of her head with one hand, pulling her mouth to his for a quick, hard kiss. "Good night, Stacy. Sleep well."

As she set the security system, she wondered if she would sleep a wink. She was more likely to toss and turn during the night, much too aware that she was sleeping in Jake's bed. And trying to convince herself that she was glad Andrew was with her this weekend so that there was no chance she and Jake would be sharing that bed before she returned to her real life back home.

CHAPTER THIRTEEN

RACE DAY WAS as frantic and fascinating as Stacy had expected. Jake hadn't been exaggerating about his entire day being scheduled in five-to-fifteen-minute intervals, beginning at 8:00 a.m. and continuing until just before the green flag.

She finally met Pam, a tall, attractive and intimidatingly efficient redhead. Pam and Jake quite obviously had a close relationship, communicating almost without words as she shepherded him through his responsibilities. And yet, Stacy realized almost from the first moment of seeing them together that there was no romance between them at all. Friendship, definitely. Mutual respect and admiration. Even some easy flirtation. But that was the extent of it.

She couldn't help wondering why nothing more had developed between them. They were both so striking, so involved in the world of racing, so driven and ambitious. Pam looked as comfortable as Jake in the public eye. On the surface, they seemed like the perfect couple. And yet she sensed somehow that neither of them had ever wanted more than a professional friendship from the other.

Maybe they were too much alike.

Watching Jake that afternoon, she realized that he was surrounded by women almost all the time. Fans, associates, people connected through his sponsors and teammates. Some were almost embarrassingly eager to catch his attention; others were much more subtle but still seemed interested in getting to know him better. He treated them all the same way. Warm, friendly, flirtatious—but at a careful distance.

She didn't believe for a moment that he'd led a monk's existence the past few years. But she got the distinct feeling that he'd been very careful in his liaisons. She supposed he had been so focused on his career goals that he hadn't let anything else distract him for long.

Only now was he beginning to think about expanding his life off the track—and she was the one he seemed to be focusing on. For now. And Stacy had no more idea why he'd chosen her than she understood why he hadn't chosen Pam, or one of the other women who traveled in the same circles he did.

Andrew loved every minute of the day, from watching autograph sessions to eating the grilled-chicken lunch served to the team outside the hauler to browsing through the souvenir trailers outside the stands. He wore his official pass proudly, almost strutting whenever one of the crew acknowledged him by name. He was so thrilled to be part of the inside crowd, at least for one weekend.

Stacy was touched to watch all of the Woodrow Racing drivers meet with several gravely ill children who were at the race through a wish-fulfilling organization. Even Andrew was somber during that encounter as he watched the wan little faces light up when the drivers in their colorful uniforms walked into the room. She wasn't at all surprised that Jake was so gentle and sweet with the kids, but Ronnie and Mike and Scott were just as kind. She supposed they had all done this before, but she could tell that none of them saw it as a chore.

Andrew perked up again when he was allowed to sit in on the drivers' meeting during which NASCAR officials laid out the rules and announcements for the evening's race. Later, they had a prime location from which to watch the introductions of the drivers, and Andrew loudly cheered the entire Woodrow Racing lineup. He had warned Stacy that all the top drivers would be greeted with a fair share of boos as well as cheers. She'd thought she was prepared for that ritual, but it still startled her to hear how fiercely fans of other drivers expressed their derision for the competition.

Jake received mostly cheers and applause for his first race back from his near disastrous accident. Both J.R. and Andrew assured Stacy that he usually had plenty of boos, but even the most ardent fans of other drivers could express their respect for Jake's determination to get back into his car. They wanted to see him lose to their personal heroes, of course, but they were glad he was back to put up a challenge.

It would have been hard to be at the track and not get into the spirit of the activities. As the national anthem played and fighter jets flew overhead and flags waved and team members lined up in their bold team colors, Stacy felt her pulse rate increasing, her muscles tensing in anticipation.

Still in pristine condition, the cars gleamed in the bright artificial lights. In response to the famous cue, forty-three engines roared to life simultaneously, sounding for all the world like restless, hungry creatures barely held under restraint as they demanded to be set free. The noise was so loud she could almost feel it vibrating inside her. Only the headset she wore kept it from being deafening.

Through that headset, she heard Wade and Jake talking, Wade giving encouragement and instructions in his calm drawl, Jake's voice bearing an edge of nerves and adrenaline. The cars began to roll behind the pace car, and Andrew glanced at her with a broad smile that made her throat tighten. He looked so excited. Happier than she had seen him in quite a while.

He felt a part of this, she realized. Special. Here, he wasn't the short, awkward teenager whose mother had abandoned him and whose father had to work such long hours to support him. Here, he was a friend of famous race car drivers, sitting in a place of honor on top of Jake's hauler where thousands of race fans envied him that privilege.

She and Andrew had been given free run of the hauler and the pit area, as long as they stayed out of the team's way. They were to help themselves to snacks and drinks in the hauler, and make themselves comfortable in the lounge area to watch on TV if they grew tired of being outside.

She might have thought she'd have felt conspicuous sitting up there herself, but she realized that there were people perched on every available surface at the venue. The stands held over a hundred thousand spectators, and the infield was filled with motor homes, campers, buses, haulers, almost all topped with race fans. Letting Andrew take the prime viewing spot, she stayed more in the background with Lisa, who also wore a headset and sat in a folding chair next to Stacy's.

Jake had kept his word about not drawing any special attention to her that day, she mused as she waited for the green flag to fall. While he'd made sure that she and Andrew had missed very little, they had watched primarily from the sidelines. Jake had looked their way fairly often, as if to make sure they were still there, but he'd been fairly discreet about it.

Stacy had been aware of a few curious glances, but she had shamelessly used her nephew as a shield, standing slightly behind him as if he were the honored guest for the weekend and she nothing more than a chaperone. She had always been pretty good at fading into the background when she wanted. She figured her average, girl-next-door looks stood her in good stead for that. She doubted that she looked like the type of woman who would captivate famous bachelor driver Jake Hinson, despite his flattering behavior toward her recently.

The pace car left the track and the race was under way.

Stacy settled back in the chair that had been provided for her for the upcoming four hours or so. The weather was nice, just cool enough for jeans and a light jacket. Andrew had brought a denim jacket, but tonight he wore a deep purple Jake Hinson jacket. The swag kept piling up, Stacy thought with a smile, and Andrew was enjoying every bit of it.

She never would have imagined that she could sit for four hours watching cars running in circles. She would have thought she'd grow bored. Restless. But that had been before she'd cared so much about one of the drivers.

That thought made her so nervous that she cleared her throat and forced herself to concentrate more fiercely on the action on and around the track. For all she knew, this could be the only race she would ever attend, she reminded herself, especially from this insider's vantage point. She shouldn't waste the opportunity fretting about why she was there in the first place.

A sudden crashing sound from the track made her jump and look anxiously in the direction of a cloud of brake smoke. Someone had hit the wall, she realized anxiously, and another couple of cars had been unable to avoid impact.

"Jake's okay," Lisa said loudly, pointing toward another section of the track where the Number 82 car was slowing for the caution. "He wasn't near it."

Relieved, Stacy sat back in her seat, trying to relax. Even if he was wrecked this evening, Jake would be fine, she reminded herself. He had assured her repeatedly that the car was safe and that he wouldn't be hurt even if he hit the wall or another car. Just in case, he had warned her and Andrew that the wrecks sometimes looked bad, but that injuries were increasingly rare, so they shouldn't get too anxious if he should happen to be involved in one that evening.

Not that he planned to wreck, he had told them with a laugh. He'd intended to win.

Jake came in for a pit stop during the caution, as did most of the other cars, and Stacy found that a fascinating process to watch from this close. The team stood poised for action as the Number 82 car made its way down the pit road, then swarmed over the wall and around the car like precisely choreographed robots, filling the tank and changing all four tires with dizzying speed.

On instructions from Wade, they made some sort of adjustment while the car was there, but she didn't have a clue what they were talking about. Andrew seemed to know what was going on; he watched the process intently and seemed satisfied when Jake peeled out of the tight space and headed back onto the track at the required pit road speed.

It was going to be a long race, she reminded herself. She really should try to relax or she would be exhausted by the time it ended. But it was hard knowing Jake was out there, knowing how much it meant to him to perform well tonight. She wanted so badly for him to win, or at least to be pleased with his finish.

The extent of her anxiety for him made her grow nervous all over again—not for Jake this time, but for herself. She was taking more than a few risks, as well. Her heart was in the danger zone, and she was afraid the damage would be irreparable if this particular challenge ended in a hard crash.

WITH THE RACE just over two-thirds completed, Jake was running very well. He had led several laps, and was currently in fourth. Andrew had gotten hungry—as the teenager so often was—so he and Stacy and Lisa had raided the hauler kitchen for sodas and sandwiches that had been set out for the team. They brought the food back up to the top of the hauler for a picnic under the artificial lights, which were bright enough to pretty much block out the stars.

Andrew never removed his headset during the kitchen raid. Stacy and Lisa left theirs behind for a while, but put them back on after they'd eaten, both to hear Wade and Jake talk and to dull some of the engine roar. Conversation was pretty much impossible during the race, though Lisa and Stacy managed to shout a few comments at each other.

Stacy thoroughly enjoyed listening to the exchanges through her headset. It was interesting to hear the way Arnie, the spotter, guided Jake around the track, avoiding other cars and problem areas with the skill of an air-traffic controller. They had developed their own shorthand for directions, in addition to the traditional "low" and "high" designations. More than once during the evening, Arnie kept Jake from being collected in wrecks, guiding him through clouds of smoke that had Jake pretty much driving blind through the melee. Stacy had to watch those near misses from behind her hands, holding her breath until Jake was clear and safe.

Wade kept Jake informed about how the race was progressing as a whole. How fast other drivers were going, Jake's own lap times and track position. They talked about wedge and track bar adjustments, about fuel mileage and pit strategies and tire wear, much of which she didn't understand. They joked around a bit, mostly on Jake's part, since Wade tended to be pretty serious while he was working.

She lifted her head when she heard her own name through the headset.

"Is Stacy doing okay?" Jake asked Wade. "Has she had anything to eat?"

"I think so." Wade turned on the pit box to glance up their way, nodding toward her and Lisa before looking back at the track. "She's wearing a headset."

"Hi, Stacy," Jake said. "You don't have to answer. Just wanted to remind you to be sure and ask J.R. if you or Andrew need anything at all, okay? Arnie, where's the Number 56 car? Is he still coming up behind me?"

The conversation in the headsets turned to business again. Stacy noticed that Lisa had grimaced in response to Jake's comments. Pulling off the headset, she asked, "What?"

Lisa hesitated, then shrugged. "Jake lets it slip his mind sometimes that the airwaves are always being monitored. By NASCAR, the media, the fans. Sometimes he starts talking and he forgets it isn't just Wade and Arnie and him having a conversation."

Stacy bit her lip as she became aware of what Lisa was telling her. Jake had just mentioned her by name over the radio, expressing concern for her well-being during a race. And though she had managed to remain in the background thus far during the weekend, she had just been thrust front and center, if Lisa's concerns were legitimate.

Andrew was grinning at her from across the hauler. She gave him a rather sickly smile in response. Sure, he thought it was great that Jake was thinking about them out on the track, but then he didn't have to worry about the potential fallout.

So maybe she was overreacting. Maybe no one would think twice about his asking about a guest at the race. He had mentioned Andrew, after all, and she'd made a point of pushing Andrew forward. Jake tended to talk a lot while he was driving, keeping up a running, almost stream-of-consciousness commentary. Much of what he'd said had been inconsequential, teasing or complaining. She couldn't imagine that anyone would make too much out of his mention of one random name.

A few laps later, she noticed a trackside reporter standing beside J.R. down on the ground. The reporter had been by a couple of times earlier to shove a microphone into Wade's face and ask about track and pit strategies and how it felt to have Jake back in the car. She assumed that as the race drew closer to an end and Jake moved steadily toward the front, sitting in second place now, the reporter was back to ask for more comments.

Her stomach sank when J.R. turned with an obliging smile and pointed toward the top of the hauler. Right to where she sat.

Lisa groaned loudly. "J.R. has the common sense of a turnip," she proclaimed in disgust.

Wade saw what was going on and made a quick summoning motion to J.R., who excused himself to the reporter and moved toward the pit box. Wade leaned down and spoke a few terse words into J.R.'s ear, after which J.R. disappeared into the hauler, not to emerge again.

Glancing apologetically up at Stacy, Wade went back to work.

"Wade really does run the whole show down there, doesn't he?" Stacy asked Lisa, leaning close to be heard.

Lisa nodded. "He's definitely accustomed to being in charge," she said. "I have to remind him every once in a while that I'm not a member of the team."

Maybe bossiness was a trait of people in the sport, Stacy mused, leaning back in her chair again. A refusal to take no for an answer. It served them well in their careers, but it could be a definite drawback in a relationship.

Watching as the reporter drifted to the next pit, she tried to assure herself that everything was still okay. The reporter had simply wanted to identify the Stacy Jake had referred to. Surely J.R. had said, if asked, that Stacy and Andrew were just friends of Jake's who were there to watch the race. Since Jake and Stacy had been extremely circumspect in front of everyone, J.R.

probably really did believe that this weekend was more about Andrew than Stacy. She hoped.

With three laps to go, Jake was still in second place, but closing fast on first. The entire crowd of spectators were on their feet, screaming for their personal favorites to win. Andrew practically jumped up and down as he cheered Jake on. Caught up in the excitement, Stacy and Lisa stood close together, eyes locked on the purple Number 82 car as if intense concentration on their part could push Jake to the front.

He almost made the pass in Turn 3. But then the frontrunner blocked frantically, taking up as much track as possible as he approached the checkered flag. Jake crossed the finish line only a heartbeat behind the other car, taking second place.

Andrew looked disappointed, but Wade and the rest of the crew seemed satisfied with the strong finish. Jake was back, they were all saying in the headsets. Still a contender, still a force to be reckoned with. His performance today had left no doubt of that.

Jake didn't seem to mind the loss too badly. In fact, he kept saying how much fun that had been, chasing down the leader and almost taking him. "I'm back, baby," he said, satisfaction in his voice, the comment addressed to anyone who happened to be listening.

Stacy's throat tightened as she realized just how happy he was to be back in his car, back in contention. Nothing in Jake's life would ever compete with his love of racing, she thought somberly. Any woman who became involved with him should understand that from the start.

JAKE FACED a barrage of postrace interviews, everyone wanting to know how it had felt to be back, whether he was pleased with his finish, if during the race he had experienced any aftereffects

GINA WILKINS 197

from his injuries. He assured everyone that he was fine, that he'd
had a great time battling for the lead at the end, that a second-
place finish for his first race in eight weeks was satisfying,
though he'd have rather had the win.

He skillfully worked his sponsors into every interview, thanking them for their support, thanking the fans for the flood of
e-mails and cards and letters he'd received after his accident,
thanking his owner and his team for their unwavering loyalty. He
thanked Pete for filling in for him and doing a great job of it,
stating each time that he was sure Pete would be back in NASCAR
NEXTEL Cup racing soon with a full-time ride of his own.

He braced himself when he was approached by a reporter who
specialized in NASCAR gossip, and who'd been trying for a
couple of years to find out more about Jake's very private personal life. He was still annoyed with himself for mentioning
Stacy's name during the race. Sometimes his mouth jumped
ahead of his brain when he was out there on the track for all those
hours of laps. He'd just wanted to make sure she was having a
good time, and he'd blurted it out before he'd thought about
anyone else who might find the comment intriguing.

"How are you doing, Jake?" the reporter, Melanie Main,
asked with rather cloying sympathy. "Was it difficult getting
back into the swing of things so late in the season?"

"It felt like I was never gone," he replied, keeping his smile
steady and bland.

"Everyone worried about you when you just disappeared the
way you did a few weeks ago."

"I took some time away to rest and recuperate, but I'm back
in peak shape now."

"I know it must have been horrible for you, losing a longtime
friend and being so badly injured yourself. Where did you find
the strength to deal with those challenges?"

Losing Eric had been more than a "challenge," Jake thought in annoyance. And a great deal more tragic than his own loss of a few races or a chance at a championship.

"Eric was a good friend," he said quietly. "I'd known him since junior high. He'll be greatly missed by his family and his friends, but we know he'd have wanted us to stay strong and go on with our lives. I'm starting a scholarship fund for his two young sons—the details will be on my Web site soon."

His attempt to lead the conversation into a new direction wasn't particularly successful. Rather than following up on the scholarship-fund announcement, Melanie said, "You mentioned someone named Stacy during the race. Is she someone who's helped you through the past few weeks?"

"Stacy's a friend," he said lightly. "She's here with her nephew, who's a big fan of the Woodrow Racing team. This was his first race, and we've made sure he's had the full experience."

Pam appeared at his elbow then, speaking with her usual air of brisk authority. "Sorry to cut this short, but you have some people waiting to speak with you, Jake."

"Okay, thanks, Pam. Melanie, it was nice to see you, as always."

"I'd love a longer interview with you soon."

"Give me a call," Pam said smoothly, guiding Jake away. "We'll see if we can set something up."

As soon as she was sure they were out of hearing, she added beneath her breath, "But, gee, I think your schedule is completely filled for the foreseeable future."

"If anyone asks you about Stacy…"

Pam nodded with the resignation of having handled sticky PR situations for Jake before. "A casual friend, here to show her nephew a good time."

"Thanks. Don't know what I was thinking out there."

Pam gave him a look that showed she knew exactly what he'd been thinking.

He cleared his throat and headed for the hauler.

CHAPTER FOURTEEN

WITH A RARE SUNDAY OFF, Jake took advantage of the extra time to spend with Stacy before she had to leave early that evening. Of course, Andrew was with them all day, but he liked Andrew well enough. And as long as Stacy was there, Jake wasn't complaining.

They visited the shop, which was unusually quiet on this off Sunday. But there was always some activity in the shop, seven days a week, and today was no exception. Andrew was fascinated by seeing cars in every stage of development from a few welded bars to a completed, painted and decaled race car, ready for the cameras. The room full of completed purple-and-silver Number 82 cars, each one slightly modified for a specific race, struck him almost speechless.

Leaving the shop, Jake drove them to his house. He reminded them on the way that he hadn't yet decorated, but he still wanted them to see the place.

Or rather, he wanted to see Stacy there.

"Jake, it's beautiful," she said when he drove through the decorative gates of his security fencing to reveal the sprawling white estate with the lake visible behind it. "Just beautiful."

His breath left him in response to her reaction. He hadn't even realized until then that he'd been holding it. "Thank you. I've got to admit, I think so, too."

It still amazed him at times that a guy who had grown up in cheap rented rooms could afford a place like this by the time he was thirty. He loved the spreading lawn and all the sparkling glass from dozens of windows. He got great pleasure out of the big kitchen with its travertine floor and quartz countertops and top-of-the-line appliances he rarely used. The big, open dining room and formal living room, both featuring gleaming wood floors and glittering chandeliers. The home office paneled in rich pecan with built-in cabinets and desks for his computer equipment. The media room with stadium seating, a wall-sized viewing screen, discreetly hidden sound system. The five bedrooms, only one of which was decorated as of yet.

Andrew wasn't quite as impressed with the house as he'd been with the shop, but he said he liked the place, especially the media room. Stacy, on the other hand, seemed to genuinely love Jake's home, chatting eagerly with him about his plans for furnishing and decorating, complimenting the choices he had made so far.

Standing in the middle of his bedroom, which he'd had done in a tropical theme in shades of green and sand with splashes of red, she turned to him with a bright smile. "This is perfect," she said, motioning toward the huge window that looked over the lake. "It's like being in the islands somewhere."

"That's what I had in mind," he agreed. "I'd like to use different themes in all the bedrooms because I like several different decorating styles, but tropical was my first choice for my room."

Andrew stood at the window, looking out at the dock and the boat garage, the outdoor kitchen and dining area and the natural-shaped swimming pool with a rock waterfall at one end and a hot tub at the other. "Looks like you could have a lot of fun here," he commented.

"I don't get to spend a lot of time here," Jake admitted, "and the time I do have off is in the middle of the winter, but I take advantage of the chances I have to spend at home."

As he'd been doing the day of his accident, he remembered. He and Eric had cooked steaks on the grill for lunch and had then gone out in the boat for a tour of the lake. Jake had been laughing at something Eric said when they'd been broadsided by the boat that had come out of nowhere. Even now, he wondered if he should have reacted faster or somehow differently. If he could have avoided the accident. If he'd only been more on the ball.

No matter how often everyone assured him that there had been nothing he could have done differently, he thought he would always feel vaguely guilty whenever he remembered that day.

ANDREW WENT OUTSIDE to explore while Jake and Stacy moved back into the kitchen. Jake had arranged to have a late lunch waiting for them. A big bowl of cold shrimp-and-pasta salad sat in the fridge along with several side dishes, requiring nothing more than uncovering them and setting them out to serve.

"This kitchen is amazing," Stacy said, running a hand admiringly over the gold-flecked green quartz countertop.

"Thanks. I'm afraid most of the cabinets are empty and the pantry's pretty sparse. I've only bought the basics of kitchenware so far. I've got my eye on a fancy new espresso maker. And my dishes are sort of mismatched right now. I haven't had time to pick a style."

"I'm surprised you haven't hired a decorator to come in and take care of all that for you. You could have every room furnished and equipped within a couple of months."

"Everyone says that," he admitted. "And I probably should just hire someone. Considering my schedule and at the rate I've been going, I might still be living in empty rooms when I'm ready for retirement. But I kind of like the idea of doing it all myself, you know? Using stuff I chose on my own because I liked it, not because some design-school graduate said it was in style."

"I can understand that." She picked up a large wooden bowl he'd found in a craft shop in Arizona, and in which he usually kept a selection of fresh fruit. "It's nice to feel a personal attachment to the things that surround you every day."

"Exactly," he said, glad she seemed to comprehend. "My mother and I lived in so many cheap furnished apartments. We never had much of anything that was really our own or that we had chosen for ourselves. Having someone else decorate this place for me, even if the stuff would be a lot nicer than anything I ever had as a kid, would still feel to me like living with someone else's things."

She studied his face for a moment, and he wondered if he'd said too much. He hadn't been trying for sympathy, just explaining honestly why he had been resistant to hiring a decorator.

"That makes perfect sense," she said after a pause. And then she turned to continue setting out their lunch.

Those few words were enough to make him believe that she really did understand. That was just one of the things about Stacy that drew him to her; he had always felt free to be himself with her. He'd never felt the need to retreat behind the public persona he had carefully developed during the past few years. Never felt compelled to hide his fears or doubts or insecurities. Somehow, she got him—even though he suspected she didn't quite realize that herself.

He knew she still had her doubts about him. About them. She worried about his obsession with racing, about his life in the spotlight, about whether he would grow bored with her and move on to the next woman. The first two issues were legitimate enough; the racing life wasn't an easy one and a woman should be very sure she was prepared for that before getting involved with a race car driver.

As for the latter—he intended to do whatever it took to convince her that he'd known almost from the beginning that she was the one woman he'd been waiting for his entire life. That she was the first to make him feel like this, and would be the last, if he had his way.

He had never needed a string of beauties to boost his ego or make him feel more like a man. But he needed Stacy to make his life feel complete. He didn't require any more time to be certain of his feelings for her. He had known without a doubt when he had seen her waiting at the hauler after last night's race.

She had smiled when he walked in, and congratulated him on running a great race, never mind that he hadn't crossed the line first. She'd told him she had enjoyed watching him and had been very impressed with his driving.

He had ached to kiss her then, wanted it so badly that he'd been sure she had seen the desire in his eyes. Her cheeks had gone pink and she had turned to congratulate Wade, implicitly reminding Jake that there were other people around them. And while Jake had reluctantly conceded that the time hadn't been right to publicly stake his claim, he had been absolutely certain that he wanted Stacy to be there to meet him after every race in the future.

They still had a way to go before he could express that wish to her. She still needed convincing that what had developed between them was worth all the effort it would take to make it last a lifetime.

Jake hadn't gotten where he was without self-confidence, determination and charm, all of which he intended to employ to win Stacy Carter's heart.

STACY INSISTED on cleaning the kitchen after lunch, sending Jake and Andrew off to play video games while she did so. She knew Andrew would love that, and to be honest, it was a pleasure to putter around in Jake's dream kitchen.

A woman could almost marry him for this kitchen alone, she thought frivolously. Stumbling, she nearly dropped the leftover pasta salad on the stone floor as she heard her own disconcerting thought. What on earth had made her think about marriage? She and Jake weren't anywhere near even thinking about that step.

They had known each other less than a month. They had shared only a few kisses—amazing kisses—but nothing more. She wasn't even sure she would see him again after she left this afternoon, though she suspected she would receive more invitations to do so.

Maybe it felt as though she were falling head over heels for Jake, but there was always the possibility that she was simply being carried away by the glamour and romance of this magical weekend. Maybe time away from him would put all of this into perspective, help her remember the reasons she had been reluctant to get involved with him in the first place.

Maybe she would come to see that Jake wasn't really as special as he seemed.

Leaving a spotless kitchen behind her, she went in search of the guys, hoping wryly that she wouldn't get lost on the way to the media room. As beautiful as this house was, it was ridiculously large for only one person.

She heard Jake and Andrew talking as she approached the media room doorway. Beeps and bams underlay their words, evidence that they played as they conversed. Not wanting to interrupt them without announcing herself, she slowed as she drew closer. She was startled to hear Andrew mention his mother, since he absolutely never talked about his mother. Ever.

"She left us," he said as Stacy moved close enough to hear. "Just took off without hardly stopping to say goodbye."

"That stinks, man," Jake said bluntly. "I know the feeling."

"Yeah? Did your mom leave, too?"

"My father. Ran off when I was just a little kid. Left me and my mother high and dry."

"Stinks."

"Seriously."

"So you had family and stuff, didn't you? Like I got my grandma and her husband, Lou, and Aunt Stacy?"

"No. It was just me and my mom. She worked really hard to put food on our table."

"My dad works all the time," Andrew muttered.

"He's probably having a rough time of it," Jake suggested. "Supporting you. Keeping his job. And all of that while dealing with the end of his marriage. Gotta be tough on him, you know?"

Andrew was quiet for a few moments, the only sound in the room the strange noises issuing from the video game. And then he said, "He could have talked her into staying."

"You're not blaming him because your mom left, are you, Andrew? Because let me tell you, chances are he did everything he could to keep the family together. From what I saw of him, family means a lot to him. I could sure tell that you mean everything to him. You're lucky, you know, to have your dad in your life. I would have liked to have had mine."

"Are you and your mom still close?"

"My mom died several years ago. I don't have any family left."

"You don't have any family?"

"No. Just my friends at work."

There was another pause and then Andrew said, "If you marry Aunt Stacy, you'd be a part of our family."

Stacy nearly fell on her face. Served her right, she thought, for eavesdropping. She deserved to be humiliated.

Making plenty of noise, she moved toward the doorway. "How's the game going?" she asked, her voice entirely too bright and cheery. "Is he beating you as badly as I predicted, Jake?"

Jake looked at her sharply, obviously wondering how much she had overheard. She gave him a smile that she hoped revealed absolutely nothing. "When should we head for the airport? We don't want to miss our flight."

THEY FLEW HOME on a commercial flight. Jake drove them to the airport, growing quieter the closer they came. He stood by as they checked their bags, then walked with them to the security check-in, which was as far as he could go. The airport was fairly crowded on this early Sunday evening after the big race, and Stacy was aware that Jake was recognized more than once as he strode with them through the crowd. She saw people pointing and whispering, but at least no one pestered him for his autograph. Maybe it was because for once, Jake didn't look particularly approachable.

He made an effort to smile when he held out his right hand to Andrew. "Well, I guess this is it."

Andrew shook his hand solemnly. "Thank you again for bringing me here this weekend, Jake. It was the best time I've ever had. I can't wait to show Dad and my friends the pictures Aunt Stacy took of me with you and Scott and in the pits and the garage and stuff."

"Tell your dad I said hi, okay? I'm sorry he couldn't join us this weekend, but I understand having to work on Saturdays. I have to do it most weeks, myself."

Andrew nodded. "Yeah, I guess you do work a lot of hours, don't you? Even more than my dad, maybe."

"A guy does what he has to do to get by. I know your father would rather hang out with you than at the office, and I know he does every chance he gets."

Andrew nodded. "We always watch the races together on Sunday afternoons."

"That's great. Watch for me next week. I'll wave like this at the camera, and you'll know I'm saying hi to you and your dad, okay?" He held up two fingers and waved them back and forth in a modified salute.

Grinning, Andrew nodded. "I'll watch for it."

Jake turned to Stacy then, moving so slowly that she could tell he was reluctant to say goodbye. She felt the same way.

Before he could say anything, she held out her hand. "I want to thank you, too, Jake. Andrew and I had a wonderful time."

He looked at that hand and then up at her face. "So did I."

Rather than shaking her hand, he took it in both of his own. "Have a safe flight home. I'll call you later, okay?"

She nodded.

He didn't immediately release her hand. His gaze locked with hers, he looked as though he had a lot he wanted to say, but wasn't free to do so. "I'm glad you came," he said finally.

"So am I."

"If I make the arrangements, will you come to another race? I don't suppose you'd want to come to Martinsville next Sunday, but maybe Atlanta in two weeks. You'd like that one, I think."

"I don't know, Jake. I can't make that decision now."

He frowned a little, but spoke evenly. "You can think about it on the way home. Let me know in a few days."

She was starting to feel a bit pressured. "I'll think about it," she said, making no commitment.

"I'll miss you every day we're not together," he murmured, making sure no one else could hear him over the noise of the terminal. Not even Andrew, who stood close by, pretending not to watch them.

She didn't know what to say, except "We'd better go."

"I know," he said with a sigh. "So, I'll see you, okay?"

Swallowing hard, she nodded. "See you."

Maybe.

Before she knew what he was going to do, he tugged at her hand, making her stumble toward him. His mouth was on hers before she'd regained her balance.

The kiss didn't last excessively long, but it was certainly powerful. Stacy heard her pulse roaring in her ears. She even saw a flash of light.

Only when he finally released her did she take a deep breath and realize that the flash had been from a camera. She even saw the photographer, a young man in a Ronnie Short jacket and cap.

She gave Jake a look of reproof, but he didn't look particularly regretful. Giving her a slight shrug, he finally released her hand and stepped back. "I'll call you," he said.

Gripping her purse so tightly her knuckles ached, she turned abruptly. "Come on, Andrew. Let's find our gate."

"IT'S INCREDIBLE. He's like a different kid."

Stacy studied her brother across the table of the little diner near his office where she had joined him for lunch on the Tuesday after her return from North Carolina. "He really had a wonderful time."

"I know. It's all he's talked about since. But the thing is, he's talking," Nick said with a stunned shake of his head. "To me. He must have shown me his pictures a dozen times. And he's told me the same stories several times during dinner. I don't care. I've just decided to enjoy it while it lasts."

"I think he came to a few realizations while we were away,"
Stacy mused. "He saw that you aren't the only man who has to
work long hours in your job. And that yours isn't the only broken
family that has to keep functioning after one parent leaves. And
he saw that it won't really matter if he doesn't grow to over six
feet—several of the racing stars are on the shorter side."

"Whatever he learned during the trip, I hope the lessons last
for a while." Nick took a bite of chicken-fried steak and washed
it down with a sip of sweetened iced tea. "I know one weekend
can't work miracles. Andrew's a teenage boy, and he's going to
go through his phases of rebellion and defiance. But maybe we
can make some headway while he's still in such a great mood."

"I hope so."

Scooping up a forkful of mashed potatoes and gravy, Nick
asked, "So what did *you* learn during your outing?"

Looking up from her chicken salad and mixed-fruit plate, she
asked, "What do you mean?"

"I guess I'm asking if you're going to see Jake again. Andrew
talks like the two of you are a serious item. I think he's already
imagining how cool it's going to be to have a famous race car
driver for an uncle."

Feeling her cheeks go warm, she frowned. "Then he's being
entirely too imaginative."

"So you haven't fallen for the guy?"

"I like Jake very much," she prevaricated. "But that's all there
is to it at this time."

Nick put down his fork and clasped his hands on the table.
"I've got to admit, I would have some concerns if you became
too involved with Jake. I mean, he's a great guy, don't get me
wrong. I'll always be grateful for what he did for Andrew this
past weekend. But...well, his life couldn't be more different
from yours."

"I know."

"You've chosen to live so quietly. So privately. He chases the spotlight as hard as he chases a victory at the track. He has to— it's part of his job."

"I know," she said again.

"Not much privacy in the life of a race car driver. And I would imagine the typical driver thrives on excitement and challenges, which doesn't exactly describe your lifestyle, either. They live for the next race, the next win. And as for women—well, there are certain types who would do just about anything to catch the eye of a rich, famous driver. They'd be so drawn to the fame and fortune that they'd have little compunction about ruining existing relationships. It would be hard for a man not to be tempted by a steady stream of attractive, willing women competing for his attention."

She knew that, too, of course. She had seen it for herself at the track last weekend. She couldn't tolerate the idea of an unfaithful mate. Would Jake be able to resist that temptation, even after the newness of a relationship wore off and time inevitably began to leave its marks?

Biting her lip, she chided herself for leaping that far ahead, despite her warnings to Andrew and to herself. After all, Jake hadn't actually discussed anything long-term. He made no secret of being interested in her now, but all he had talked about was the next racetrack where he wanted her to join him. And he hadn't invited Andrew to that one.

Jake wouldn't be content for long with the kisses they had shared thus far. He was already making his impatience clear. And she knew herself too well to believe she could indulge in an affair with him that wouldn't lead to her giving her heart to him.

Deep down, she was about as traditional as a woman could get. She wanted a family. One man, one woman, a couple of kids and a dog. Maybe even a minivan. She had never pictured a race car. Could she really have any of those things with a man like Jake?

"You're Stacy Carter, aren't you?" a diner employee asked, pausing by the table to study her.

Swallowing a sigh, Stacy nodded. "Yes."

She expected questions about her encounter with the courthouse gunman. While the interest in that story had waned considerably during the past few weeks, she was still recognized occasionally.

She didn't expect the woman's next comment. "Are you really dating Jake Hinson? Is he as good-looking in person as he is in the racing magazines?"

"How did you—? Um, what makes you think I'm dating Jake Hinson?" she asked weakly. How could someone from Little Rock know about last weekend?

"I saw it on the Internet. At one of the Jake Hinson fan sites. There was a picture of you and him kissing at the airport and some people were saying how he wanted to meet you after he heard about you taking down that criminal at the courthouse a few weeks ago. They said he saw your picture and looked you up. That's so romantic, you know?"

"And so untrue, I'm afraid," Stacy replied, trying to keep her tone light. "It sounds as though you've been reading some Internet gossip."

"I saw the picture," the waitress insisted. "You were at the race last week, weren't you?"

"I was there with my nephew," Stacy agreed somewhat coolly.

"People on the message boards are all wondering about you and how serious you and Jake are. They've been wondering when he was going to hitch up permanently with someone, instead of just dating a string of models and beauty queens, you know? I think it's cool that he's seeing someone from around here. A hometown girl. Especially one who could whup his butt if he gets too full of himself, you know?" The waitress laughed loudly at her own joke.

The young server who'd been waiting on Stacy and Nick appeared at the table with a pitcher of tea in her hand. "Marla, you've got an order up. Better get on it before Mack gets mad again."

Marla sighed heavily. "All right. But I sure would like to hear more about Jake Hinson."

"I really don't have anything else to tell you right now," Stacy assured her firmly.

Sighing again, Marla shuffled off.

"Sorry about that," the newcomer—whose name tag read Jill—murmured as she refilled their drinking glasses. "Marla's, like, the biggest gossip on the planet. Anytime we have anyone even remotely famous in here, like a TV news anchor or somebody who's been in the society pages or something, she's all over them. Mack's warned her that if she doesn't stop it, he's going to have to fire her."

"You'd think I'd get used to that," Stacy said to her brother after Jill moved on. "Jake certainly takes it in stride that total strangers want to know all about his personal life. I don't know that I could ever handle it as smoothly as he does."

"It's certainly something to consider," Nick agreed somberly. "I mean, you and I both remember what it was like to see our family's name splashed all over the local newspapers."

She winced at the memory. "All too well."

"Of course, there is a difference," he seemed compelled to point out. "Dad was always in the middle of some sort of scandal or controversy. Jake's press is mostly the admiring type. But his is on a larger scale, of course. Dad was pretty notorious here in the state, but not so much outside. Jake's famous nationwide, and he's got the Internet grapevine to contend with, which wasn't even around at the height of Dad's shenanigans."

None of which made her feel much better. "I was really hoping I could go to the race without making it onto that grapevine."

"I doubt that Jake can sneeze without someone commenting about it on one of his fan sites. That's something you'd better just get used to if you're going to keep seeing him," Nick said bluntly. "I know you don't follow race gossip, but one of the drivers was involved in an ugly and very public divorce last year. The Internet practically buzzed with gossip about it. People actually took sides between the two, and each side trashed the other pretty thoroughly. I couldn't help thinking then that it would be hard to live like that. It was hard enough when Deb took off and I knew people were probably gossiping about us. But at least that was on a much smaller scale."

Stacy moistened her lips. "I met quite a few happy couples among Jake's racing friends. Several of them seemed to live relatively quietly, keeping their private lives out of the spotlight."

Nick nodded. "I suppose that's possible if they make the effort. Of course, those guys might not be the kind who draw attention like Jake does. There's just something about Jake that seems to intrigue people—especially the women."

Remembering Marla's comments about models and beauty queens, Stacy pushed her plate away, her appetite suddenly gone.

"WELL, I DON'T CARE what anyone says. If you want to see Jake Hinson, you ought to do so," Mindy insisted stubbornly Thursday afternoon, as she and Stacy stuffed small toys and individually wrapped candies into tiny, colorful gift bags. They had volunteered to run a game booth at their church's fall carnival, which would be held on Halloween, just under two weeks away. Because both of them liked to prepare early for that sort of thing, they'd agreed to meet this evening to start preparations and make sure they had everything they needed.

Taking her time about answering, Stacy tied a ribbon around a filled bag, leaving a loop at the top. Their booth would be a fishing pond. Children at the carnival would cast a fishing rod—or a wooden dowel with a string and a plastic hook—over the top of a sheet of plywood painted with a cheery lake scene. Stacy and Mindy would take turns hiding behind the plywood, attaching gift bags to the plastic hooks and then tugging lightly to let the young fishermen know they'd made a catch. The plywood stood nearby in Mindy's living room, waiting to be painted, and they had several other things to do before the night of the carnival, but at least the prizes would be ready by the end of this evening.

Setting the bag in a large basket that already held quite a few, Stacy reached for another to fill. "That's easier said than done," she said finally. "Considering that we live in different states, and that Jake is usually on the road at one track or another, it's hardly possible for us to date in a traditional sense."

"He calls you, doesn't he?"

"Yes." He'd called every day since she'd left North Carolina. The calls lasted a long time, and they never seemed to run out of things to say. Jake told her all about his days—which, of course, were much more interesting than her own—but he also seemed genuinely interested in what she'd been doing since she'd returned home.

They talked about world news and philosophies, about their friends and coworkers, about childhood memories and future goals. And yet, Stacy was aware that she was still holding back in some ways, still protecting herself from being hurt by him, still resisting any suggestion that they were a couple and not just long-distance friends.

Jake was growing more frustrated with that hesitation. He told her he wanted to know that he would see her again. Soon. He told her how much he missed her. He told her he wanted to kiss her again—and he implied that he hoped for much more the next time they were together. And even though he was trying to be patient, she could tell he wanted a concrete answer to when she would join him again.

And it would have to be her joining him, she mused glumly. His schedule didn't allow him to be the one to come to her. A life together would always revolve around Jake's career. His moods would always be connected to how well he performed on the track and where he stood in the points. He would always have to be concerned about keeping his owner and his sponsors happy. Not to mention his fans.

"So when are you going to see him again?"

Stacy pulled a knot tighter than she had intended, then made herself go back and loosen the ribbon a bit. "I don't know. He wants me to join him in Atlanta a week from Sunday."

"Are you going?"

"I don't know," she repeated.

Tucking a lock of brown hair behind her ear, Mindy turned to study her thoughtfully. "Let me put it this way, do you want to go?"

"I want to see him," Stacy replied after a long pause. "I just don't know if I can handle everything that goes along with him."

Mindy smiled fondly at her. "I think you can handle anything you want badly enough. And as much as I hate the thought of you not living close to me all the time, I really want you to be happy. If gorgeous, successful, charming Jake Hinson makes you happy, then I think you should take the risk."

Her brother was warning her away from Jake. Her best friend

was practically pushing her into his arms. Everyone seemed to have an opinion about her future with Jake. Everyone except Stacy herself.

CHAPTER FIFTEEN

JAKE LOOKED at the telephone in his hand and scowled. It was early Friday evening, and the first free fifteen minutes he'd had that day. Qualifying had gone well; he had taken the pole for Sunday's race, having run the fastest qualifying lap by less than one-hundredth of a second. His team had been elated, of course. Even Wade had whooped into the headset.

Jake was pleased, as well. Ecstatic, he assured himself. Finishing second in last week's race, taking the pole for this one—he was leaving no doubt in anyone's mind that he was back in peak shape. Though his owner and sponsors had expressed no concerns to him, he knew they'd had their private questions. He hoped he had successfully addressed them all during his brief time back.

It would have felt even better if Stacy had been there to greet him with a smile of congratulation when he'd climbed out of his car.

He dialed her number, thinking of how unsatisfactory these calls were becoming. He wanted to see her. Touch her. Hold her. Though he would take what he could get, hearing her voice on the phone was little consolation.

Their last call hadn't ended particularly well. He had tried to push her into giving him an answer about when they would see each other again, and she'd gotten defensive. He'd backed off before it had turned into their first quarrel, and they had disconnected the call civilly enough, but that didn't mean he was giving up on them. Why couldn't she admit that they had something very special between them, too valuable to let it fizzle for lack of persistence?

"Hello?"

He could tell from her tone that she already knew who was calling, probably thanks to caller ID. The slight reserve in her voice let him know she hadn't forgotten last night's call, either. "Hi. I got the pole."

"That means you'll start in first place for the race, right?"

"Right. And I'll get to choose my pit stall. Not to mention that it's considered quite an accomplishment to take the pole."

"Congratulations."

He could hear the smile in her voice, the one he'd fantasized about seeing. "Thanks. I wish you'd been here to celebrate with us."

The smile faded when she replied, "I had a couple of meetings today that I couldn't miss."

"I know. You told me. I just wish you could have been here," he repeated.

"I do have a job of my own, you know. I can't be on call to be your personal cheerleader."

He scowled again. "That isn't fair, Stacy. I've never asked for that."

He heard her sigh through the airwaves. "I'm sorry. I was out of line. I just…"

He wasn't really angry with her, and he tried to make that clear with his gentle question. "You just what?"

"It's getting to be too much. Apparently my name is all over the Internet. I'm getting calls from reporters again, this time wanting to know how I met you, and whether I'll be seeing you again. Had I not just been in the news over the courthouse incident, it probably wouldn't have been such a big deal that you and I were together last weekend, but now they have a new hook."

Pushing a hand through his hair, he said, "I'm sorry. But you do get used to it, eventually. You learn how to give a brief, polite statement that reveals no more than you want, and then refer the callers to a spokesperson. As for the gossip that's out of your control, you learn not to care, eventually. People can say what they want—*you* know what's true."

"Yes, well, that's easy to say. Especially for someone who likes living in a fishbowl."

"I didn't say I like it. But it is part of the job I love and that I've dreamed about for most of my life."

"I know. It isn't part of my job."

"I know that, too." As understanding as he was trying to be, he was getting annoyed, and he was having a difficult time disguising it.

She sighed again. "I'm sorry, Jake. I keep saying that, but it's really true. I don't mean to take my stress out on you."

"I keep telling myself you wouldn't be so conflicted if there wasn't a part of you that wanted to give us a chance. I understand that you're worried about the repercussions, but you wouldn't even be considering it if you weren't at all interested."

"You know I'm interested," she said in a low voice.

He probably shouldn't press his advantage, considering her mood this evening, but he couldn't resist asking, "You're admitting that you have feelings for me?"

"I said I'm interested," she answered with renewed asperity.

"You're afraid," he suggested. "Afraid of the attention, afraid of the uncertainty, afraid of being hurt."

"Among other things," she muttered. "I know it's hard for you to understand, considering you're never afraid of anything."

That took him aback. "Who said I'm never afraid?"

"Well…you're a race car driver. It takes a lot of confidence to be a success at that, both on the track and off. You even told me once that you're never afraid because you trust the people around you."

"I'm not afraid on the track, no. And the publicity doesn't usually bother me. But that doesn't mean I'm never scared. I was terrified that I wouldn't be able to drive again after my accident. I couldn't imagine what my life would be like if I couldn't race. Racing is more than what I do, Stacy. It's who I am."

"I know that."

Which, he realized, was part of her problem. He could see how it would be daunting if she thought she had to compete with something that important to him.

"There's something else that scares me," he said.

"What is it?"

"Losing you without ever having a chance for us to see how good we could be together. Not just physically, though I think that could be dynamite. But in every other way."

He heard her catch her breath as he spoke, and he knew he'd taken a big risk to speak so boldly. He knew she still thought it was too soon for such statements, but he was tired of waiting. He'd known she was the one for him from the beginning. Why should he wait an arbitrary amount of time until the proper moment to say so?

"Come to Atlanta, Stacy," he said softly. "Let me show you that we can handle the obstacles."

"I'll…think about it."

She had been saying that for almost a week. And he didn't think he was making any headway at all in convincing her.

The call didn't last much longer. It was the shortest time they'd ever talked when he'd called her. And as he set his phone on the table in the hauler office, he hoped it wasn't a sign of things to come.

Someone tapped on the closed door. "Jake? It's time to get ready for your shopping-channel spot. Time to push the licensed merchandise."

He let out a breath and pushed himself to his feet. "Okay, Pam, I'll be right there. Just give me a minute."

He needed that time to put himself back into "Jake Hinson, NASCAR star" mode. It was getting harder to do so all the time after talking to Stacy, he realized with a ripple of nerves that might have surprised his associates.

CHAPTER SIXTEEN

IT WAS VERY LATE that evening when Jake's cell phone rang. Tired to the bone, he was just about to turn in. He'd already turned out the light in his motor home bedroom. Yawning, he reached out to snap it back on as he dragged the phone to his ear. Probably Pam again, he thought without bothering to check the screen. He wouldn't put it past her to have another addition to his already crazy schedule for the next day. "Yeah?"

"Jake, it's Stacy."

That brought his heavy eyelids completely open. "Stacy?" He looked at the clock, frowning when he saw the time. "Is everything okay?"

"I'm sorry, I just remembered the time difference. I hope I didn't wake you."

"No, I'm still up." Mostly. "Are you sure nothing's wrong?"

"Nothing's wrong. I've just been thinking about what you said earlier."

He felt his stomach muscles tighten. He wasn't sure what he would do if she was calling to tell him she had decided she wasn't interested in pursuing anything further with him. If she'd come to the conclusion that whatever she felt for him wasn't enough to offset the drawbacks of a relationship with a race car driver. Would he have enough grace to let her go without an argument? Enough pride to do so without begging?

"What have you been thinking?"

"I'd like to come to Atlanta."

The breath he'd been holding escaped slowly through his nose. He smiled in relief. "Yeah?"

"Yeah. But you don't need to send the private jet. I'll get there on my own."

"I'll make the arrangements," he said firmly. "I'll have someone contact you with the details."

"All right. But, Jake, I still want to take our time with this, okay? I mean, there's no need to rush into anything, is there?"

"Absolutely," he promised. "I'll let you set the pace, whatever makes you comfortable, as long as I can see you."

"And let's try again to keep it low-key. It will be harder, I know, especially because it will be my second race with you and this time Andrew won't be there, but I'd rather not go too public as yet."

"You've got it."

"Okay. Then I'll be there."

"I'm glad."

"Just one more favor?"

"Name it."

"Try to win, okay? I want to see you do that burn-out thing you and Andrew were talking about."

He laughed, amused by her sudden teasing tone. "I'll give it my best shot."

"Do that. Good night, Jake."

"Good night, darlin'."

"Um, okay." She hung up abruptly, and Jake laughed again. The lazy endearment had obviously startled her. He would have to use them more often.

Suddenly in a very good mood indeed, he snapped off the light and fell back into the pillows. Tonight he would dream of Stacy—not that there was anything new about that.

STACY COOKED lunch after church on Sunday and invited Nick and Andrew to join her to eat and watch the race. Andrew was still in a pretty good mood overall, though he had his moments. Nick told Stacy that he hadn't even complained too much about having to get up for church that morning, which was unusual in itself.

Her heart leaped when she saw Jake on the screen prior to the race. Reporters surrounded him as he walked to his car, his helmet beneath his arm, looking so handsome and proud. He joined his team for the prerace prayer and anthem, then climbed into his car for the event.

Andrew informed Stacy that this was the shortest track and that she could expect lots of bumping and banging. It was a good thing that Jake had qualified so well, he added, because passing was difficult there. And it would serve him well to stay in front as much as possible, since there was little room to avoid a crash if someone spun or hit the wall in front of him.

All of which only made her very nervous for Jake's sake, though Andrew seemed to be looking forward to the melee.

There were many heart-stopping moments during the next few hours, most of them avoiding near misses by Jake as others wrecked around him. Disaster seemed to be inevitable when he was tapped from behind late in the race, sending him flying up the track toward the wall, but he made a miraculous last-minute save, emerging with only a few dents that seemed to have no effect on the car's handling.

At least, that was what Andrew assured Stacy. She had retreated behind her hands when it had looked as though Jake would wreck, and she didn't emerge again until she was sure he was safe.

Nick shook his head doubtfully. "If you're going to watch him race very often, you're going to have to get over this squeamishness. Trust me, he is going to wreck at some point. It's highly unlikely that he'll be injured, but it'll likely look scary to you."

"I know," she said on a deep breath. "That's just one of the things I'm going to have to get used to. It'll just take me some time."

Nick nodded gravely. "No need to rush into anything," he agreed.

Both Stacy and Andrew were on their feet by the time the race ended. After dominating the entire event, Jake crossed the finish line first, barely a nose ahead of his nearest competitor. It was another breathtaking, close finish—just the kind he claimed to like best—and both Stacy and Andrew cheered the win like excited kids.

Nick watched them hug and high-five, smiling indulgently but with a worried look in his eyes that Stacy noted but chose to ignore. Even Oscar was studying her odd behavior as if he wondered if she'd lost her mind. Maybe she had, but she was just so happy for Jake.

The camera panned to Jake's team, celebrating jubilantly in the pit with fist bumps and shoulder thumps and silly dances.

"Look at Wade," Andrew pointed out, laughing, so proud to claim acquaintance with the winning team. "Bet they aren't calling him 'Ice' now."

Stacy had to agree. Wade was grinning from ear to ear, high-fiving and hugging with the rest of them. They were all so happy to have Jake back behind the wheel, back in Victory Lane. Stacy felt her throat tighten at this evidence of how close Jake's team were to each other. She couldn't help wondering if there was room for one more among the tightly knit crew.

While Jake made his way to Victory Lane, reporters interviewed Wade and other drivers who'd finished in the top ten, including Ronnie, who had moved ahead in points with a strong finish of his own. The Chase was still close, but Ronnie had a good chance of claiming his first championship, the announcers agreed, making Stacy smile again. Ronnie and Katie must be thrilled, she thought, almost as proud as Andrew that she knew those interesting people.

Back in Victory Lane, a reporter waited for Jake to climb out of his car. Looking flushed and sweaty and satisfied, Jake boosted himself out of the tight opening, sliding a sponsor cap onto his mussed hair and reaching for the official soft drink of his team to take a long swallow. He made sure, of course, that the brand name was prominently displayed. Jake was nothing if not sponsor savvy, she thought with a shake of her head.

Behind him, his rowdy team shook up champagne bottles, spraying Jake and everyone around them with the bubbly liquid. Jake hardly seemed to notice the champagne pouring off the brim of his cap and wetting his shoulders as he stepped up to the reporter with a broad grin.

"How does it feel to be back in Victory Lane, Jake?" the reporter wanted to know.

"Fantastic," Jake answered fervently. "Really great. I want to thank the Woodrow Racing team for giving me an amazing car today. That Number 82 Vaughan Tools car was just awesome."

He worked in the names of a few more sponsors, thanking all of them with the same enthusiasm, and the reporter patiently allowed Jake to earn his pay before breaking in with another comment and question. "That was an extremely close finish, Jake. Looked like the Number 76 car had a shot at taking you there at the end. Did you ever get worried?"

Having turned to exchange congratulatory man-hugs with Wade and Woody, who had just made their way to him, Jake turned back to answer, "Yeah, the Number 76 did an awesome job out there. Raced me clean and gave it everything he had. It was a lot of fun."

"Anything else you want to say, Jake?"

"Just that I'm really glad to be back and I want to thank all my fans again for their support. And a special shout-out to Stacy Carter. This win was for her."

All of the stiffness going out of her legs, Stacy sat down on the couch with an inelegant plop. Her heart in her throat, she looked at her brother. "Tell me he didn't just say that."

Nick nodded sympathetically. "I'm afraid he did."

"Man, that was so cool!" Andrew crowed. "Did you hear, Aunt Stacy? He dedicated his win to you. Aren't you excited?"

She thought she might be sick. "I, uh, think I need some more coffee," she said, hoping her legs would hold her now as she stood.

By the time she made it into the kitchen, her temper was burning as hot as the fresh coffee in the carafe.

STILL BUZZING with the excitement of the close win, Jake and Wade were finally able to break away from the photographers and reporters, sponsors and fans and make their way back to the hauler in preparation to head back to North Carolina.

Ronnie Short joined them halfway there, his own hauler being parked next to theirs. He congratulated Jake on the win, and Jake congratulated him in return for his promising points lead. Both of them were quite satisfied as they approached the haulers and the people who waited for them there.

Jake's steps faltered when he saw Lisa and Katie standing with their heads close together, both of them frowning. They looked at him as he approached, and rather than congratulating him, they both looked as if they wanted to strangle him.

"Wow," Ronnie murmured, looking taken aback himself. "What did you do?"

"Not a clue," Jake answered honestly, wondering if they were only imagining that the women looked furious with him, for some reason.

But Katie put an end to that question the moment he came within her hearing. "What on *earth* were you thinking?" she demanded.

Jake looked cautiously behind him, to see if there was any chance she was talking to someone beyond his shoulder. "Uh, when?" he asked when he accepted that he was the object of her irritation.

"You dedicated your win to Stacy," Lisa said, looking as exasperated as her friend. "Please tell us she knew you were going to do that."

"Well…no, I guess she didn't. But what's so bad about it?" he asked defensively. "Most people would consider it a compliment."

Lisa and Katie groaned loudly in unison.

Annoyed with the way they were acting, Jake turned to Ronnie. "Do you have any idea what they're talking about?"

"No, not really," he confessed, looking nervously at his wife. "I mean, I thought it was kind of, you know, romantic."

Planting her hands on either side of her hugely pregnant belly, Katie stared at both of them in apparent disgust. "I can't believe you two. There are things that are more important than a race, you know. Even a winning race."

"After all the trouble we went to last week to keep Stacy low profile at the track so she wouldn't be the subject of gossip while you and she were in the early stages of a relationship, you go and do something like this," Lisa added curtly. "Didn't you learn anything from blurting out her name in the car last week? You knew that bothered her. But she forgave you for that because we all assured her that was inadvertent. This was deliberate."

"Neither of you understand," Jake insisted, beginning to secretly worry that he'd messed up again. "She called me last night and said she's coming to Atlanta next week. I mean, we're sort of officially seeing each other now. We couldn't really keep it a secret much longer, anyway."

"When she agreed to see you again next week, did she give you permission to announce it on national television?" Lisa asked archly, sounding like the cutthroat prosecutor he knew her to be.

He didn't like being on the witness stand in front of everyone like this, on the defensive and sweating with guilt he was trying not to show. "That isn't what I did," he muttered.

"You might as well have," Katie said with a shake of her head. "All the fan sites are going to be buzzing with gossip about whether you and Stacy are getting serious and whether she's going to take you out of the eligible-bachelor pool. Whether she's good enough for you or pretty enough for you or whether she's just after your money and your fame. Trust me, I've been there. But at least I was a little more prepared for it, since Ronnie and I had been dating a while before we made it public."

"A while? You and Ronnie were married six months after you met."

"That's true," she agreed coolly. "But he never once pushed me into the spotlight against my will."

"It isn't like that," Jake insisted again, knowing he sounded less certain every time he said it. "Uh, I've got to go make a phone call, okay? I'll talk to you all later."

Looking at him with as much pity as vexation now, they watched him hurry away.

CHAPTER SEVENTEEN

STACY'S CELL PHONE rang incessantly that evening. Most of the calls were from Jake, but others were from reporters, friends and passing acquaintances who wanted details about her relationship with the famous race car driver.

She didn't answer any of them. She would have turned the phone off entirely, but she knew her brother and mother would worry if they couldn't reach her. She didn't have a land line, using her cell phone as her only means of communication.

She was still so angry with Jake that she couldn't stop pacing. Oscar stayed discreetly out of her way, sitting in his doggie bed with his squeaky toy and a wary look on his furry face.

Finally cooling off enough to check her messages, she listened as Jake grew more and more insistent that she call him back. He'd started out all cheery and jovial, but he must have finally figured out that she was deliberately ignoring his calls.

"Look, Stacy, I hope you aren't mad about what I said after the race," he said into her voice mail service. "Lisa and Katie thought you might be, but Ronnie and I couldn't really understand why there would be a problem. I mean, most people like having a win dedicated to them. I was excited and I was wishing you were there to see it all, and…well, I just blurted it out, okay? Darn it, I hate talking into these recording things. Call me, will you?"

So Lisa and Katie both understood exactly why she would be

furious with him. Why she would feel betrayed by his thoughtless actions. If they, who barely knew her, could see how much that would hurt her, why couldn't Jake, who claimed to have a special bond with her? Who knew exactly why she had been so reluctant to find herself and her family back in the aim of the gossipmongers?

He quit calling at midnight, her time. Either he'd accepted that she wasn't going to talk to him that night or he'd gotten angry himself and decided she wasn't worth the effort. Maybe that would be best, she thought, lying wide awake on her bed with Oscar curled beside her, snoring softly. Maybe she'd been foolish to convince herself that she and Jake had even a slight chance of a lasting relationship.

Okay, so maybe she had fallen head over heels in love with him. Oddly enough, she had acknowledged that only today, when she'd realized that what he'd done wouldn't have hurt nearly as badly if she hadn't started to love him. To trust him.

But she couldn't let that matter now. There could be nothing between them if he couldn't respect her wishes. Her feelings. If he saw her only as someone to be there to support him in his career, then he'd chosen the wrong woman.

As she had pointed out to him recently, she had a life of her own. A satisfying life. He needed to understand that she would be sacrificing the contentment she had found for herself if she became involved with him, and that her life here was as important to her as NASCAR was to him.

She had finally decided she was willing to take that risk because he had convinced her he genuinely cared for her. But now she was questioning him all over again. And as badly as it hurt now, she told herself it would have been much worse if she had let this go any further, only to discover that Jake didn't even know her, much less really love her.

STACY HADN'T EMERGED from her apartment by midmorning Monday. Her phone kept ringing, but she answered only a few of the calls. Her mother. Her brother. Mindy.

Jake didn't call again. She told herself she was relieved about that. Apparently, he'd gotten the message loud and clear. She hadn't had to spell it out for him. Lisa and Katie must have done an adequate job of that.

When someone knocked forcefully on her door at just before noon, she was almost afraid to answer for fear that it could be a particularly persistent reporter. But then, deciding that it must be Nick, she moved to answer, looking through the security viewer just to be sure.

She nearly stumbled against the door when she saw who stood on the other side. It took her several long moments to get up the nerve to answer, during which time he knocked again.

"Stacy, it's me," he called out, "Jake. Please open the door."

Drawing a deep breath and keeping her face impassive, she turned the knob.

At least he wasn't holding flowers, she thought when she saw him standing there in his gray polo shirt and jeans, looking more like the guy she'd met at the river than the famous driver who had broken her heart. She could do without the clichéd apologies.

"Shouldn't you be in North Carolina?" she asked without inviting him in.

"I should be at a meeting with my sponsors," he answered bluntly. "Followed by an ad I'm supposed to shoot for spicy potato chips. After which I had an interview scheduled with the cable racing channel. Pam's doing her best to reschedule everything, though she may not talk to me for a while after this."

Shaken by the list of important responsibilities he had shirked to come here, she bit her lip. She supposed the least she could do was ask him to come in. It would be somewhat more civil to end their relationship in her living room than with him out in the hallway.

Accepting her invitation, he stepped inside, bending to greet Oscar, who almost attacked him in a frenzy of welcome. "It's good to see you, too, buddy," Jake murmured, rubbing the dog's ears and making him roll over in bliss. "I've missed you."

He certainly said those words easily, Stacy thought, trying to hold on to her anger. He'd missed her. He'd missed her dog. He'd totally missed the point.

Straightening from the dog, he pushed his fingertips into the front pockets of his jeans and studied her gravely. "You could have called me back."

Her eyebrows rose. He was criticizing *her* actions? Maybe this wasn't going to be as difficult as she had anticipated. "I could have," she agreed coolly. "I chose not to. I had so many messages on my phone last night and this morning that I couldn't possibly return them all. A lot of them were the same reporters who bugged me after the courthouse incident."

He grimaced. "I'm sorry about that. I guess I just spoke without thinking."

"Something you apparently do a lot. Especially where I'm concerned."

"Look, I know you're mad—"

"Yes, I'm mad," she shot back at him before he could make excuses. "I asked you to keep me low profile. You said you would. And then you broke that promise."

"I guess I did," he said grimly. "I was just so excited about the win. I wanted to share it with you. I didn't—"

"The win," she repeated irritably. "It's all about the win to you, isn't it? You warned me that racing was more than a job to you, but I guess I just didn't realize that it's the only thing that matters to you at all."

"If that were true, I wouldn't be here now," he replied evenly, his eyes narrowed. "Do you know how annoyed everyone is going to be with me for cutting out today?"

"Then why did you come?" she asked wearily. "There really wasn't any need for you to."

"I came because I realized I screwed up. And I wanted to tell you in person that I'm sorry. I know I betrayed your trust and I feel lousy about that. I can't believe I was so stupid and thoughtless. I don't really have an excuse, except for the adrenaline rush of the win. All I can do is ask you to give me another chance to prove that we can do this. That I can be what you want me to be."

He still didn't get it. She shook her head sadly. "I'm not trying to make you into someone you aren't, Jake. You shouldn't have to guard every word you say when you're celebrating a hard-fought win. Even though you spoke without thinking this time and accidentally broke a promise by doing so, the real problem is with me, not you. I'm not cut out for your life. I don't fit there. Ignoring that is only going to make us both miserable in the long run."

"I don't believe that. There are lots of different personalities represented in NASCAR. Wives and girlfriends who enjoy the spotlight, and others who avoid it. Couples who are never more than a few feet apart, and others who pretty much go their own ways most of the time. We don't have to be like anyone else. We can make our own rules for our relationship. Just give us a chance."

He would probably never know how tempted she was to take him up on that. How touched she was that he had risked so much to come to her today. How hard it was for her to shake her head in the negative. "I'm sorry. I can't."

"You were willing to try Friday, when you accepted my invitation to Atlanta," he reminded her. "Was dedicating the win to you really so bad that it made you completely change your mind about us?"

She sighed and crossed her arms in front of her. "I've accepted your apology. I know you didn't mean to hurt me. But all of this has made me think hard about what I was about to do. To realize that I was on the verge of making a mistake that would affect both of us. I'm not right for you, Jake. It would be easier if we both just accept that now. If we say goodbye as friends, and enjoy the memories we made together."

He shook his head with a stubborn expression she had come to recognize all too well. "I won't accept that. We could have a lot more than friendship. And we could make a lot more memories together. A lifetime of memories, if you'd only take a chance on me."

How could he be talking about a lifetime when they'd known each other less than two months? When they hadn't even been able to make it that long? "I can't."

He looked stunned. A little sick. "You're ending it? Just like this? Now?"

"I suppose I am," she whispered. "I think it's for the best."

He stood without moving for a long time, his expression suddenly closed to her. And then he nodded curtly. "I told myself I wouldn't beg," he muttered. "I guess I have to accept your decision."

Oh, no, please don't beg, she thought with an inner shudder. She wouldn't be able to bear that. Not from Jake. "Thank you. I think you'll agree eventually that I've made the right choice."

He looked briefly angry then. "No, I damned well don't agree," he said. "And I won't change my mind later. We could have been great together, you and I. I'll always believe that."

Because she couldn't believe that he wouldn't come to his senses eventually, if not soon, she said nothing.

He moved toward the door, his shoulders slumped, his head down. He looked miserable, and she felt the same way. This was the hardest thing she had ever done. Maybe someday he would understand that she had done it as much for his sake as for her own.

He paused at the door to look at her with tortured eyes. "I really am sorry, Stacy."

"I know," she whispered. "So am I."

"If you ever change your mind…well, I'm not that hard to find."

She nodded, certain that she wouldn't go looking for him.

"Tell Andrew I said goodbye, will you? Anytime he wants to write to me or call me or anything, he's welcome to do so."

"That's very kind of you."

Her words only seemed to annoy him more. He turned abruptly toward the door, putting his hand on the doorknob. She steeled herself to watch him walk out.

And then he paused, his head down. "I just want you to know that if I handled everything all wrong, it was because I'd never been in love with anyone before. Maybe I got carried away. Maybe I shouldn't have tried to rush you into something you weren't ready for. But I did it all because I fell in love with you during that week at the river and I wanted so badly to make you a part of my life."

He swallowed and gave her one fulminating look. "You said racing is my life, and you were right. It has been my life until this point. I was hoping that, with you, I'd found something more to live for. I'm more sorry than you'll ever know that you couldn't feel the same way about me."

He let himself out before she could reply. He didn't see the tears that welled in her eyes and streamed down her cheeks, or hear the incoherent sound she made. As she threw herself onto the couch and buried her face in her hands, she tried to convince herself that she hadn't been trying to beg him not to go.

JAKE COULDN'T HAVE SAID how he made it through the next week. Somehow he managed it. Oddly enough, the pain he was going through didn't affect his performance on the job at all. He qualified on the pole for the race in Atlanta, which wasn't even one of his strongest tracks.

He supposed if racing was the only life he was ever going to have, he needed to make sure he did it better than anyone else.

"Heck of a qualifying run," Wade said later, when it was just the two of them in the hauler office. "You ran darned near a perfect lap out there. Right in the groove. Set a record qualifying speed. I'm proud of you."

"Thanks," he replied without much enthusiasm. "I think I'll go to my motor home for a while. Call me if you need anything, okay?"

Wade caught his arm when he would have brushed past to the doorway. "I know this is none of my business, but are you all right?"

"No," Jake answered simply. "I'm not."

"I know how it feels, you know. When Lisa left me and went back to Chicago…well, I felt like I'd been hit by a bus. Like something was broken inside, and I didn't know how to go about fixing it."

But Lisa had come back. Stacy had no intention of ever doing so. "Yeah. That pretty much sums it up."

"Is there anything I can do?"

"Hell if I know." He tried to smile, knowing he failed miserably. "I've never been dumped before, you know. I don't quite know how to go about getting over it."

"Some people would say you were pretty lucky to go this long without ever being dumped."

"Yeah. Lucky." Pushing his hand through his hair, he said, "I've got to go. See you later, Wade."

"Yeah." Sounding unusually morose, Wade watched him leave. "See you later, pal."

"I STILL DON'T UNDERSTAND why you broke up with him," Andrew said, giving Stacy a searching look from beneath his shaggy bangs. "I don't see how what he did was so bad."

"It wasn't just that, Andrew," she replied awkwardly. "Even though he knew I didn't want him to talk about me on the television. You know how much I hate having attention called to me that way."

"Well, yeah, but it was only because he wanted to share his win with you. We were all so excited about the win. Remember how you and me were jumping around and yelling and everything? Jake was sort of doing the same thing, all carried away and stuff."

"I understand that." It was exactly the excuse Jake had used, after all. "I just…well, it annoyed me. But as I said, that wasn't the only reason I thought it best to stop seeing him."

"Aren't you even going to watch the race with Dad and me tomorrow?"

She shook her head. "I doubt it. I've never been a race fan—you know that. Besides, Mindy and I are going to be working here tomorrow afternoon to get ready for the carnival Wednesday night."

She and Andrew were in the large fellowship hall of their church, which was in varying stages of decoration for the annual fall festival. Andrew had helped her carry in the large plywood board, now painted bright blue with happy-looking fish swimming across it, and they were trying to make sure it fit steadily on the stand Nick had built for it. They didn't want it falling on any little costumed "fishermen" Halloween night.

This was the first she'd spent any time with Andrew since the breakup with Jake, and she had dreaded the questions she knew would come. She hadn't been able to talk about Jake to anyone else all week, other than to tell Nick and Mindy that it was over between her and Jake.

She wondered if she would ever stop feeling as though a part of her had been ripped away, leaving an aching hole behind.

Andrew sat cross-legged on the floor, threading heavy fishing line through a plastic hook. "Some of my friends have been telling me that I've been talking too much about that weekend in Charlotte. You know, sort of bragging about my NASCAR friends."

Setting the big laundry basket of prizes behind the board, Stacy asked, "Are they right?"

"Yeah, probably. It's the first thing I ever really had to brag about, you know? The first thing that ever meant that much to me."

"I'm glad you have those memories," she told him gently. "And I'm glad I was able to share them with you."

"Maybe it's the same way with Jake, you know? He was sort of bragging about you because he knew how lucky he was to be dating you. I mean, any guy would feel that way about you."

Startled, she dropped a gift bag, having to bend to pick it up and place it carefully in the basket. "That's a very nice thing to say, Andrew."

He shrugged self-consciously. "It's true. And it's probably the way Jake felt, too. Why he said what he did."

"Maybe," she muttered, not wanting to discourage the conversation but growing uncomfortable with its direction.

"He just wanted to share his win with you, Aunt Stacy. It was the thing that mattered most to him right then—and maybe you were the person who mattered most to him. Does that make sense?"

She swallowed hard. "Yes, sweetie. It makes sense. But could we talk about something else now, please? I...well, I just can't talk about Jake right now, okay?"

He nodded glumly.

Throwing herself into her decorating, Stacy tried not to think about what her nephew had said, though she knew his sweet words would haunt her later.

SHE WATCHED the end of the race. Not with her brother and nephew, but alone in her apartment after she'd returned from decorating with Mindy. Mindy, thank goodness, had carefully refrained from talking about Jake, as Stacy had begged her to do for the afternoon.

Jake finished third, and everyone seemed to think that was pretty good at this track. According to the announcers, he might have even won had he not had a flat tire early in the race. She was glad she hadn't been there to see that. It would have upset her very badly for his sake.

Though she knew she was torturing herself, she watched the postrace interview with him. He looked fine, she decided. Relaxed and comfortable as always on camera. Tired, of course, but he always looked a bit worn after so many grueling hours in the car. No one could tell by looking at him that he'd had a rough week emotionally.

Maybe he hadn't taken the breakup as hard as she had, after all, she thought with a rather resentful glare at his breezy smile.

But then he looked directly into the camera, and her heart squeezed tightly in her chest. Forget what she'd just thought.

Despite his light tone and bright smile, Jake's eyes were as sad now as they had been the first time she'd gazed into them. And she had the feeling that she might be one of the few people in the world who would recognize that.

Clutching a small purple plastic car in her hand, she thought of what Andrew had said to her the day before. *He just wanted to share his win with you, Aunt Stacy. It was the thing that mattered most to him right then—and maybe you were the person who mattered most to him.*

And then something Jake had said. *I just want you to know that if I handled everything all wrong, it was because I'd never been in love with anyone before.*

Stacy gripped the car so tightly it dug into her palm and lowered her head to her fists. Oscar whined in sympathy from beside her, obviously wishing he could help her.

She wasn't sure that was possible, even for her beloved pet.

EVEN ON THE FIRST SUNDAY in November, Texas was comfortably warm. *Uncomfortably* warm in a race car barreling around the pavement. But it could have been worse, Jake figured, strapping on the fire-resistant shoes and heat shields that every driver wore for a race. It could have been Indianapolis in July. Or Tennessee in August. Now, those were hot races.

He had a little while before he had to go outside for the prerace activities, and as was his habit, he sat in the hauler office alone, mentally preparing himself for the upcoming contest. He'd won at this track before; he could do it again. He wanted that win.

Winning races was the one thing he had to look forward to, he thought in a moment of self-pity that he quickly shook off.

He wondered if Stacy would be watching today. And then he wondered if he would ever be able to race again without wondering if she were watching.

He wondered if he would ever think of her without feeling as though someone had just kicked him squarely in the chest.

Someone tapped on the door, and he scowled. Everyone knew he didn't like to be disturbed until the very last minute before he had to go out there. He had a good fifteen minutes left yet, and he had planned to spend them putting Stacy out of his mind so he could concentrate on the race.

One look at the person who entered, and he knew that wouldn't be possible.

"Stacy?" he said, wondering for a moment if he'd hallucinated her. "What—?"

She looked like a petite angel in a pure white long-sleeved blouse and fitted jeans. Hardly the usual track couture, but so very right for her. "J.R. tried to stop me from coming in, but Wade said it would be okay. He told J.R. that you could be mad at him if you didn't like it."

"I'm not mad at anyone. I just…can't believe you're here," he said, rising slowly to his feet. Seeing the pass around her neck, he asked, "How—?"

"Lisa," she explained briefly. "She took care of everything for me."

"Why are you here?" He wondered if she thought maybe she hadn't dumped him hard enough the first time and was here to finish him off—but she couldn't be that cold, could she?

She moistened her lips, looking nervous for the first time. "When I took down Alvetti at that courthouse? Everyone talked about how brave I was. They made a big deal out of that in the news stories afterward. They called me a lion in a kitten's clothing. A hero. But I knew all along that they were wrong. I'm not brave. I've never been brave. I just acted on instinct. Later, when I was alone, I started shaking so hard I could hardly stand up unassisted."

"Why are you telling me this?" he asked, folding his hands into fists to keep them from reaching for her.

"You scared me," she answered simply. "More than I'd ever been scared before, I think. You accused me of being too afraid to take a chance on us, and you were right, but I don't think even you realized just how terrified I was. I was afraid of the publicity, afraid of competing with your career, afraid of the other women who would throw themselves at you. Afraid of not measuring up to your expectations, or that you wouldn't measure up to mine. Afraid of losing myself in your shadow. Afraid of having my heart broken again—only not being able to recover from it this time the way I had before."

Maybe it was the way she had worded that somewhat disjointed explanation, but for the first time Jake truly understood why she had been so hesitant to get involved with him. "Those are all legitimate fears," he said, his voice not quite steady. "I can see why you needed time to confront them. I shouldn't have been so impatient."

"And I shouldn't have been such a coward," she answered evenly. "I'm sorry, Jake. I hope I haven't let my fear ruin everything between us."

Hope began to blossom inside him, but it hurt almost as badly as the anguish he'd felt before she'd come in. He knew how much it would hurt if she changed her mind again just as he'd allowed himself to start to believe...

"You aren't afraid now?"

"A little," she admitted. "It's going to take me a while to get used to this crazy life you live, and to find a place for myself in it. But I got to thinking about something you told me, and it gave me the courage to try."

"What—" He had to stop to clear his throat. "What was that brilliant thing I said?"

Her smile was a little strained around the edges as she searched his face, trying to read his emotions. "You said you weren't afraid on the track because you trusted the people around you. Your spotter, your team, the other drivers."

He nodded.

She shrugged. "I trust you," she said simply. "It just took me a while to figure that out."

His throat tightened so hard he had to force his voice out. "I let you down. I stupidly broke my promise to help you stay in the background until you were ready to go public."

"I didn't say I think you're perfect," she reminded him gently. "You aren't. Neither am I. We'll both make a lot of mistakes, since it's so new for both of us. But I trust you not to hurt me deliberately. And to respect my wishes from now on, just as I'll try to respect yours. I trust you not to stop loving me, even when I get scared and defensive, just as I won't stop loving you the next time you say something stupid. Which you probably will."

He tried to laugh. "Count on that. But I will try to keep my foot out of my mouth. It's got a real nasty taste."

He cleared his throat, then asked hesitantly, "Did you just say you love me?"

She tilted her head, the movement reminding him a bit of Oscar. "Should I count that as a stupid question? Yes, Jake. I love you. I wouldn't have found the courage to be here if I didn't."

"You don't need more time?"

"Not to be sure of that part," she answered steadily. "As for the rest of it…we'll take that as it comes. As you said in my apartment, we have a lifetime to figure it all out."

"A lifetime." It was almost too much to take in. He had gone from the depths of despair to the heights of happiness in such a short time that his head was sort of spinning. "Is that a promise?"

"It is if you want it to be."

"Oh, yeah." He reached for her then, unable to resist touching her for another minute.

The kiss was long, deep, hungry, joyous. It ended only when they both surfaced for oxygen, and then they dived feverishly into another. Jake's hands were already starting to roam when another tap came on the door.

"Uh, Jake?" J.R. sounded nervous when he spoke through the closed door. "It's time for you to come out for the race."

"Oh, man." Jake drew a deep, shaky breath, resting his forehead against Stacy's. "For the first time in my life, I'd rather stay in the hauler than go out on the track. That couch looks awfully inviting."

She reached up to kiss him again, quickly, and then she pulled herself out of his arms. "Go," she said. "You have a race to run. I'll be waiting for you afterward."

They were the most beautiful words he'd ever heard. And if he didn't get out of there quickly, the cameras were going to catch a macho race car driver with tears running down his face, he thought wryly.

"You can stay in here if you like," he told her, moving toward the doorway. "You can watch the race on the screen."

She shook her head and laced her hand with his. "I can take it," she assured him. "Let's go win a race."

As far as Jake was concerned, he had already won.

* * * * *

*For more thrill-a-minute romances set against the exciting
backdrop of the NASCAR world, don't miss:*

*OLD FLAME, NEW SPARKS by Day Leclaire
ALMOST FAMOUS by Gina Wilkins
Available in August*

*THE ROOKIE by Jennifer LaBrecque
LEGENDS AND LIES by Katherine Garbera
Available in September*

*A CHANCE WORTH TAKING—by Carrie Weaver
TURN TWO—by Nancy Warren
Available in November*

*And for a sneak preview of TURN TWO, featuring a cameo by
real-life NASCAR driver Carl Edwards, just turn the page....*

SUNDAY WAS A PERFECT DAY for racing. Sunny but not too hot, the sky so clear and blue there was no danger of rain, and the air shifted with only a slight breeze. Taylor hoped that a perfect day was a good omen for Hank's first NASCAR NEXTEL Cup Series race.

She was so nervous she could barely stand still. She felt as proud of Hank as if he was her brother or son, and so nervous she thought she might throw up.

Her driver was fortunately made of sterner stuff. If he was nervous it didn't show. He stood proudly in his brand-new fire suit with the name of the chain of hardware stores sponsoring him prominently identified.

"How are you feeling?" she asked him.

He grinned at her, and she could see the excitement shining in his eyes. "I feel good," he said. "Real good." He glanced around as though he couldn't believe that he was here. "Today is going to be a great day."

They made their way to the staging area where drivers were milling around, each with his PR manager. Fans watched from the perimeter.

Carl Edwards caught sight of Hank and immediately walked over.

"How you doing?" he asked Hank.

"I'm doing fine. Not too nervous." He stood there for a second and asked, "Do you have any advice for the rookie?"

"Yeah. Drive fast. But not faster than me."

They laughed and even that little release helped dim Taylor's stress level. She took a quick glance around and thought that most of the PR managers looked more tense than their drivers.

"Really, what I would say is just, you know, enjoy the moment. I'm guessing you've dreamed of this day since you were a little kid."

Hank nodded. She could picture him hanging around cars as a little guy, watching races, finally getting a chance to try a cart and falling in love with the sport.

"There's a lot more guys who dream of going out there than will ever get the chance. You have to drive like you mean it. Drive with your heart and your guts and all your dreams right out there. Keep your focus and—" he shrugged, looked up at the sky as though for inspiration "—do what has to be done."

"Okay."

"What we do is amazing, right?" He looked like he'd pumped himself up with his pep talk. "This is so cool."

"It sure is. I've been practicing my backflips, in case I win."

Carl treated him to his toothy grin. "Stick to something you can handle. Like a cartwheel."

The picture of Hank in his blue-and-yellow suit, turning cartwheels was so ridiculous she had to laugh.

He appeared to take the suggestion seriously. "Think that's too flashy? Maybe I should stick to one of them…what do you call them? Somersaults."

Carl gave him a mock punch. "You're going to be okay."

Then the drivers were being introduced. She heard Hank's name called and felt another swell of pride. This was it. While he made his introductory lap, she walked back to the garage.

The air was buzzing with excitement. She took a moment to look up at the stands and enjoy the spectacle of one hundred and sixty-eight thousand or so fans all set for one of racing's premier events. The stands were a sea of color. Fans sported racing gear, most of which was in bold, primary colors. It was a rainbow of caps, jackets, T-shirts, coolers.

Hank arrived, looking pretty colorful himself in his brightly hued fire suit. He stood by his car, chatting with his crew chief. Photographers were everywhere, snapping photos from every conceivable angle. Hank, like most of the drivers, did his best to pretend he didn't notice.

As drivers walked by, they'd give him a good-natured shove or mumble something that she assumed meant good luck in some incomprehensible sports-guy speak.

As he continued talking to his crew chief, Taylor was thrilled to see a broadcaster walk by for a quick interview.

"How do you think you're going to do out there today?" Hank was asked. A no-brainer question and one she'd prepared him for.

"I'm going to do my best. I've got a great team behind me, a company I'm proud to race for and sponsors and fans who believe in me." He broke into his infectious grin. "I have to tell you and everybody out there who's rooting for me today that I feel ready for this."

Taylor stood by while he climbed into his car, put in earplugs, pulled on his helmet and plugged it in. She watched him strapping in, putting the steering wheel on—getting ready to go.

When she heard the words *Gentlemen, start your engines,* she thought she might hyperventilate. This was it. Not only Hank's rookie race, but hers, too.

* * * * *

Available November 2007, wherever books are sold.

HARLEQUIN *Super Romance®*

Welcome to Cowboy Country...

TEXAS BABY

by *Kathleen O'Brien*

#1441

Chase Clayton doesn't know what to think.
A beautiful stranger has just crashed his
engagement party, demanding that he not
marry because she's pregnant with his baby.
But the kicker is—he's never seen her before.

Look for TEXAS BABY and other fantastic
Superromance titles on sale September 2007.

Available wherever books are sold.

HARLEQUIN *Super Romance®*

**Where life and love weave together
in emotional and unforgettable ways.**

Love Inspired
SUSPENSE
RIVETING INSPIRATIONAL ROMANCE

SECRET AGENT MINISTER
Lenora Worth

Things were not as they seemed...

The minister of Lydia Cantrell's dreams had another calling.
As his secretary, she knew the church members adored him,
but she was shocked to discover Pastor Dev Malone's past as
a Christian secret agent. Her shock turned to disbelief when
Pastor Dev revealed he'd made some enemies—
and that he and Lydia were in danger.

Available September wherever you buy books.

Steeple
Hill®

LIS44258

REQUEST YOUR FREE BOOKS!

2 FREE NOVELS PLUS 2 FREE GIFTS!

Silhouette®

SPECIAL EDITION®

Life, Love and Family!

YES! Please send me 2 FREE Silhouette Special Edition® novels and my 2 FREE gifts. After receiving them, if I don't wish to receive any more books, I can return the shipping statement marked "cancel." If I don't cancel, I will receive 6 brand-new novels every month and be billed just $4.24 per book in the U.S., or $4.99 per book in Canada, plus 25¢ shipping and handling per book and applicable taxes, if any*. That's a savings of at least 15% off the cover price! I understand that accepting the 2 free books and gifts places me under no obligation to buy anything. I can always return a shipment and cancel at any time. Even if I never buy another book from Silhouette, the two free books and gifts are mine to keep forever.

235 SDN EEYU   335 SDN EEY6

Name	(PLEASE PRINT)	
Address		Apt.
City	State/Prov.	Zip/Postal Code

Signature (if under 18, a parent or guardian must sign)

Mail to the **Silhouette Reader Service™**:
IN U.S.A.: P.O. Box 1867, Buffalo, NY 14240-1867
IN CANADA: P.O. Box 609, Fort Erie, Ontario L2A 5X3

Not valid to current Silhouette Special Edition subscribers.

Want to try two free books from another line?
Call 1-800-873-8635 or visit www.morefreebooks.com.

* Terms and prices subject to change without notice. NY residents add applicable sales tax. Canadian residents will be charged applicable provincial taxes and GST. This offer is limited to one order per household. All orders subject to approval. Credit or debit balances in a customer's account(s) may be offset by any other outstanding balance owed by or to the customer. Please allow 4 to 6 weeks for delivery.

Your Privacy: Silhouette is committed to protecting your privacy. Our Privacy Policy is available online at www.eHarlequin.com or upon request from the Reader Service. From time to time we make our lists of customers available to reputable firms who may have a product or service of interest to you. If you would prefer we not share your name and address, please check here. ☐

SSE07